The
PRINCETON
IMPOSTOR

Ann Waldron

BERKLEY PRIME CRIME, NEW YORK

THE BERKLEY PUBLISHING GROUP
Published by the Penguin Group
Penguin Group (USA) Inc.
375 Hudson Street, New York, New York 10014, USA
Penguin Group (Canada), 90 Eglinton Avenue East, Suite 700, Toronto, Ontario M4P 2Y3, Canada
(a division of Pearson Penguin Canada Inc.)
Penguin Books Ltd., 80 Strand, London WC2R 0RL, England
Penguin Group Ireland, 25 St. Stephen's Green, Dublin 2, Ireland (a division of Penguin Books Ltd.)
Penguin Group (Australia), 250 Camberwell Road, Camberwell, Victoria 3124, Australia
(a division of Pearson Australia Group Pty. Ltd.)
Penguin Books India Pvt. Ltd., 11 Community Centre, Panchsheel Park, New Delhi—110 017, India
Penguin Group (NZ), Cnr. Airborne and Rosedale Roads, Albany, Auckland 1310, New Zealand
(a division of Pearson New Zealand Ltd.)
Penguin Books (South Africa) (Pty.) Ltd., 24 Sturdee Avenue, Rosebank, Johannesburg 2196, South
Africa

Penguin Books Ltd., Registered Offices: 80 Strand, London WC2R 0RL, England

This is a work of fiction. Names, characters, places, and incidents either are the product of the author's imagination or are used fictitiously, and any resemblance to actual persons, living or dead, business establishments, events, or locales is entirely coincidental. The publisher does not have any control over and does not assume any responsibility for author or third-party websites or their content.

PUBLISHER'S NOTE: The recipes contained in this book are to be followed exactly as written. The publisher is not responsible for your specific health or allergy needs that may require medical supervision. The publisher is not responsible for any adverse reactions to the recipes contained in this book.

THE PRINCETON IMPOSTOR

A Berkley Prime Crime Book / published by arrangement with the author

PRINTING HISTORY
Berkley Prime Crime mass-market edition / January 2007

ISBN: 978-0-425-21362-9

BERKLEY® PRIME CRIME
Berkley Prime Crime Books are published by The Berkley Publishing Group,
a division of Penguin Group (USA) Inc.,
375 Hudson Street, New York, New York 10014.
The name BERKLEY PRIME CRIME and the BERKLEY PRIME CRIME design are trademarks belonging to Penguin Group (USA) Inc.

PRINTED IN THE UNITED STATES OF AMERICA

10 9 8 7 6 5 4 3 2 1

One

❧

THE SUN WAS shining on the wisteria vines that clung to the walls of the Gothic buildings on the Princeton University campus the day the police interrupted McLeod Dulaney's writing class to arrest her star student. It shone in the west windows of the seminar room in Joseph Henry House where McLeod was teaching.

A proctor from the university's Office of Public Safety, escorting a plainclothes policeman from the Borough of Princeton, opened the door from the Joseph Henry House's dim corridor and came into the sunlit seminar room. McLeod sat at the head of the long table, and sunbeams danced on her white hair. She recognized the man with the proctor—he was a sergeant with the Borough Police Force. What was a policeman doing in her classroom?

"Sorry to interrupt," he said. "I'm Sergeant Popper from the Borough Police. I'm looking for Greg Pierre. I believe he's in this class." His gaze went down one side of the long table and up the other, examining the face of each student who sat around it.

McLeod frowned at him and said nothing. Then she watched the students as they stared at Popper and the proctor, puzzled. Only Greg Pierre, McLeod's favorite class member, down at the far end of the table, did not look at Popper. Instead, he looked around the room, out the window, down at his notebook on the table in front of him. He laid his pencil beside the notebook, turned a page in his notebook, and kept his eyes lowered.

He was a tall young man, somewhat older than the other students, thin—almost gaunt—very tan, with longish brown hair, gray eyes, and a thin mouth. He had never said much in class, but had written copiously and fluently.

As McLeod watched him, Greg sighed heavily, and shrugged. He picked up his pencil again and put it in a pocket in his notebook, closed the notebook, picked it up with his manuscript, and put them in his backpack. Nobody said a word while he zipped the pack, stood up, took his jacket from the back of his chair, and said, "Okay, Officer, that's me." Slinging his pack over one shoulder, he walked—slowly—the length of the table to where the men stood.

"Pierre?" asked Popper.

"That's me," said Greg again. He turned to McLeod. "Sorry, Ms. Dulaney. I know I should say, 'That's I.' "

McLeod stood up and went over to him. "What is it, Greg? Can I help?" She turned to Popper. "What's going on, Sergeant?"

"I'm sorry, ma'am. I can't talk now. Come along, Pierre. I apologize for interrupting the class." And the three disappeared through the door into the dim corridor. The sun went behind a cloud, and McLeod's white hair looked duller.

McLeod turned to face the eleven other students. "Do any of you know what's going on?" she asked.

Eleven heads shook from side to side.

"He's an odd duck," said Olivia Merchant, breaking the silence. "I know that much. He's a real loner."

"He sleeps on the floor," Clark Powell said. He grinned. "That's all I know."

"Sleeps on the floor?" said McLeod.

"That's right. He said he was used to sleeping outdoors

when he got here. So he slept on the floor—at least he did his freshman year when he lived in Holder. That's what his roommate told me."

"That's interesting, but not a crime," said McLeod. "Not something you get arrested for. But they didn't say they were arresting him, did they? I'll have to find out about this. He's a very talented young man. Isn't he a friend of any of you?"

"He really is a loner," said another student.

"He runs cross-country," somebody else chimed in, shrugging.

"That's right," said Clark Powell. "He's good at it."

"I've found him to be very nice," McLeod said. "And he's a great writer." She paused. "Well, let's get on with the class. Let's finish talking about the next assignment . . ."

McLeod's class was a seminar on nonfiction writing, with emphasis on writing about people, offered under the aegis of Princeton's Council of the Humanities, and she loved spending one semester a year in Princeton. The rest of the year she spent in Florida, where a series of articles for the Tallahassee *Star of Florida* had once won her a Pulitzer.

"Maybe we could all write an article about somebody who gets arrested," said Clark Powell, grinning again.

McLeod frowned at him. "We'll certainly keep Greg in mind. Maybe we will write something about this. And we certainly need to find out how we can help him. On to the current assignment—an interview with a person from a foreign country, or any person whose background is completely different from your own." She resolutely soldiered on with the class.

Finally, it was four-thirty, time to leave. "We're halfway through the semester and it's time to begin to think about your final paper," McLeod said. The final paper was supposed to demonstrate the sum of all they had learned about research on people, interviewing, and writing lively personality pieces. "We'll talk more about it next week. No, next week is break week. We'll talk about it after we all get back."

Two

❦

WHEN THE CLASS was over and the last student had trailed out the door, McLeod rushed upstairs to her cubicle on the third floor of Joseph Henry House and called the Borough Police. Her friend Lieutenant Nick Perry was busy, but the officer answering the phone took McLeod's telephone number.

Her next logical step, she thought, would be to talk to George Bridges. George was her old friend, her current landlord—she was staying this semester in the spare bedroom in his house on Edgehill Street—and also vice president for public affairs at the university. She looked at her watch. It was almost five o'clock, and George would still be in his office. Was he coming home tonight, or did he have a meeting? She could not remember. She tried never to call him at the office, but this was an emergency. It was an outrage that the police could walk into a classroom and take away a student. The university should prevent things like this from happening. She punched in the numbers of his extension.

Gina, George's secretary, answered the phone and, when McLeod identified herself, said, "George is in a meeting with President Blackman," said Gina. "Can I have him call you when he comes back?"

"No, that's all right, Gina. Do you know if he has a meeting tonight?"

"Nope, no meetings," said Gina cheerily. "He might be late getting home, though. Big crisis today about a student who got arrested." McLeod was glad to hear Gina say that—it surely meant George and President Blackman were as upset as she was. Gina was talking: "I guess you want to know when he'll be home."

"I guess that's what I want to know," said McLeod, wondering why Gina would act as though she were a possessive wife after all these months during which she had scrupulously refrained from calling George when he was at work in Nassau Hall. "I'm in my office if he comes back anytime soon," she said. "I'll be home shortly. If he's going to be late, ask him to call me there, will you?"

"I sure will," caroled Gina, still cheerful to a fault.

When she had hung up the phone, McLeod felt no better about the arrest of her student. She chewed her lower lip, and realized she was clenching her fists. Better to do something, she decided, than to sit there and let the tension take over. She would tidy her cubicle while she waited for Lieutenant Perry to call her back. When she had done everything she could think of—taken every scrap of paper off her desk and put it either in the wastebasket or in a drawer—she realized, for her own sanity if for no other reason, that she had to stop waiting and start moving. She would go to Borough Hall—it was not far out of her way home to walk there now—and find out what was going on.

Outside, she noted that, although it was after five, it was not dark yet, and the air was definitely warmer than it had been. Spring was almost here, she thought with great relief. The winter had been terrible.

At police headquarters she asked to see Lieutenant Perry and was surprised when almost immediately he came out to the hall to meet her. He did not smile.

"Come in here," he said, opening the door to a small interview room. "I was just about to call you. I know why you're here. I had no idea this man would be in your class when we nabbed him."

"Well, he was," said McLeod. "And he's one of the best students I've ever had. What on earth is going on?"

They sat down facing each other across a table in the little interview room. McLeod liked Nick Perry. She had known him for several years, first encountering him in connection with a couple of murder investigations. They had become friends and occasionally went out to dinner or the movies, when his work allowed it. She looked at him now, taking in his bald head, his bright blue eyes, his navy blazer and gray flannel trousers.

"Popper was upset when he got back here with Billings—or Pierre, as he calls himself," Perry said. "He really hated it when he found out it was your class he would be interrupting. To answer your question, a lot is going on, McLeod. It's a very serious matter. In the first place, his name is not Gregory Pierre; it's Bob Billings. He's wanted for breaking parole in Wyoming. We'll hold him here. He'll be arraigned at Mercer County Superior Court in Trenton in a few days."

"You mean there are local charges against him? What are they?"

"Forgery, theft by deception, wrongful impersonation, and falsifying records. For starters."

"I can't believe this, Nick."

"You better believe it. It's true."

"How did he get into Princeton University if he was on parole in Wyoming? I don't understand."

"I'm not sure how he got into Princeton."

"What's going to happen to him?"

"He's going back to Wyoming and go to jail."

McLeod digested this. "Can I see him?" she asked after a pause.

Perry hesitated. "I guess so. I've been talking to him, but we need a break. I'll bring him in here and Popper will be outside."

"Thanks, Nick."

When Perry reappeared with Greg, McLeod was happy

to see that her student still wore the clothes he had had on in class. At least he wasn't in those awful orange pajama things that people seemed to wear on television when they were in police custody. She stood up and hurried toward him. "No, McLeod," said Perry. "Sit down, please."

McLeod sat. She looked at Greg, who sat down across the table from her beside Perry. It took all her strength and determination to produce what she hoped was an encouraging smile for him. She wanted to howl in despair, not smile encouragement. "How are you?" she asked. "Are you all right?"

"I guess so. It's cool of you to come here to see me."

"What on earth has happened? How did you end up here?"

"It's a long story," Greg said.

"I'm very concerned, Greg. But what is all this about? Do you have a lawyer?"

"No, I don't."

"What about your family? Is somebody coming to see about you?"

"I'm an orphan," Greg said.

Perry cleared his throat and McLeod noticed he was frowning at Greg.

Greg glanced at Perry and then looked back at McLeod. "Well," he said, "I might as well be an orphan. I don't have anything to do with my parents."

"Wouldn't it be a good idea to get in touch with them now?" asked McLeod.

"Not really," said Greg. He looked thoughtful. "You might say I'm a runaway."

"Do they know where you are?"

"At Princeton, you mean? Or here, right this minute?"

"Both."

"Actually, neither."

"Tell me what you were charged with in Wyoming," she said. "I want to know the worst."

"I was charged with possession in Jackson," Greg said. "But I didn't do it. I was framed. I know that's what every man who ever gets arrested says, but I really did get framed. And I went to jail. When I got out, I had this chance to come to Princeton. And I took it. I thought I could begin a new life after I got here. And I did. I like to run cross-country. I like my classes and I like your class especially. But I guess it's over. I'll go back to the old life."

McLeod knew very well that life wasn't fair. As her Aunt Maggie used to say, "Fair, fair—fair's in September." But it seemed extraordinarily unfair that this talented young man would have to leave Princeton and go to jail in Wyoming.

Perry stood up. "Afraid your time's up, McLeod," he said.

"Greg, do you have everything you need?" McLeod asked hurriedly, as they stood up. "Can I get you anything?"

"Nothing now, I guess, Ms. Dulaney. I'd like to have my laptop, but I don't know whether they'll let me use it or not."

"You can have a laptop," Perry said. "But no modem."

"I'll get it for you," McLeod said. "Where is your room?" They worked out the details—McLeod was to call Greg's roommate and arrange to pick up the laptop.

"I'll be happy to do that," McLeod said. "And anything else. "There must be something we can do. Besides the laptop, I mean. I'll call my friend Cowboy Tarleton, the lawyer. As I said, there must be something we can do. Truly. Do not despair. The darkest hour is before the dawn—that's something my Aunt Maggie used to say."

She reached out to shake his hand, but Perry touched her arm in warning and he shook his head. "Let's go, Billings," he said and took Greg out. Greg looked back over his shoulder as he left, smiling wanly.

McLeod waited until Perry returned. "This is dreadful, Nick. I'm very upset about this."

"I know you are. But he's trouble, McLeod. Real trouble."

"But he's a college student," said McLeod. "Can't you cut him some slack?"

"Cut him some slack?" Nick was outraged. "What about his college, his alma mater? Ask your pal George about Princeton's role in this. I have really got to get back to work. I'll see you later. We'll talk."

"All right," said McLeod wearily and left Borough Hall. As she walked down Stockton Street toward Edgehill, she thought of all the questions she wished she had had time to ask Greg. And Perry. Then she faced another dilemma: What about supper? she wondered as she reached the front door of George's house. Should she go to the grocery store? Was there anything in the house to cook? First she would call Ted Vance, Greg's roommate, and then she would call Cowboy and then she would worry about dinner. Ted Vance did not answer.

She called Cowboy Tarleton and, as she had expected, got his voice mail. Frustrated, she left a message.

Three

AS SOON AS she hung up, the phone rang. It was George. "What on earth is going on?" she demanded. "The Borough Police came to my class today and arrested my best student. I've been down to Borough Hall to see him, and Nick Perry told me to ask you about it. I'm very upset about this."

"I can tell you are," he said. "I'm ready to leave the office and I'll be right home. Is there anything there I can cook for supper?"

"I have no idea," she said. "I just walked in myself. I can't really think about dinner, George."

"Calm down," he said. "I'll go by Wild Oats and get some steaks on my way home."

"Fine," she said, and hung up the phone. Why was it so infuriating when somebody told you—very kindly—to calm down? And why did men think of steaks every time there was a crisis? As though cholesterol were a panacea?

When George came in with his big brown paper bag from Wild Oats, she followed him into the kitchen. "Tell me what is going on," she said.

"First, let's get this straight. I had no idea he was a student of yours. Not that it would have made a difference. What was done had to be done."

McLeod was about to scream at him, but he held up his hand. "Let me hang up my coat and I'll make us a drink—"

"Don't tell me to calm down again," warned McLeod.

"I'm not about to waste my breath like that," George said. "I've never seen you so exercised."

"I have seldom been so exercised," said McLeod, following him to the hall coat closet then back to the kitchen, where he quickly made two martinis. Automatically, she opened a bag of chips and put some in a bowl, then followed him into the living room.

"I'll build a fire," George said when he had handed her a martini. "I can do it in a New York minute. I'll go get some wood. And then we can talk."

McLeod, who wanted to talk instantly, before the New York minute was up, sat down and tapped her foot.

At last, with a fire blazing away, George sat down, too, drink in hand, and began to talk. "The university got a call from the police in Wyoming. They had reason to believe—"

"Wait a minute," McLeod interrupted. "Who got the call? You?"

"They called the president's office. They said they had reason to believe that a Princeton student was using a false name, that he was really Bob Billings, who was wanted for parole violations out there. Somebody in the president's office referred them to Public Safety. Sean O'Malley—the director of Public Safety—called the dean's office. The dean called the president. Tom took this very seriously and talked to me and the dean and the lawyers and some of the trustees. Well, the upshot was that we called Pierre in and talked to him. And we heard the most amazing story. We decided we had no choice but to cooperate with the Wyoming authorities and to file charges ourselves for forgery, theft by deception, wrongful impersonation, and falsifying records."

"Oh, George!"

George ignored her. "So today, it was arranged for the Borough Police to arrest him. Sean and Lieutenant Perry checked with the registrar and got Billings's class schedule, and Popper and a proctor went to get him out of class this afternoon. As I said, I had no idea that it was your class he was in this afternoon."

"But George, I don't see why the university is so full of vengeance. I think you should protect him from the Wyoming authorities—not throw him to the wolves. And certainly not file charges of your own against him. What does it matter if he got into Princeton under false pretenses? He's doing the work. And he's on the cross-country team."

"McLeod, if we protected him, as you put it, from the Wyoming authorities, we'd be guilty of obstruction of justice. And as for our own charges, the more we found out about him, the more convinced we became that he was a bad lot. He deceived Princeton thoroughly. Deceived the dean of admission, the track coach, everybody. Everything he told us about himself before he was admitted was a pack of lies."

"He's had a terrible life," said McLeod. "He seemed very open with me this afternoon. From just the little he told me, I know it's been hard for him. Alienated from his family. Framed for possession. No lawyer at his trial in Wyoming. And then when he was admitted to Princeton, he knew he had a chance at a new life. And he is a good student, George. He is a wonderful writer. I didn't notice him so much at first. I was distracted by Clark Powell and Olivia. Greg was so quiet he was easy to overlook. Then what he wrote was so good that I couldn't ignore it."

"Are you sure that he wrote it himself?"

"Of course I am." McLeod was indignant. "Are you accusing him of plagiarism along with everything else?"

"It wouldn't surprise me at all."

"It would surprise me a great deal if he plagiarized his very good article on the track coach." McLeod sat with her back very stiff and one eyebrow raised in a look of scorn.

"A lot has been written about Spike Lilly. Maybe you should do a Nexus search to make sure Billings didn't pick up his article from some newspaper or magazine."

"George, I certainly will check it out. But I don't believe for a minute he stole it. I saw his first draft, and he had a notebook full of notes."

"Maybe I'm wrong about that article," said George. "But check. I'm sorry you're so upset about this. I'll go cook supper. Sit here and simmer for a while and then maybe you'll cool down." He smiled at her as he left for the kitchen.

"I'll simmer, but I don't think I'll cool down," she said. "Oh, I'll come make the salad." If she didn't make the salad, supper would be pure cholesterol, no doubt.

"Good," said George. "I bought an avocado."

They were silent as they worked in the kitchen, George broiling steaks and reheating baked potatoes he had bought, McLeod making a salad and setting the table in the dining room.

When they sat down to eat, George poured wine from a bottle of Bordeaux into their glasses. "That's good," McLeod said when she sipped the wine.

"I got it out because I thought it might cheer you up," George said.

"And divert me?"

"Well, that, too."

"But I can't be diverted. All I can do is worry about Greg Pierre."

"You know his name is not really Greg Pierre?" said George.

"I know. Nick Perry told me. Is that what upsets Princeton? That he used a false name?"

"It's one of the things," said George. "You know he was in jail in Wyoming and got out on parole and broke parole?"

"He told me he wasn't guilty, that he was framed. I can see why he would grab at the chance to start a new life and get out of Wyoming, parole or no parole."

"They all say they were framed," said George.

"Maybe they do," said McLeod, "but I'm willing to believe Greg. He certainly doesn't use drugs now. He couldn't, could he, and run track and keep up with his classes, and look trim and neat?"

"Beside the point. He's got more nerve than anybody I

ever heard of. He actually got admitted to Princeton before his trial. When he was convicted and sent to jail, he had the nerve to write to the Admission Office and ask for a deferment."

"Did he say why?" asked McLeod.

"He said his mother was dying in Utah and he wanted to look after her. Said they had been estranged and now he owed it to her to stay with her. And the dean of admission granted the deferment!"

McLeod laughed out loud. She couldn't help it. It was so outrageous, so clever, so brave. She admired Greg Pierre. "That's wonderful," she said, wiping her eyes with her napkin. "I love it."

"Laugh if you must," said George. "Think it's wonderful, if you want to. We think it's deplorable."

"But how did he get caught? How did they know where he was?"

"Somebody from Wyoming recognized him here and called his old track coach at Wyoming and told him Bob Billings was at Princeton. Under an assumed name. Somebody in the coach's office knew about the trial and conviction and got busy and called the newspaper. The newspaper called the district attorney, and he called us."

"So it's all out now," said McLeod.

"I'm afraid so," said George.

"Nothing can be done now?"

"Nothing," said George. "The wheels of justice are turning."

"I see," said McLeod, and tried to give her full attention to the steak and the salad, rich with avocado and Roquefort cheese.

But after supper, she climbed the stairs to her room and sat down in the comfortable little wing chair and thought about her student. If he hadn't been in jail and had not broken parole, the university wouldn't be so upset about false names and all the other stuff. And she believed Greg when he said he was innocent of the original charge. No matter what George said.

She hated to see George acting the role of the Avenging

Angel. She liked George. They had had a brief romantic fling when McLeod was teaching at Princeton for a semester a few years before. This term, she was his sedate front room boarder. They shared a very amicable existence, with George occasionally going out with other women and McLeod seeing Nick Perry when Nick had time for her. This was the first occasion on which she had ever disagreed with George on a university matter. There had never been anything before that she could disagree with him about—he was really such a bright, levelheaded man that he did an admirable job, she thought, as vice president for public affairs.

Oh, well, nobody could be right all the time, and this time she thought he was wrong. The thing to do was to get Greg cleared of that charge in Wyoming. But how to do that? She had been to Wyoming once, to Jackson, and had thought the Jackson Hole area and the Grand Teton mountains beautiful beyond compare. But what had that to do with all this? She didn't even know where in Wyoming Greg had lived, much less where the trial had been.

Tomorrow, she would get his laptop and take it over to Borough Hall and demand to see Greg again. Then she would get details out of him. And she would talk to Cowboy Tarleton.

Then she remembered to call Greg's roommate again. It was late to call anybody else, anybody but a student, that is. Students were late to bed and late to rise. Sure enough, Ted Vance sounded wide awake when he answered the phone.

She introduced herself and told him about Greg and where he was. "I knew something was up," Ted said.

She asked him where she could meet him to pick up Greg's laptop, but Ted told her not to worry. "I'll take it to him now, if that's okay. Tomorrow, if it's not okay tonight," Ted said.

He sounded like a very nice boy, McLeod thought. A little disappointed that she wouldn't meet him—she wanted to ask him questions about Greg—she explained where the police department was at Borough Hall. She told him to ask for Lieutenant Perry and to call her if he had any problem with his errand. She gave him her office phone number, as well as her home phone, and went to sleep feeling that she had accomplished one tiny thing—and enormous tasks lay ahead.

Four

FRIDAY MORNING, MCLEOD was up early, but not as early as George, who had left for the university by the time she came downstairs. She called Greg's roommate—she knew it was too early to call a student, but she also knew that an early hour was a good time to catch a student in his room, even if he was asleep.

Sure enough, Ted sounded groggy from sleep when he finally answered his phone, but he tried his best to be polite when he found out it was a member of the faculty. Yes, he said, he had delivered the laptop the night before and been given a receipt. No, he had not seen Greg.

"Does Greg really sleep on the floor?" McLeod could not stop herself from asking this.

"What?" Ted asked. "Oh. I get it. No, not anymore. He said he did when he first came his freshman year because he was used to sleeping outdoors. But he's been sleeping in his bed this year."

(So it had been true that Greg used to sleep on the floor, McLeod thought.)

"What's going to happen to him, Ms. Dulaney?" Ted continued.

"I don't know," she said. "I want to get him a lawyer." Then she added on impulse, "Can you meet me for lunch, Ted? I'd like to know more about Greg."

"What's today? Friday? I guess so." Ted did not sound enthusiastic, but agreed to meet her at the student center at noon.

When she hung up, she made some tea and toast and ate breakfast while she read the newspapers. *The Times*, the Trenton paper, had no story about Greg's arrest, she was happy to see. Finally, after she had attempted, fruitlessly, to do the Friday crossword in *The New York Times*, it was nine o'clock and time to call Cowboy Tarleton.

When he came on the phone, McLeod told him about Greg Pierre and his plight and asked if Cowboy could represent him. "He's a student," she said, "and he has no money."

Cowboy said he was sorry, but he had no time to take on another pro bono case right now. "But it's so unfair," McLeod said. "He's a good student."

"You've had him in class?" asked Cowboy.

"I have him in class this semester, and he's very good," she said.

"Look, I just don't see how I can do it, McLeod, but I'll try to get by there today somehow. And I'll tell you if there's anything that can be done at this point."

McLeod had to leave it at that. She decided she would go back to Borough Hall and see if she could talk to Greg again. She went upstairs and dressed—it was a day to dress in something that would cheer her up. Since it was warmer, she would wear a skirt, for a change, instead of long pants. Accordingly, she put on a gray flannel skirt and a blue sweater she had knitted years before. It made her feel quite springlike, even with a warm jacket topping it all off.

NICK DID ALLOW her to see Greg briefly. Sergeant Popper sat with them this time and Greg seemed to be more relaxed around him than he was with Nick. He thanked

McLeod for calling Ted and said that since he had been re-united with his laptop, he had been working on his paper for her class.

"Do you need any books for any other classes?" she asked.

Ted was going to drop them off today, he said.

"Good," said McLeod. "George Bridges told me something about what happened to you. But I don't understand how you got into Princeton if you were on parole," she said.

"It's wild," he said. "I got in Princeton before I was on parole. As I told you, I was pretty much on my own. My father walked out on my mother and me when I was a baby. She was a drunk and on drugs, and I always knew if I wanted to have half a life, I had to manage my life myself."

"Did you still live with your mother?"

"I lived in the house or the apartment with her, but I hustled from the time I was in elementary school. I got odd jobs. I had paper routes. I had to hide my money from my mother or she would have spent it on drugs or alcohol, and I needed the money for school supplies and for lunches and occasionally a decent pair of jeans."

McLeod listened, appalled.

"I was lucky," Greg went on. "In middle school I went out for track because I liked the words 'long-distance running.' It sounded romantic. Like I could run away from my awful life with my mother. And it turned out I was pretty good at running. In high school the coach took an interest in me, and one time I lived with him and his family for a while. And I was good at English, and an English teacher took an interest in me. Between them, they got me a full scholarship to the University of Wyoming."

"So you've been to college already?" asked McLeod. "No wonder you're such a good student."

"I didn't finish," said Greg. "I was ambitious. Wyoming was just a taste of what I wanted. I wanted to be the best runner in the world, and I wanted to be a writer. I knew that long-distance runners are at their best when they're in their late twenties, after college age. So I dropped out of Wyoming and I got a job on a ranch where I could run all I wanted to and I read a lot and I learned to live outdoors. And after a couple of years, I applied to Ivy League schools."

"You didn't apply just to Princeton?"

"Oh, no. I explained on my applications that I grew up in a commune in Utah, and I said I didn't have a transcript since I had not gone to high school. I did well on the SATs and on the achievement tests, though—I'm good at tests. I told them in my applications about my running speeds, and Princeton flew me here for an interview with the Admission Office and with the track coach. Their best runner took me out running and I was faster than he was. The upshot was they admitted me. Ms. Dulaney, I thought I had died and gone to heaven. And then I got arrested."

"What were you arrested for?" McLeod asked.

"For possession."

"Possession of what?" asked McLeod. "What kind of drugs? Marijuana, crack, cocaine, heroin?"

"Ms. Dulaney, I'm impressed with your knowledge of drugs."

"Thanks," said McLeod, "but what was it?"

"It was methamphetamine. Crystal meth, and the stuff for making it. I kept telling everybody that I didn't know how the stuff got there. It was the truth, and I thought somebody would believe me, but they didn't. I was convicted and sent to jail for six months. So I wrote Princeton and asked to defer my admission."

"Did you tell them why?" McLeod thought she would like to hear Greg's version of this part of his story.

"Not likely," said Greg. He went on to tell a story substantially the same as the one George had told her last night. "I told them my mother was dying and that I wanted to take the year off to stay with her in Utah and look after her. They granted the deferment. And so I went to jail and then got out on parole and I came to Princeton."

"Was your mother dying?" asked McLeod, just to make sure.

"I don't know. I really haven't been in touch with her for some time."

"When did you change your name?"

"That was when I decided to apply to Ivy League schools. I was afraid if I used my real name, old SAT scores and track records might surface and they wouldn't take me. They don't want older students who have already been to college."

"Now tell me about the Wyoming charge—the one you were framed for," said McLeod.

"Time's up," said Popper.

McLeod stood up. "Oh, yes, a lawyer named Cowboy Tarleton is going to try to get by to see you," said McLeod. "He's a good sort."

"Thanks, Ms. Dulaney. I don't have any money, you know."

"He won't charge for this visit," said McLeod. "Tell him everything."

"Okay. Thanks," said Greg, leaving with Popper. He looked very docile as he went out.

McLeod was shaken by the story. By and large, she preferred honesty. A straightforward, truth-telling person was what she liked to deal with. The kind of prevaricating that Greg did was outside her experience. She tried to think of it as something like a sitcom on television in its cheerful mendacity. The nerve of it! Last night it had made her laugh out loud. And today it was still, well, remarkable.

Greg had had a hard life. He had been tough and clever enough not only to survive, but to get himself out of a rotten situation and into Princeton. If he had had to cook up a few fantasies along the way, was that so bad?

She knew what George would say: "You don't know that he's telling the truth about his mother. She might be the nicest woman in the world." But somehow McLeod thought Greg had not made that up about his mother.

WHEN SHE MET Ted for lunch at the Frist Center, he said he had not seen Greg when he went back to Borough Hall. "They said he was with his lawyer," said Ted. "I didn't know he had a lawyer."

"He doesn't really. That was Cowboy Tarleton, a friend of mine, who said he'd try to drop by and see Greg. I'm glad he got there," McLeod said. "I think I'll go get a salad." Frist operated like a food court, where people went to different areas to get different kinds of food. Ted said he'd get a burger. "I'll come pay for it," said McLeod. "My treat."

Finally, they had full trays and sat down at a small table. "Tell me about yourself," said McLeod. "Where are you from and what are you majoring in and what do you want to do when you get out of Princeton?" McLeod's curiosity about people was unquenchable, and even though she had set up this lunch so she could ask Ted about Greg, she still wanted to know about Ted.

"I'm your typical preppie," said Ted. "I grew up in Greenwich, Connecticut, and I went to Andover and now I'm at Princeton. I'm majoring in the Woodrow Wilson School, and I want to be secretary of state when I grow up."

"Well, that's quite impressive," she said. The Woodrow Wilson School taught politics and policy and public affairs. "Good luck." She took a bite of salad. "That's quite a different background from Greg Pierre's."

"Couldn't be more different," said Ted cheerfully. "We fascinate each other. He's from the West, an outdoorsman, a long-distance runner. I'm an effete Easterner. I play hockey."

"How did you meet?" asked McLeod.

"Last spring during bicker," Ted said.

Bicker, McLeod knew, was the rush season for Princeton's eating clubs for upperclassmen.

"We both joined Ivy," Ted continued.

McLeod was impressed. Ivy was perhaps Princeton's most exclusive eating club. Ted pressed on. "Ivy was pursuing the chimera of diversity, and a Western wild man was just what they needed. No, that's not fair to Greg. I'm just being pompous and Eastern. A record-breaking track star from the West with good grades to boot was a plum for them. I got in because I was a legacy."

"A legacy?"

"My father and my grandfather were both Ivy," he said.

McLeod had begun to like Ted immensely. "Did you know anything about his, er, history?" she asked.

"I did not. I was hoping you would tell me."

"I can tell you what little I learned from George Bridges—the vice president—who is a friend of mine. Lieutenant Perry at the Borough Police told me a little. And Greg has told me more." She told Ted everything she knew.

"But what was the crime that got him in jail? What was it exactly?" Ted asked after she had explained Greg's history.

"Possession," McLeod said. "Methamphetamine. He insists he was framed. But I don't understand why that wasn't revealed at the trial in Wyoming. As smart as Greg is, it does seem he could have found a way to prove his innocence."

"Yeah," said Ted. "That's the puzzle."

"Maybe I can talk to Cowboy Tarleton—the lawyer who went by to see Greg today—this afternoon."

"Is he going to represent Greg?"

"He does a lot of pro bono work, but he said he couldn't take on another pro bono case right now. He's good. I wish Greg or I or somebody had the money to hire him."

"Maybe the money can be found," said Ted vaguely.

McLeod looked at him sharply. Was he indicating that he might know where the money might come from? She didn't know. She could only hope.

"Is his name really Cowboy?"

"Everybody calls him that," said McLeod.

Ted, who had finished his hamburger and Coke, stood up, and thanked her for lunch. "I'm meeting my folks at the airport—we're going to St. John for spring break."

They parted, promising to keep in touch. "But try not to call me so early in the morning," Ted said, smiling as he said it. McLeod laughed and agreed to mend her ways.

Five

❧

COWBOY TARLETON CALLED her later at her office. "McLeod, I'm sorry, but I don't see how we can do anything. Pierre—or Billings—violated patrol. The state of Wyoming has issued a fugitive warrant for him."

"But what if he was innocent of the original charge?" asked McLeod. "He says he was, and I believe him."

"McLeod, he pleaded guilty."

"Pleaded guilty? In Wyoming?"

"He did. He was sentenced to six months and got out early on parole. But then he left the state."

"Well, this is a surprise."

"He told me a song and dance about protecting a friend, but the fact remains that he pleaded guilty and got a very light sentence."

McLeod was baffled. "Thanks a million, Cowboy. I owe you a lot. Will you come to dinner sometime? I'd love to cook some Southern food for you." McLeod had lived most of her life in Tallahassee, and shamelessly exploited her background when she thought it would be helpful.

"Sounds good to me, as long as it's not grits," said Cowboy.

"No grits," she promised. Why didn't Northerners like grits? she wondered. Personally, she thought her cheese grits casserole had no peer. She hung up the phone, and sat in her cubicle. Greg Pierre's case was complicated, to say the least. But she reminded herself of Aunt Maggie's axiom that the darkest hour is before the dawn.

She decided to check out Greg's very good profile of Spike Lilly, the track coach, and called up Nexus on the computer. George was right—a lot had been written about Spike Lilly. After several hours of looking at hundreds of articles, she felt confident that Greg's work was original, as well as better written than many of the professional profiles. With that settled, she felt renewed zeal to help her student.

Could she possibly get in again to see Greg? she wondered. Well, she could only try. It would be better to appear at Borough Hall in person, she thought, than to telephone for permission. Accordingly, she took care of all the chores—e-mails and voice mail messages and snail mail—and much later than she had intended, set out again for Borough Hall.

Nick Perry looked none too pleased to see her, she thought, when he led her to the interview room. "What do you want to talk to him about?" he asked her. "You saw him this morning. He needs a receptionist. Cowboy Tarleton came to see him, and I let his roommate in for a little while just now."

"I talked to Cowboy and I need some information from Greg before I can really start to work to clear him of the Wyoming charge," she said.

"Clear him of the Wyoming charge? You'll have your work cut out for you there, McLeod."

"I know he pleaded guilty," she said. "But he says he wasn't guilty, and I believe him."

"Then why did he plead?"

"That's what I want to find out," McLeod said reasonably. "To protect a friend? To get a lighter sentence? Why?"

"Oh, all right," said Nick. "Regard me as his social secretary. I'll bring him in."

He returned with Greg, and they all sat down around the table. Greg had been in jail only twenty-four hours, and he already seemed much paler. He looked older, too. Well, who wouldn't? she wondered.

"Greg, I'm very much on your side," said McLeod. "I want to see you out of here and back in class. If we can get rid of the original Wyoming charge, I'm sure they'd drop the fugitive charges. Please tell me why you pled guilty to the possession charge in Wyoming."

Greg was quiet a long time. He looked from McLeod to Nick Perry and back to McLeod. "Can I tell you in confidence?" he asked. He turned to Perry. "Can you promise me you won't use what I say against anybody?"

"You mean yourself?"

"No, I mean against anybody at all."

"Yes, I promise," said Nick. "That seems safe enough. As long as you talk about the Wyoming charges, that's not my affair."

"Word of honor?" asked Greg.

"Don't be childish," said Perry. "I've told you."

"Oh, all right," said Greg. "I don't have a lot of clout—or even credibility, I know. Anyway, what happened was the classic plot. You know: The friend asks you to keep a package and the cops come and the package is full of contraband and you get busted. In this case, it was a knapsack, with stuff in it."

"Come on," said Perry. "I swore I wouldn't say anything, but I can't help it. You don't expect us to—"

"No, I don't expect you to believe it," said Greg. "I don't expect anybody to ever believe anything I say again. But let me tell you about it. It was a girl. A girl I liked a lot.

"I was working on this ranch that summer, and I slept outdoors most of the time. I loved it. She used to come out to see me sometimes. And sometimes she spent the night. She liked to sleep outdoors, too. There was an old pickup truck parked out there—it had a cover on the back—and I could keep stuff in there, and if the weather was bad, I could sleep in it.

"So one day she was out there and she spent the night and the next morning she was getting ready to leave, and I said, 'Don't forget your pack,' and she said, 'Can I leave it here for a while?' and I said, 'Sure, but why?' And she said, 'I think my roommate is stealing some of my stuff, and I put my mother's locket and some books in there, and I'd love to leave it someplace safe.' So I said, 'Cool.' And she left."

"Did it feel like it had books in it?" McLeod asked.

"I didn't even touch it," Greg said. "It didn't matter to me. I just left it in the truck." He paused, and stared at McLeod before he sighed and went back to his story. "Then the next day somebody from the sheriff's office came, and they had a search warrant. That was pretty funny if you think about it. All I had was a sleeping bag and a little food and a gasoline stove. Anyway, they found the knapsack. And they went through it and it had ephedrine inhalers and all this stuff for making ice."

"Ice?" said McLeod.

"Crystal," said Nick Perry. "Or meth. Whatever. Methamphetamine. It's the drug of choice these days—especially in the Northwest. It's easy to make, and the whole laboratory for making it can fit in a suitcase—or a knapsack." Perry turned to Greg "And you had a camp stove to use."

"Yeah, I know. But so help me, I had never used it for making ice. I told the sheriff's men that, and told them somebody had left it there. They asked who left it, but I wouldn't tell them who. They arrested me and took me to jail. I still didn't want to incriminate the girl. I liked her a lot. I didn't know what was going on, but I knew I couldn't rat on her. I kept thinking she'd turn up and clear it all up, but she didn't. It went on and on. Finally they persuaded me to plead guilty and get a light sentence, so I did."

"How old were you at the time?" asked McLeod.

"Twenty-five," said Greg. "I wasn't a juvenile, if that's what you're getting at."

"You never told them who left the knapsack?" asked McLeod.

"I never told anybody."

"Don't you think it's time you did?" asked McLeod.

"You may be right," Greg said. "My life seems to be thoroughly fucked up right now."

"Who fucked it up?" asked Nick Perry. "You did, that's who."

McLeod and Greg both stared at him. "You said you wouldn't—" McLeod began, and Nick said, "I know. I said I wouldn't say anything. Go on, Billings."

McLeod had to admire Nick. He was a police officer, and this was his turf. She had no right to reprimand him but he had taken it well. He was really a nice guy. She turned back to Greg. "Well, who was she?"

Greg gazed into space for what seemed a long time before he spoke. "Isabel was her name," he said, looking directly at McLeod. "Isabel Pittman."

"Tell me about her," said McLeod.

"She was a really cool girl," said Greg. "Like I said, I liked her a lot. I guess you might say I was in love with her. I really thought she would turn up and get me out of the mess I was in. " He looked wistful—sad, McLeod thought. For a young man who had clawed his own way out of one life and into another, he was incredibly naive.

"Could you get in touch with her now?" asked McLeod.

"I don't know how."

"Don't you know anything about her?"

"Not much," said Greg.

"How did you meet her?"

"Oh, around Jackson. She was working there for the summer. She had a job in the Million Dollar Cowboy Bar—that's the famous one that has saddles on the bar stools."

"You mean the customers sit in saddles at the bar?" asked McLeod, fascinated.

"That's right," said Greg.

"I'd love to see that," said McLeod. "Greg, you must know something about her. Did she use drugs?"

"I guess so. Everybody did." He paused. "Everybody but me. I never could afford them. And I had to work too hard. I didn't dare."

"Was she from that area?"

"I don't think so. She said she went to the University of Texas—you know, in Austin."

"Okay, that's something. That was a couple of years ago—right?" said McLeod.

"Right."

"Isabel Pittman—that's her name? You don't have an address of any kind?"

"Nope."

"Give me the names of some people you knew in Jackson," said McLeod.

"I didn't know anybody," said Greg. "I mean, not really."

"You must have known some people that knew Isabel. Some of them might know where she is now."

"I don't want anybody to know I'm a rat fink," said Greg.

"You're not a rat fink," said McLeod. "There's no honor code in the world that says you have to go to jail so you don't betray somebody who deliberately planted drug paraphernalia on you."

"I guess that's one way to put it," said Greg. "It has taken me a long time to see it that way. But I guess you're right. Okay. Mark Bloom might know. I think he's still there. He worked for this ranch . . ."He talked on, but in the end could give McLeod only two names with vague addresses.

That was all McLeod had to go on when Nick Perry called a halt to the visit. "I've stretched the rules as it is," he said.

"Well, goodbye, Greg. I'll see what I can do. I'm a pretty fair researcher. Keep your chin up. We'll do something."

Greg did not look too hopeful as Nick led him away.

Six

❦

"LOOKS GOOD," SAID Nick when he came back to see her in the little interview room.

"Looks good? I don't see much chance of finding Isabel Pittman and getting her to clear Greg," said McLeod. "I'm glad you think it looks good."

"I meant it looks good for law enforcement," said Nick.

McLeod hated the way he was grinning. "That's cruel," she said. "But never mind. 'The wheels of justice grind slowly, but they grind exceeding fine.'"

"Yeah," said Nick. "What are you going to do?"

"I'm going to Jackson," said McLeod.

"WHAT DO YOU mean, you're going to Jackson? You must be insane." This was George Bridges at home that night.

McLeod was in the process of stir-frying scallops with onions and sweet red peppers. She stared at the skillet, and spoke slowly and distinctly. "I am not insane," she said. "This kid is innocent and I want to clear him of all these charges."

"In the first place, he is not a kid, and he is not innocent. He did defraud the university."

"Oh, that," said McLeod. "I'm talking about the drug charge. If it hadn't been for that, none of this would have come up."

"But it did come up," said George.

"I'm still going to try to clear him. Look, these scallops are done. Let me stir in the walnuts. Is the rice ready?"

"The rice is ready. The salad's on the table. Shall we serve the plates in here?"

"Yes. We can eat. And I'm hungry."

They carried heaping plates into the dining room and sat down. George poured wine from a chilled bottle of pinot grigio and they ate.

"Would you like more?" asked McLeod, when she had cleaned her plate.

"I think I will," said George, getting up. "And I'll put on the coffee while I'm in there."

It was while they were drinking coffee in front of the living room fire that George brought up her trip. "Why are you doing this?" he asked. "I don't understand."

"Because I feel like I must. He's my student. He's good. And he has no one else to take up his cause. Besides, I'd like to get my hands on that Isabel Pittman and strangle her."

"Don't do that. Then I'd have to go to Wyoming and I don't have time," said George.

McLeod smiled. "That's nice of you, George."

"You're my front room boarder," said George. "I have to make sure you can pay your rent."

"Thanks. I think I'll go call and see if I can get a reservation tomorrow."

When she got off the phone, George had gone upstairs, and she plodded up to find him. "Well, I don't know what to do," she said, as she stood in the open door of his study. "I'm afraid I can't go. I can't even get a reservation to Jackson until Monday, and then the fare would be eleven hundred dollars. I can't get a cheap fare—and the cheap fare's not cheap, really—

for three weeks. And time is of the essence. I really
don't know what to do. If I go Monday, I'll only have
Tuesday and Wednesday to poke around. I have to be
back by Thursday."

"Well, you'll know you did your best," said George.

"How much would it cost to hire a private detective?"
she asked.

"Too much," said George.

"I guess so," said McLeod, and went sadly to her room.

WHEN SHE WENT to bed, she was still worrying about
her student. Just before she went to sleep, she had a great
idea. Why hadn't she thought of it before? Lyle Cramer.
He was a former student of hers. And he had just moved
to Salt Lake City to work for the newspaper there. Wasn't
Utah right next to Wyoming? She got out of bed and, at-
tired in her fuzzy slippers and woolly bathrobe, padded
into George's study to find the atlas. Yes, Salt Lake City
wasn't right next to Jackson, but it looked like an easy
drive. She would call Lyle. He had been in the first class
she had taught at Princeton, and had helped bring a murder to light and the murderer to justice. He had just gone
to Salt Lake City as a reporter. She looked at her watch—
eleven o'clock. But it was earlier out there in the West
than it was on the East Coast. Wasn't it three hours earlier? Only eight o'clock? She didn't have Lyle's telephone
number but he might still be at work. She padded downstairs to call him.

Lyle was indeed still at the newspaper and his usual
cheerful self, although it was nine o'clock in Utah, not
eight. "We're only two hours behind you," he explained.
"But that's all right—I was just about to leave. I'm glad
you called. What's up?"

McLeod told him about Greg. It took a while.

"That's awesome," Lyle said. "I mean that he could get
into Princeton when he was on trial for possession."

"I know. And Lyle, he's good. He really is. I can't let

him get kicked out of Princeton and sent back to face jail in Wyoming."

"I can see that. What can I do?" This was what McLeod had hoped for—that Lyle would be impressed with Greg's daring and interested in helping him.

"Can you see if you can find this girl—Isabel Pittman? Maybe she will realize what she's done to Greg and will take responsibility for her actions."

"Yeah, and maybe hell will freeze over tomorrow."

"Well, you never know. It's worth a try, don't you think?"

"I guess so. And I'm off work tomorrow and Monday. Where is she now?"

"That's the problem. I don't know. Greg doesn't know. She was working in Jackson two years ago. Oh, and he gave me a couple of names of people he knew up there— Mark Bloom was one." She fished out her notebook and gave him the other.

"Oho. This is easy. One woman somewhere in the world. Two names of people who might have known her. And I'm in Salt Lake City, not exactly the hub of the universe."

"But it's close to Jackson, isn't it?"

"Ninety miles, more or less."

"I didn't realize it would be that far."

"Let me see what I can find on the telephone," said Lyle. "I'll let you know if I think it's worth a trip to Jackson."

"Okay. Oh, Lyle, Greg Pierre's name used to be Bob Billings."

"What?" Lyle was almost screaming, so McLeod had to explain about the name change. That took more time.

"I have to say this is intriguing," Lyle said. "But I think I'm stupid to get involved in this."

"It's not stupid to help right a wrong," said McLeod. "You know what a good deed in a naughty world does?"

"What?"

"It *shines*."

"Okay. I'll call you tomorrow if I decide to go."

"Thanks, Lyle."

Lyle didn't wait until Saturday to call. Before McLeod could get upstairs to bed, the phone rang. It was Lyle calling to say he couldn't resist her. He would leave for Jackson early the next morning. McLeod went to bed and slept very soundly, confident that everything would work out. Sure.

Seven

LATE SATURDAY NIGHT McLeod was on her way upstairs to go to bed when the phone rang. George answered it downstairs. "It's for you," he said, looking up the stairs to make sure she heard him.

"Who's calling me at midnight?" she said.

"Pick up in my study if you like," George said.

It was Lyle, calling from the West, where it was only ten o'clock. Things did not look so good, he said. "I'm in Jackson. I got on the phone this morning and I found a deputy who had worked on the methamphetamine case. So I drove up here. But it's not very promising. The deputy said they never understood Billings. They almost believed him when he said the ephedrine and stuff wasn't his, but they went ahead and charged him and thought he would crack and give them some names, but he never would. He even pleaded guilty. They thought he was protecting somebody but they weren't sure who. Blah, blah, blah."

"Oh, dear," said McLeod.

"Yeah, I know. It looks bleak."

"Did you find any trace of Isabel Pittman?"

"Not a shred. Nor of those other names you gave me. I even went by the Million Dollar Cowboy Bar to look for Isabel Pittman."

"How was it?"

"Well, they do have saddles for seats on the bar stools, but nobody remembered Isabel Pittman."

"I'm sorry, Lyle. A wild-goose chase. But thanks a million."

"Oh, well. I always wanted to see the Grand Tetons. I'll stick around tomorrow and go back home tomorrow night. I may drive up to Yellowstone tomorrow."

"Have a great time. At least you'll see more of the Wild West."

"That's right. The Wild West is all over the place. I'm staying in a motel that has individual log cabins for rooms. The Episcopal church is made of logs. Did you know Wyoming has a bucking bronco on its license plates?"

"I did not. Amazing," said McLeod.

"You'll have to come out and see the wonders of the West," said Lyle.

"I'd love to. Keep in touch." McLeod hung up the phone. When George appeared in the door, she told him the depressing news. "I thought it was a wild-goose chase," he said.

"Sometimes a wild-goose chase turns up pretty good foie gras," said McLeod.

"That's a real bon mot," said George. "Good night. Sleep tight."

McLeod lay awake for some time trying to think of a new tack to take, with no success.

The next morning she made waffles for breakfast, which pleased George no end, but did not soften his heart toward Greg Pierre. Full of waffles and strawberry jam, she decided to go to church. If man could not help Greg, maybe God would, and she trudged off to Nassau Presbyterian Church, where, alas, she failed to find an answer to her fervent prayer for Greg's exoneration.

• • •

AS SHE CAME in the front door at home, George appeared at the top of the stairway and said, "Lyle Cramer called. He said for you to call him right back. Here's the number."

"Thanks. Maybe he found something." She hung up her coat and hat, and made for the phone in the kitchen.

"Well, McLeod, you got the answer to your prayer," he said. "It was in the newspaper this morning. I don't suppose it made the papers in the East."

"What about?" said McLeod, confused.

"It's all over the Casper *Star-Tribune*," said Lyle.

"What is?"

"Isabel Pittman has found God. She has become a born-again Christian and has confessed to any number of things, but especially working with a group that made and sold methamphetamine a few years ago. But it's not just that. What she feels worst about is letting somebody else take the blame. She came up here to clear Bob Billings, she says."

"For heaven's sake, there is a God," said McLeod. "Talk about the answer to a prayer. It really is. I prayed about it in church this morning. How did you know?"

"Oh, you always pray," said Lyle. "I remember."

"Well, are they dropping the charges against Greg, or Bob, whoever?" asked McLeod.

"The prosecutor says they'll investigate."

"That means time, doesn't it?"

"That's right. I'm not going to Yellowstone. I'm going to see if I can talk to the prosecutor. This is a good story for me in Salt Lake City. I've already talked to my editor. I'll let you know how it goes. So thanks, really, for sending me up here."

He read her the entire news story about Isabel Pittman and they marveled again at the timing of it all.

"It's just too good to be true," McLeod said. She hung up the phone and went to look for George, who was coming down the stairs. Even after she told him the news, George was skeptical. But he reluctantly agreed that the university might reconsider the case against Greg Pierre if it turned out he was indeed innocent of all charges and that there was a good reason for the deception and false identity.

"Meanwhile, he sits down there in jail," said McLeod. "He should be back in his classes."

"Well, it's spring break," George pointed out.

"You know, I forgot it was spring break. Maybe I should go to Wyoming, after all."

"Don't be silly," said George. "It would cost the earth. And aren't you going to New Haven this week?"

"That's right. I forgot about Harry."

McLeod's son, Harry, a perennial graduate student in the history of art at Yale, was, finally, near the end of the long, hard trail to a Ph.D. He was supposed to defend his dissertation on Thursday, and McLeod was going up for the defense and the party afterward.

"How could I forget?" she asked. "I thought it was so unlucky that they scheduled it on a Thursday when I had a class, and then I realized it was the Thursday of spring break week. Oh, I'm so excited about Harry. How could I have forgotten him?"

"You got distracted by Billings/Pierre," said George.

"And he's still on my mind. I've got to go to Borough Hall and tell him about Isabel Pittman."

"Eat some lunch. We have some good stuff for sandwiches. And I opened a can of tomato soup."

"Your favorite," said McLeod. "Great."

"Want to go over to Lambertville for dinner when you get back from visiting the prisoner?"

"Sure," said McLeod.

Greg had a hard time grasping McLeod's news. The fact that he was probably about to be cleared seemed to be eclipsed by Isabel's motivation. "She got religion?" he kept asking. "Isabel?"

"That's what Lyle said the paper said."

"It just seems so unlike her," said Greg. "She had great contempt for churches. And religion. And anything spiritual. Anything supernatural, really."

"Be glad she changed her mind," said McLeod.

"I am," said Greg. "I am. Believe me. But it will take a long time for the effects to reach me, I'm afraid."

"I'm afraid so, too. Nick Perry's not here today. I'm anxious to see what he's going to say about this development."

She did not stay long, but hurried back home very soon.

Eight

❧

MCLEOD WENT TO New Haven on Wednesday, taking her time on the drive. She wanted to have a full day on Thursday so she could visit the Yale Art Gallery and the Center for British Art before Harry's defense. And she wanted to see Harry on Wednesday night when he wouldn't be surrounded by friends and colleagues.

It all worked out very nicely. Harry looked radiant when he came to her motel. He was tall and, she thought, handsome, and his hair, like hers, was turning white far earlier than it should. It didn't bother Harry.

"It makes people take me more seriously, and girls think it's romantic," he said, when she commented on it.

"I always found it an advantage because it made people talk more freely to me when I interviewed them for the newspaper," she said.

They went for dinner at a seafood restaurant out by the Sound. "Did you know Rosie's coming tomorrow?" asked Harry.

"I didn't know. That's wonderful." Rosie was McLeod's daughter, who worked for a newspaper in Charlotte, North

Carolina. She and Harry were only thirteen months apart
and had always been very close.

"She can't get here for the defense, but she'll come to
the party at Mory's afterward."

"That's wonderful. She's very fond of you."

"Likewise," said Harry.

"And I'm very proud of you," McLeod said. "You've
stuck to it."

"And stuck to it and stuck to it and stuck to it. It's taken
forever. I know you've been worried about me."

"But you've been self-supporting for the last few years,
what with teaching and all," McLeod said. "I just feared
that you weren't leading a real life. Graduate students are
insulated in a way from the real world."

"The Ivory Tower?"

"Something like that. Anyway, I'm proud of you."

"I may even have a job," said Harry. "I mean a real job."

"Really? I thought you didn't really go on the job market until January."

"I don't. But actually, my advisers seem to think highly
of me. And one of them has recommended me to USC for
a one-year post."

"USC?" McLeod was almost screeching. "But that's in
California!"

"That's right. The University of Southern California is
indeed in California."

"But that's three thousand miles away."

"Planes fly it all the time."

"I know. I'm sorry. That's great—to have a job right
away, isn't it? What would you be doing?"

"It's not tenure track or anything. It's only a one-year
appointment as an instructor, but I'd be teaching. I'd have
to teach the introductory art history course, and I'd get to
teach a course on medieval architecture."

"Your specialty," said McLeod.

"Yes, they have a very strong presence in European art
and they need a medievalist in a hurry. It's for only one
year—even so, I'll be very happy if I get the job."

"Let's keep our fingers crossed," said McLeod, deciding privately that she would not just keep her fingers crossed, but would pray for Harry and his job. Her apparent success in the prayer line where Greg Pierre was concerned had gone to her head.

Reminded of Greg, she said, "Let me tell you about my student. The police came into my classroom last Thursday and arrested him . . ." And she told the whole tale.

"That's the most amazing thing I've ever heard," said Harry. "This girl got religion and confessed all."

"That's right," said McLeod. "It was a miracle."

"You and your students. A former student saves the day for a current student. So he applied for Princeton when he had a jail sentence hanging over his head."

"He did," said McLeod. "And he changed his identity and got in without high school transcripts."

"He must be very bright."

"He is," said McLeod. "And he's a first-rate writer. Furthermore he's a long-distance runner."

"Superman. But he's in jail right now?"

"Waiting for Wyoming to clear him," said McLeod. "I hope he'll be able to finish the semester."

The next day was glorious. It was cold, but clear and sunny. McLeod was on her own, visiting museums and admiring Yale's towering Gothic buildings—Sterling Library was like a cathedral—until two o'clock when she met Harry in front of the Center for British Art.

They crossed Chapel Street and turned in a door on High Street. Stairs led to the offices of the Department of the History of Art in Street Hall. Harry led her through the offices and into a long and narrow room with a very, very long conference table running its length. Three tall Gothic windows opened onto Chapel Street. Faculty members and Harry sat at the table. A few spectators sat in chairs along the wall.

The defense, as McLeod had expected, was a formality, but very cheering for a mother's heart. Harry's advisers each offered up praise for his dissertation on the domestic architecture of medieval Cluny and each had an idea of how it could be revised slightly and published to great acclaim. It all ended with applause and an invitation from Harry for everyone to join him at Mory's.

He introduced McLeod to his advisers, smiled complacently while they praised his work again, and led everyone off to Mory's, the restaurant/club that occupied a small white-frame house nestled amid all that stately Gothic. They filed past the downstairs rooms with the blackened booths and went upstairs to a large room for private parties. Its walls were lined with ancient black-and-white photographs of old Yale football teams. Tables were loaded with hearty hors d'oeuvres and a bar stood ready in one corner. "Should I go meet Rosie?" McLeod asked Harry. "I didn't even think about that."

"No, she's coming on her own. Come here. I want you to meet Lindsay," said Harry.

Lindsay was Harry's girl of the moment. McLeod looked at her and liked what she saw. Hope swelled: now that Harry had his Ph.D., maybe he would settle down. . . . Full of hope and glory, she took the glass of champagne Harry offered her and downed it. She talked to Lindsay and went into her interrogatory mode, discovering that Lindsay was from Baltimore, had gone to Bryn Mawr, and was working on a dissertation on Renaissance frescoes.

"So you've spent a lot of time in Italy, I take it," McLeod said.

"Two years," said Lindsay. McLeod felt a brief flicker of sympathy for Lindsay's parents. Two years in Italy! Harry had spent a year in Cluny, and gone back to France for some cleanup research, but that wasn't as bad as financing two whole years in Italy. Art history was wonderful, she thought, if you liked to travel.

Lindsay melted away as the party got bigger and louder. Rosie arrived, hugged her brother and mother, and was introduced to everyone there. McLeod noticed her at one point in serious conversation with Lindsay.

Meanwhile, McLeod met art historians in every stage of life—distinguished professors with world-famous names, struggling assistant professors, and hopeful, youthful graduate students. Always curious, she asked each one about his or her field of specialty and was most interested in the man who taught a course on American maritime painting in the eighteenth and nineteenth centuries. But then there was the woman who knew all about Byzantine architecture and the young graduate student studying Islamic art who wanted to do his dissertation on Mughal art. And everybody always praised Harry as much as they talked about their own work. It was a mother's paradise, and McLeod, happy as any clam, arranged to have breakfast with Harry and Rosie and floated off to her motel room.

The next day, slightly hung over, she ate breakfast with the children, drove Rosie to the airport, and then made her way back to Princeton.

She hummed all the way home. What splendid children she had. Harry had finished his graduate work. He would get a Ph.D. at commencement. He was on the job market. He probably even had a job. Rosie looked beautiful and happy.

SHE PULLED INTO the driveway on Edgehill Street and took her small bag inside and upstairs to her room. She checked her mail, unpacked, and set out for the university. Although it was Friday afternoon, she thought she had better check her e-mails and her snail mail at the office. And Greg. How was Greg? She had forgotten about him. What had happened while she was off having so much fun? She walked up Edgehill to Stockton Street and crossed over when it sort of faded into Nassau Street. Walking past the nail salon, a real estate company, and the American Express travel office, she noticed the blue mailbox on the curb. That was the very mailbox where the letters with anthrax powder in them had been mailed in 2001. It was one of those odd points about Princeton that McLeod treasured, like the fact that Princeton was one of the few places in the country that could fly the United States flag at night. (Princeton had once briefly been the nation's capital, and Nassau Hall the seat of government.)

When she reached her office, she found e-mails and

phone messages from Lyle Cramer. She called him immediately, and he told her that law enforcement people found Isabel Pittman's story quite credible. She had provided circumstantial facts that made everyone believe her story. It would take time to officially clear Greg Pierre, or Bob Billings, as he was known, but the state of Wyoming was willing to ease its demand for his immediate return.

"That's wonderful, Lyle. What a good job you've done."

"I didn't do anything," Lyle said. "It all happened without any help from me."

"But you held their feet to the fire. I'm sure it would have taken much longer if you hadn't been out there and cheering for him."

"I wish I could take credit," said Lyle. "Anyway, things look pretty good. And Isabel Pittman is quite a treat. She says that she sinned but that she has truly repented. She will never use drugs again and she wants to right every wrong she's ever committed. The major one, apparently, is dumping that backpack on your pal. And then, apparently, when the law was breathing down her neck and her buddies' necks, she tipped them off about where they could find the portable lab. She thought that was better than just ditching that backpack in a river or something. She wanted to provide a perpetrator for them."

"She sounds like a nasty piece of work," said McLeod.

"You ought to see her, though. She's very glamorous. Blonde. Small, but a great figure. In great shape."

"Why did she really come up there and confess years later?"

"She says she found Jesus and he told her to do it. She wants to be a witness for God. She says, 'I'm a hundred and ten pounds of firecracker exploding for the Lord.'"

"That's good, I guess. Good for Greg, anyway. You know he says he was quite taken with her. So she must be attractive, but she sounds a little kinky."

"You said one time—I remember it—'Kinky's good. People I like are kinky.' So don't we all sound kinky?"

"I guess we do. Now I've got to persuade the university

to drop their charges and get him out of jail here and back in classes on Monday."

"Good luck, McLeod. You can do it, if anybody can."

"I'll do my best," she said.

She walked back home, thinking of the best way to win George over to her point of view. George's opinion would carry weight at the university, she knew. Lots of weight. It was essential that he was on her side.

First, a good dinner wouldn't do any harm, she thought, so she drove to the grocery store to get everything she needed for her coq au vin. She invested in a few flourishes, such as goat cheese and a delicious-looking camembert, two big, gorgeous artichokes, a chocolate mousse cake from Chez Alice, and two bottles of claret from Corkscrew.

What if George wasn't coming home tonight? What would she do with all this stuff? Invite the president of the university and try to win him over? That wasn't practical. She'd think of something.

Fortunately, she didn't have to. George came home about six—early for him—and mixed martinis. He was suitably impressed with Harry's accomplishments and agreed that it was marvelous that Rosie had come to New Haven.

When she brought up the subject of Greg Pierre, he was amazingly compliant. "Actually, one of his other teachers—Stern in history—called Tom, begging for clemency. I told Tom all you had said, and we're going to drop the charges for now. Let him at least finish this semester. Then we'll reevaluate the situation."

"Oh, that's wonderful," said McLeod. "I'm so glad." She poured wine in both their glasses.

"When will he get out of jail?"

"He got out today," said George. "He's back in his dormitory."

"What a nightmare this has been for him," said McLeod.

"Oh, it wasn't so bad. I went down myself to see him yesterday and apparently he has had a steady stream of company. Your friend Nick Perry said he had never seen anything like it. And you know his roommate's family hired a lawyer in Wyoming to help push things along."

"I'm so glad I wasn't the lone crusader."

"Not by a long shot."

AFTER DINNER, MCLEOD sent Greg an e-mail congratulating him on his release. He replied, thanked her for her help, and asked for an appointment for a conference on Monday afternoon. He was catching up on his work, he said, and he needed to talk about the assignment he was working on for her class. She went to bed that night thinking that all was right with the world. And it was—for two whole days.

Nine

ON MONDAY A graduate student was found dead in Frick Chemistry Laboratory. The news swept the Princeton campus, percolating even into the offices and cubicles in Joseph Henry House. Frieda, the Humanities Council's secretary, came upstairs to the third floor to tell McLeod the news, but McLeod had a hard time taking it all in because Frieda went off on one of her poetic tangents.

"Edna St. Vincent Millay said, 'Death devours all lovely things,'" Frieda said. "Do you suppose the graduate student was lovely?"

McLeod shook her head in bewilderment. Frieda's quotations were often puzzling. Then her phone rang. It was Greg Pierre.

He had to break his appointment for a conference with her that afternoon. "That's all right, Greg," she said. "Is anything the matter? You sound strained."

"I am. The police have come for me. It seems I'm the chief suspect in a murder case on campus."

"What?" asked McLeod.

Greg told her again.

"But who was the victim? I heard it was a graduate student. Did you know him?"

"No, but the police think I did. Look, I've got to go. Put me down for tomorrow. If my luck changes, maybe I'll be able to get there tomorrow afternoon."

"I will," said McLeod. "Thanks for calling."

Thanks for calling, she thought. Is that all you can think of to say to a kid who just got out of the clutches of the law and now is back in them? she asked herself. What could she do? She put in a call to Nick Perry, but had no hope of its being returned anytime soon.

"WHY ARE THEY picking on Greg?" McLeod attacked George when he came home on Monday night "He's such an easy scapegoat. It's an outrage, a cheap shot."

George was tired. As vice president for public affairs, he had had to deal all day with the campus security people, the Borough Police, the president of the university, a few trustees, and the press, the ever-hungry, never-satisfied press. It had been a long day. He pulled off his tie, unbuttoned his collar, and reached for the gin. "Hush," he said.

"I'm sorry," said McLeod. "You look exhausted."

George had quickly mixed a martini on the rocks in a glass, and stirred it vigorously. He took a gulp. "Let's sit down in the living room," he said. "I am indeed exhausted. How did you find out about the murder—and Greg?"

"Greg had to cancel a conference we had scheduled. We needed to talk about the article he's writing. He said the police wanted to talk to him about a murder on campus, and they were taking him down to Borough Hall. That was the first I really knew about the murder and I tried to call Nick Perry, but of course, he was busy. So I called Chuck Hammersmith and asked him."

"Poor Chuck," said George. "Newspapers and television hounded him all day." Chuck Hammersmith was the university's director of public relations, the one who dealt most often with the press, but when there was a big event—like the president of the United States receiving an honorary degree or a murder on campus—George had to provide in person an even weightier institutional presence.

"I know, but I couldn't help it. I *had* to know what was going on. Why did they pick on Greg? Because he'd been in custody last week?"

"That was only part of it. Do you know who the murdered person was?"

"Chuck said it was a graduate student in chemistry, I forget his name."

"His name was Owen West, and he was from Wyoming. He's the one who alerted the university to Greg Pierre's true identity," said George.

McLeod was silent. She was stunned. George watched her as he sipped his drink.

"How did he know Greg's 'true identity,' as you put it?"

"He was from Wyoming, as I said, and he had known Bob Billings at the University of Wyoming. He got here a year ago last fall and he didn't run into Billings—or Pierre—until last year when he went to a cross-country meet."

"For heaven's sake," said McLeod. "And he had to squeal, did he?"

"McLeod, I wouldn't call it squealing. He knew that Billings had been convicted on a drug charge. And he was appalled that he was here on campus, on the varsity track team, in Ivy Club, all under false pretenses."

"None of that hurt Owen West! What a difference between him and Isabel Pittman. Owen West goes out of his way to ruin the life of a young man, and Isabel goes way out of the way to help him get his life back."

"I see what you're saying," said George. "The woman sounds like she's crazy, though. Owen West wasn't. And now he's dead."

"And the police think Greg was so incensed at having his identity blown that he killed Owen West?"

"That was their first thought. Can you blame them? And Billings/Pierre could not prove he didn't go over to Frick Lab on Sunday night. Come on, be reasonable, McLeod.

Billings/Pierre is a bad lot. He's a lost cause. I'm going to
have another martini—don't you want one?"

"I guess so," said McLeod. "But surely Greg's not a lost
cause. He can't be; he has too much talent."

George didn't answer, just took his glass and left the
room.

The phone rang. George answered it in the kitchen, and
McLeod heard him talking.

"That was Chuck," George said when he came back in
the living room with two martinis. "The press is driving
him crazy."

"Poor Chuck, " said McLeod, rather insincerely. As a
reporter, she was always on the side of the journalist.
"How was this graduate student murdered?" McLeod
asked.

"I don't think the police have released what the murder
weapon was."

"Maybe it was some mysterious chemical that only a
chemist would know about," said McLeod.

"I don't know," George said. "Have we anything in the
house for supper? I feel better since I had a martini and a
half."

"You know we have leftover coq au vin," said McLeod.
"We were dashing about all weekend so it's still there."

"Good, I'll heat it up," said George.

They didn't talk much over dinner. George answered
two more phone calls—one from the president and one
from a reporter from the *New York Times* who knew his
home phone number—while McLeod was trying to think
how she could find out more about the murder. The trouble
was that she knew no one in the chemistry department. Science was not her forte. She knew that Frick Lab, a Tudor
building with impressive double doors, stood on Washington Road, but its interior was unknown territory as far as
she was concerned.

Later, upstairs in her own room getting ready for bed,
she remembered Forrest Meriwether. Forrest was the son
of Phyllis Meriwether, McLeod's doctor and good friend in
Tallahassee. And he was a first-year graduate student in the

chemistry department at Princeton. McLeod had scarcely seen him since she had been at Princeton this semester, so it was certainly time she did something about Forrest, wasn't it? she asked herself. She looked at her little clock and decided it wasn't too late to call a graduate student.

Forrest was in his room at the Graduate College. He said he'd be happy to see McLeod tomorrow, and lunch would be fine. When McLeod suggested Prospect, the faculty club, Forrest sounded quite pleased and agreed to meet her at noon.

After McLeod was in bed, she had another idea. She would start research for an article on some work that was going on in the chemistry department. She did not have the least idea of what such an article could be about, but she would find out tomorrow. And with that pretext, she could surely win admission to Frick Lab.

And once her foot was in the door, she would surely find out who *really* killed Owen West.

Ten

❧

THE NEWSPAPERS ON Tuesday had stories about the murder of the Princeton graduate student. *The Times* of Trenton splashed it all over the front page, while *The New York Times* played it more sedately. The Philadelphia television stations were full of it, with news people—men and women—reporting what crumbs they could pick up from the sidewalk in front of Frick Lab, which was closed off with yellow police tape. Undergraduate chemistry classes were being held temporarily in nooks and crannies all over campus. Undergraduate classes would go on, McLeod thought, even if the world was ending. The television people interviewed Chuck Hammersmith, George (who looked very handsome and competent, McLeod thought), chemistry graduate students, any professor they could prevail on to provide a sound bite, and even undergraduates, who pontificated knowingly about the widespread grief and unease on campus, the uncertainty of life, and the importance of organic chemistry in the modern world.

McLeod turned off the television and walked to the campus. She sniffed the air and found it good. It was still chilly—after all, it was March—but it was warmer than it had been. She was glad it was again warm enough to wear a skirt instead of long pants, and felt quite cheerful clad in a short wool coat instead of her heavy shearling. Then she remembered the murder and the plight of her student, and plunged into appropriate gloom. She tried to think of what she could do to help Greg, and racked her brain—fruitlessly—for story ideas in the chemistry department.

At the office, she found an e-mail from Greg confirming his conference appointment that afternoon, and she quickly wrote him back that she would expect him at three. She took care of all the other e-mails, phone messages, and snail mail, and set out for Prospect for lunch.

Prospect was an Italianate house, formerly the residence of the university presidents, set in the midst of gardens laid out by Ellen Wilson when her husband, Woodrow, was president of Princeton. The gardens looked quite bleak and bare that day, but they would soon be bursting forth with blooms.

She encountered Forrest Meriwether on the walkway up to Prospect's portico and greeted him with genuine affection. He was Rosie's age, and she had known him since he was an infant.

"Forrest, my dear, how good to see you. I'm so sorry I haven't seen much of you this semester. I can't believe how busy I've been."

"That's all right, McLeod, I understand. I've been busy, too."

"How's it going? Do you like graduate school?"

"I do."

They were inside Prospect's domed center hall and McLeod led him to the coatroom, where they could hang up their wraps, and then into the big dining room overlooking the gardens.

"This is awesome," said Forrest. "I've never been here before."

"It is nice, isn't it? I'm glad you give me an excuse to come here."

"And this is a good day for me to come to lunch here—Frick is closed temporarily so I can't work in the lab."

"Because of the murder, I suppose."

"That's right."

They ordered, and McLeod focused on Forrest. He was a very wholesome-looking young man, with rosy cheeks, reddish hair, blue eyes, and right now smiling happily. "You know, I always thought you'd go to medical school," she said.

"Like my mom? I thought so, too, but I really liked chemistry in college, and I decided I wanted to spend my life in a laboratory, not in a hospital where I'd have to make life-or-death decisions about people."

"You've always been such a good-tempered lad, I thought you'd be marvelous at dealing with patients."

"I'm good tempered because I don't have to fool with idiots who are either hypochondriacs or too lazy and stubborn to do the things the doctor tells them they have to do for the sake of their health. You ought to hear the stories Mom tells about patients."

"I've heard the stories Phyllis tells. She used to get particularly furious with patients who demanded sleeping pills but wouldn't start on an exercise program. But she's survived, and feels like she's doing good things practicing medicine."

"I know. I know," said Forrest. "It just wasn't for me."

"I understand. It's a good thing you found this out before you finished medical school and did a residency and established your practice."

"Yeah. And that's another thing. I don't want to go back to Tallahassee and practice medicine. And I would have felt bad going somewhere else, I guess. I don't know. Anyway, I like chemistry."

"Tell me what you like about it." McLeod's curiosity was always bubbling away, making her ask questions of everybody she talked to, and making her genuinely interested in the answers she got. This concern came through, she had decided long ago, and made people respond to her questions. And she always insisted that her white hair helped make people talk. Not that there was a problem with Forrest Meriwether, whom she had known all his life, and she really wanted to know why anybody, anybody in the whole world, would like chemistry.

"I liked it in college because it's well defined. You always get an answer. And it's logical; it balances. The equations work. Of course, now that I'm doing research, it's more open ended. The results aren't always what you expect. But you get to do what nobody else has done."

As he talked, Forrest's face seemed transformed. He really does like that stuff, McLeod thought. It was wonderful to talk to somebody who loves what he's doing.

Their food came and Forrest began to eat heartily. "This is wonderful," he said. "I don't get many meals like this."

"You're living at the Graduate College?" she asked.

"Yes, and I eat there when I can get there, but it's so far away from Frick that I end up eating most of my meals at Hoagie Haven or the Thai place." These were the two restaurants closest to Frick.

McLeod asked no more questions for the time being. Let the boy eat, she thought. Forrest was, after all, only twenty-three years old. By the time she finished her Cobb salad, Forrest had eaten every bit of his roast beef and oven-browned potatoes, plus a large Caesar salad. He wiped his mouth carefully—"Cloth napkin!" he said appreciatively—and smiled at McLeod. "Best meal I've had in a long time," he said.

"How about dessert?"

"Sure," said Forrest and, presented with a menu, ordered chocolate cake with coffee ice cream.

McLeod ordered coffee and mango sorbet and wondered if she had ever been able to eat as much as Forrest did. Then she remembered that she wasn't exactly a finicky eater even now. She did not care to pursue this line of thought any further. Finally getting down to the business of the day, she asked, "Did you know Owen West?"

"Slightly. He's ahead of me. Was ahead of me, I should say."

"Did you like him?"

"I didn't know him that well. I don't think anybody

liked him much, but I don't know. We weren't in the same research group."

"What research group are you in?"

"I'm in Professor Hollingsworth's group."

"And Owen West?"

"He was in Sandy Berman's group."

"Do you stay in the same group the whole time you're in graduate school?"

"That's right, with rare exceptions."

McLeod made a mental note to find out about the "rare exceptions" sometime—rare exceptions, no matter where they applied, were often very, very interesting. This whole scientific milieu was a world entirely new to her; she could tell it was far different from the humanities.

Their desserts arrived. She gave Forrest a few minutes to attack his enormous piece of cake topped with an equally enormous serving of coffee ice cream before she plowed on. "How do you get assigned to a group?"

"You choose the professor you want to work with."

"You choose the professor, or the work he's doing?"

"It's one and the same thing, really," said Forrest.

"Tell me what Professor Berman's group—the one Owen West was in—is working on?"

"They're working in medicinal chemistry and organic synthesis."

"Forrest, what does that mean?"

"It means roughly that they're trying to synthesize molecules."

"Why would anybody want to synthesize molecules?"

"I'll give you an example. There's a natural product called Taxol that's used against cancer. A company out in Colorado made it out of yew tree bark and it was a long, slow process, but they were making tons of money from a pharmaceutical company. Then you know the great chemist at home at FSU—he figured out how to synthesize Taxol. And you talk about money! A pharmaceutical company paid him millions and millions."

"That's right. Of course, I knew about that. I just didn't realize he was synthesizing molecules. He made millions

and gave FSU the money to build a new chemistry building and then he sued them because they didn't build the
kind of building they had said they would. So, synthesizing molecules to find a cure for a disease—that's what
Berman's group is trying to do?"

"They're working in that direction," Forrest said.

"It would be wonderful if they succeeded, wouldn't it?"

"It sure would."

McLeod had finished her sorbet, but Forrest was still
polishing off his cake. Nevertheless, she asked him what
his own group—Professor Hollingsworth's group—was
working on.

"We're working on fuel cells."

"Fuel cells?"

"It's electrochemistry," Forrest said patiently, "where
hydrogen and oxygen react to make electrical energy."

"I see," said McLeod, who did not see at all. She had
thought hydrogen and oxygen made water.

"Hollingsworth is trying to make it possible to have cars
that run on hydrogen," Forrest was saying.

"That sounds exciting," said McLeod. She didn't really
think it sounded very exciting. She knew she should be
concerned about the consumption of fossil fuels, but somehow she couldn't stir up much enthusiasm. Especially
since she spent so much time in New Jersey, where the law
forbade self-service gasoline stations. She always felt
much fonder of gasoline during the semesters she spent at
Princeton, where she didn't have to get out of her car to fill
up the tank.

"It is very exciting, especially if he's the first person to
manage it," Forrest said. He had scraped his plate and almost licked it. "Look. I have to get back. I've really enjoyed this, McLeod. Thanks so much."

"I've kept you a long time," she said. "I'm sorry. Let me
get the check." The payment taken care of, they left
Prospect, walking briskly out of the gates. Forrest headed
off toward Washington Road; McLeod went back to her office to get ready for her conference with Greg Pierre.

Eleven

GREG HAD A hunted look when he arrived at her cubicle on the third floor of Joseph Henry House that afternoon. McLeod. who could understand why he might feel pursued, took him downstairs to the sun porch, where it would be more pleasant—and more private—to talk.

"How's it going?" she asked him, after she had offered him coffee or tea, both of which he refused.

"I finally wrote the story about the person with a completely different background from mine. I hope you approve of my choice of subject. I know most of the guys probably went down and talked to some of those Guatemalans who live off Witherspoon Street or somebody else that couldn't speak English, or something. But I'm kind of like the people from Guatemala; I'm an outsider, too. Besides I couldn't talk to anybody like that last week," he said. "I was in jail."

He paused, and McLeod smiled sympathetically.

"So I did Sergeant Popper. He was very helpful. Here, I brought it with me." He fished a pile of paper from his backpack and handed it to her.

"Fine. I'll read it immediately. I applaud your devotion

to duty, your eagerness to keep up with your writing assignments under the most adverse circumstances, but when I asked you 'How's it going?' I was really asking about your life in general. I was appalled yesterday when you told me what was happening, but I assume you're cleared now and everything's okay."

"I'm not exactly cleared," said Greg. "I'm still their prime suspect."

"But that's absurd." McLeod paused and looked sharply at Greg. "It *is* absurd, isn't it? You didn't kill him, did you?"

"I did not kill him." Greg looked straight at McLeod, his eyes flashing.

McLeod believed him. Still . . . "I guess, though, that the police think you really have a motive," she said slowly. "Owen West did cause you great harm."

"I don't go around killing people that cause me trouble," said Greg. "If I did—well, the homicide rate would be higher than it is."

"Did you even know Owen West?"

"I knew him a little bit at the University of Wyoming— he wasn't one of my favorite people. He wasn't ever Mr. Congeniality. But he was off my radar, believe me, after I got in Princeton. Then when Princeton got upset about my identity, I found out it was West who had blown the whistle."

"Do you know exactly what he did?"

"Yeah."

Greg clearly did not want to talk about it, but McLeod thought he absolutely must tell her as much as he could— if she was going to be any help to him.

"What did he do, exactly? Did he go to the administration at Princeton or what?"

"First he called the track coach at Wyoming and told him he'd seen Bob Billings, reminded him about the drug charge. And told him that Billings was at Princeton. That I was on the cross-country team. That I was using the name 'Greg Pierre.' "

"Did anything happen because of that?"

"Not right away. But then West went to the track coach here."

"What did Coach Lilly say?"

"Not much. Nothing, I guess. He certainly never mentioned it to me."

"Then what happened?" McLeod felt as though she was working very hard indeed to get each syllable out of Greg.

"West went to the president's office here. They took a dim view of it, I think. West can be sort of a fanatic, and it made him mad, I guess, that nobody was doing anything about me. So he called the sports editor of the newspaper in Laramie. They investigated and found out Bob Billings was now Greg Pierre and was now at Princeton. They ran a story. The state got interested because I'd broken parole. One thing led to another. The university filed charges. And the Borough police arrested me."

"It's a sorry tale," said McLeod.

"It is a sorry tale. And you saved me from the really tragic ending to the story," said Greg. "I can't get over that."

"I didn't save you. Isabel saved you."

"I know. It's amazing, isn't it? Hooray for Isabel—and you—and God, I guess. You said you prayed."

"I did," said McLeod. "But who knows whether that did the trick? I guess I keep trying it because I figure it can't do any harm. I mean, if there is a God, he's not going to get mad at somebody like me and do the opposite from what I asked, is he?"

"I'm sure I don't know," said Greg. "Nobody I knew ever prayed before."

"But people helped," said McLeod. "I know that. Lyle Cramer helped. He was out there. And the lawyer that Ted Vance's parents hired. See, there are a lot of people on your side."

"But you helped with the university," said Greg. "I really appreciate it. I feel battered senseless."

"I know how you must feel," said McLeod. "They suspect you because Owen West revealed your true identity and got you in trouble. It sounds like a pretty good motive. Why else would anybody kill a harmless graduate student?"

"I have no idea," said Greg.

"You didn't kill him, did you?" she asked again.

"Of course I didn't kill him," he said.

"If you didn't, you should be able to convince the police," said McLeod.

"Yeah. Like I was able to convince the Wyoming cops that I didn't make meth."

McLeod was silent. "I see what you mean. But this is different. In Wyoming, you didn't want to incriminate Isabel. Are you protecting somebody now?"

"No."

"Are you sure?"

"I'm sure. I swear I'm not."

McLeod was quiet again. "Greg, do you have an alibi for Sunday night?"

"No. That's the problem. One of the problems."

"Where were you? You didn't go to Frick Lab, did you?"

"No, I've never been in Frick Lab in my life."

"Where were you then?" McLeod asked again.

"That's just it. I was running."

"Running? At night?"

"Yes, at night. I'm on the cross-country team, you know."

"I know."

"In the winter we have to train indoors a lot, but I run outdoors whenever I can. And I was really out of condition after a week in a jail cell. And we have a track meet Saturday. I need the training. Even though I won't be running cross-country Saturday—it's not the season and this will be indoors."

"What will you run Saturday?"

"The mile."

"I see. But back to Sunday night. I didn't know you could run cross-country at night, and as you say, it's not the season. I always think of cross-country runners running across fields and down country lanes."

Greg smiled. "That's right, and cross-country is my first choice. That's sort of what I did Sunday. I ran out and along the canal towpath for a little bit, and then when I got to the golf course, I cut off and ran up the fairways. It was great. I felt clean at last."

"And nobody saw you?"

"I didn't see a soul. I don't know if anybody saw me."

"Maybe somebody saw you and we can find them and they can back you up."

"No such luck, I'm afraid," said Greg.

"Don't give up."

"Well, it's hard not to."

"I know," said McLeod. "But Greg, let me ask you one thing. You got out of jail on Friday. Didn't you run on Friday or Saturday?"

"I didn't run Friday. My roommate, Ted, you know him, bought champagne and we had a party. On Saturday, I had a hangover. I hadn't had a hangover in years. You know I don't do drugs, and I don't drink. I mean ordinarily I don't drink. I don't want to lose control, and I'm always in training. So I just don't do drugs or alcohol. But this was an extraordinary occasion and I drank tons of champagne. Saturday afternoon, I did go out for a brief run. That was all I could do, and I slept like a log. And Sunday, I caught up on my classwork." He looked to McLeod for approval at this, and McLeod obligingly commended him on his industry.

"And finally I went out for a long run Sunday night."

"I see," said McLeod.

"Look, thanks a lot," said Greg, as he stood up and began to sling on his backpack.

McLeod started to stand up, then sat back down. "Wait a minute, Greg. What makes you say you're the prime suspect for the police?"

"Who else is there? They act like I'm a suspect. They said don't leave town. They said they'd be in touch. And like I said, who else is there? As everybody says, 'Who would want to kill a graduate student? They're such nerds.'"

McLeod stood up. "They're not all nerds," she said hastily, thinking of Harry and also of Forrest Meriwether. But who would want to kill either one of those nonnerds? She went on thoughtfully: "Graduate students would seem to be the least offensive people on earth. They have no power. They work hard. They live in ivory towers, or steel towers, divorced from reality. They have no money. But I must say, Owen West doesn't sound like a very nice person, judging from the way he squealed on you—not just to the university but to people in Wyoming."

Greg shrugged. "I never knew him very well."

"Somebody here must have had reason to kill him," McLeod continued. "Do you know anything, anything at all, about his life here?" Greg was shaking his head. "Listen, I'm not going to let them pin this on you," she added with determination.

"I hope you're right. Thanks anyway. I appreciate your support."

"And I look forward to reading your piece on Sergeant Popper."

He smiled, shrugged on his backpack, and left.

Twelve

❧

AFTER GREG LEFT, McLeod went slowly back upstairs to her cubicle overlooking Chancellor Green hall. She sat down at her desk and looked at Greg's interview with Kevin Popper, that blond, phlegmatic police sergeant.

Popper had talked—and talked and talked—to Greg. He talked about police work, which he loved, and about his childhood in a strict churchgoing family in Trenton, where his mother had always been at home, baking cookies, working in her garden, or ironing shirts for her husband and five sons. His father was a fireman, coached Little League, and believed the Bible was literally true, every word of it. "If the Bible said the whale swallowed Jonah and Jonah lived inside that whale for days, Pop believed it. He was a great man. I thought about being a fireman and then decided I'd rather be a policeman." Popper had even gone to Mercer County Community College for two years before he went to the police academy, and he loved being on the Princeton Borough force. "Man, it's sure different from Trenton!" he had told Greg.

The lives of Kevin Popper and Greg Pierre had indeed been different, as different as lives could be, McLeod thought. She was relieved that the article was as fresh and lively as it was. It was so much more fun to praise a student's work than to point out faults. She laid it aside and looked up a number in the campus directory, then punched it in.

"Chuck," she said when Chuck Hammersmith, the head of public relations for the university, answered. "McLeod Dulaney. I have a question."

"You always have a question," said Chuck. "Or two questions, or three."

"I know. It's my style, I guess. My cross, maybe." She liked Chuck. He was new this semester, but already McLeod had become his fan because of his poise, his cool relaxed manner, and his marvelous spontaneous laugh that always surprised and delighted her.

"Oh, that's all right. It's my job to answer journalists' questions. So go ahead."

"I want to do a story about the chemistry department."

"Great!" said Chuck. "Nobody ever writes about the chemistry department. Nobody. Until they have a murder and then every two-bit writer in the United States—I don't mean you're a two-bit writer, McLeod—wants to do a story about the Princeton chemistry department."

"Why does nobody ever write about the chemistry department in normal times?"

"Nobody knows what they do anymore. Since biochemistry split off from chemistry, Frick is all spectroscopy and redox polymers and God knows what. Anyway, how can I help you?"

"Actually, I wanted advice from you about what kind of story to do," said McLeod.

"Who's the story for?" asked Chuck.

McLeod was at a loss. She didn't have an assignment from a newspaper or a magazine. "Er, I'm not sure," she began tentatively.

Chuck was quick on the uptake, as usual. "I see, McLeod. You just want an excuse to go over and poke around the chemistry department." He laughed uproariously. "But why not? Let me think."

"Chuck, it's not just idle curiosity," she said. "One of my best students is a prime suspect in the murder. I thought I just might be able to find out something that would be useful to clear him."

"I expect you might," said Chuck. "Why is an undergraduate who's taking a high-level writing class a suspect in the murder of a chemistry graduate student?"

McLeod told him about Greg Pierre and his past history and his connection to Owen West.

"I see," said Chuck. "I had heard about Greg Pierre and was praying that the story wouldn't break. I was very relieved when I heard the university was dropping charges and letting him stay. But I didn't know he was a murder suspect."

"Well, he is. The police interrogated him yesterday at some length. Anyway, Chuck, Greg is a great writer, and I'd like to help him if I can. And listen, I bet I can sell a story out of it, too. So can you think of something going on over there that I could write about? What did you say about redox polymers?"

"Hmmm. Let me think. McLeod, forget about redox polymers. Chemistry is really so complicated nobody can understand it anymore. I tell you what—write a story about a person."

"Anything," said McLeod.

"This is not just anything. This is a real personality, a towering figure in the scientific world. You can write about the person and finesse the science."

"That sounds perfect. Who is he? Or she?"

"Not a she. It's a man."

"Are they all white men in chemistry?"

"No, but there aren't many women on the chemistry faculty. I'm talking about Earl Shivers. He teaches organic chemistry, has taught it for thirty years, I guess. It's required for all chemistry majors and for all premed students. It's a tough course. Shivers gives three lectures a week, at eight o'clock in the morning. Then there's a precept—students are divided into small groups for this—once a week, plus a three-hour lab every week. Students groan and curse over orgo, but they love Shivers. When they're through with the course, they always play jokes on him."

"What kind of jokes?"

"Messy ones. They've thrown cream pies at him, shot water pistols at him, dressed up in gorilla suits to try to manhandle him. One time during a final exam, six streakers came in and tried to hug him."

"Good heavens," said McLeod. "He does sound interesting."

"And right now is the time to do it," said Chuck. "He's in his seventies and he's going to retire at the end of the semester."

"Great. I'll get right on that, Chuck. Thanks so much. How do you know so much? You just started work here, didn't you?"

"I went to Princeton. Class of 1985. Shivers was teaching orgo then."

"Did you take the course?"

"No, but I had friends who did."

"Thanks so much for your suggestion."

"Sure," said Chuck. "This was comparatively easy."

"Good," said McLeod, "but if you want me to be more difficult, I'll try to oblige."

"Not at all. You're okay. Go for it. Good luck."

MCLEOD HUNG UP the phone and called Earl Shivers, identified herself, and told him she'd like to interview him for an article. He was brusque and said he was very busy, and because of a nasty affair in one of the laboratories (he pronounced it lab-O-ra-tor-ies with the emphasis on the O), the department was in disorder, so no, he was afraid he wouldn't be able to spare time for an interview. "There are two many inquiring reporters around here now. I dislike personal publicity at any time," he said, "and right now, I feel that it would be in the worst possible taste."

"I understand," McLeod said. "But look at it this way, Professor Shivers. You won't like what the press writes about the chemistry department and the murder of a graduate student." She spoke firmly—years of experience in dealing with unwilling legislators, sheriffs, and civic leaders had taught her to be resolute when she was up against the recalcitrant. Rudeness or bluster never worked, but it paid not to be too humble. "But a piece about you—a distinguished professor, a world-class scientist—would be good for the department's image, good for Princeton's image, good for the image of science." Compliments didn't hurt, either, McLeod had learned.

"You're very flattering, Ms. Er—"

"Dulaney," McLeod interjected. "McLeod Dulaney. It's not just flattery. It's the truth."

"I see what you're saying. Hmmm."

McLeod waited, not speaking.

"Ah, when would you want to—ah interview me?" Shivers asked after a few seconds had passed.

McLeod wanted to say, "Right this minute," but knew she had to be more diplomatic. "What about late Wednesday afternoon?" she said, deliberately using the word "late" to distract Shivers from the fact that she was pushing for an interview the next day.

Then he surprised her. He said that Wednesday was hard—the organic chemistry lab-O-ra-to-ry was on Wednesday afternoon. "Things look difficult this week," he said, apparently scanning his calendar. "I'm about to go out of town."

"How about tomorrow morning?" asked McLeod. "Before the lab."

"I have an organic chemistry lecture at eight o'clock," he said. "I'm afraid it will have to be next week."

"I'm sorry. I'd love to get started before next week."

"And I'm sorry, too. The only time I can possibly see you this week would be at seven o'clock tomorrow morning."

McLeod said nothing for a moment. She hated early morning interviews, or early morning appointments of any kind. But this cantankerous old man was not going to outfox her and delay the interview for a week. If this was the only time she could see him, she would make the best of it.

"That's fine," she said through clenched teeth. "I'll be there."

Shivers sounded quite cheerful as he gave her directions for reaching his office in Frick. "I believe that at least most of the building will be open by then," he said.

McLeod thanked him, hung up, and sighed. What a conversation—it had taken longer to arrange the interview than the interview itself would take.

She went home and set her alarm for five o'clock. She wanted to be on time for her appointment with Earl Shivers; she wanted to have time for breakfast before she met him, and plenty of time to find his office.

Thirteen

❧

THE NEXT MORNING she walked to the campus and crossed Washington Road to reach Frick Laboratory, the eighty-year-old stone Tudor building that housed the chemistry department. To reach one of the two front doors, each under its Gothic arch, you went up a few steps to a broad terrace edged with a balustrade. The thick trunk of ancient wisteria vine climbed across the front of the building, its buds pale in the early morning light. A policeman stood beside the doors.

"This building is closed to all but authorized personnel," he said.

"I'm authorized," McLeod said, smiling at him. "I'm a visiting professor at the university and I have an appointment with a professor in the chemistry department at seven o'clock." She showed him her university ID.

"Go right ahead," the policeman said. "We just have to watch out for the press."

She felt guilty, as though she had betrayed her colleagues in the media, but she also felt rather proud of herself and went on to find Shivers's office on the second floor. He was already there, smiling as he rose from behind his desk. He had made coffee and offered her some. She refused it but was impressed with his cordiality and the ease with which he greeted her. It was all quite different from the way he had sounded on the telephone.

She looked at him as she sat down in the spartan straight chair he indicated. He was white-haired and plump and wore the uniform of the older Princeton professor—ancient but well-cut tweed jacket, striped tie, and gray flannel trousers.

"It's good of you to come this early," he said. "You know I'll have to stop before eight o'clock. I have a lecture then," he said.

"I understand," said McLeod. "So I'll plunge right in. Is eight o'clock a popular hour with students?"

Shivers stared at her, his dark eyes sharp under frowning white eyebrows. "Of course not," he said. "Princeton students like to stay up all night and sleep until noon. My aim is to frustrate them at every turn."

"I'm sure you succeed," said McLeod, who was beginning to like this man. "But I didn't know there were any eight o'clock classes at all anymore."

Shivers smiled. "There aren't many. It's quite different from the way it was when I went to college. There are very few classes on Friday now, but I have a lecture on Friday. Of course, frustrating students is not my aim, but I'm an early riser, always have been. I care about the course. I want to teach it while I'm fresh. And scheduling it at eight eliminates a lot of students who would sign up for it and not take it seriously. And organic chemistry must be taken seriously. It is the foundation for everything."

"Can you explain to laymen why organic chemistry is so important?"

"Organic chemistry is the basis of everything. Organic chemists have produced synthetic dyes, antibiotics, explosives, perfumes, paints, inks, pesticides, and plastics. Name it—organic chemistry is responsible."

"I see. Let's talk about you. I looked up your résumé yesterday, and I know you grew up in Rhode Island and went to Groton and then Brown. When did you decide to become a chemist?"

"That happened early on. I got a chemistry set for Christmas one year when I was a little boy and I loved it. My father was a doctor and he encouraged me and bought me more chemicals and helped me set up a little lab at home. He took me to meet a friend of his who was a chemist. I never looked back. I quite liked chemistry in prep school and at Brown, and I went on to get a Ph.D. in chemistry at Yale."

"You were very lucky to know what you wanted to do from the very beginning."

"It's true," he said. "But being single-minded has its limitations. I never had time to learn about art, for instance. I tried to take a course in painting at the Arts Council here in Princeton, but I was hopeless. I did manage to learn a little about music—but I can't play the violin like Einstein. I did play the drums when I was a boy, but now I just listen. Still I like being a chemist and I'd probably settle down and specialize early if I had a chance to do my life over."

McLeod steered him back to biographical facts. After graduate school, he had taught at a couple of other places but had been at Princeton for decades, and loved it, he said. He liked teaching orgo.

"Why do the students play those jokes on you?"

"I have no idea," said Shivers. "But they do. It drives other people in the department crazy. They think it's 'unsuitable,' or maybe they're jealous. Nobody throws pies in their faces. Do you think that's it?"

"I'm sure they're terribly jealous," said McLeod. "But I think it's wonderful tradition, if you can stand it. You don't ever get mad?"

"No, they're really quite inventive. That is good for scientists. It demonstrates exuberance on the part of young people."

McLeod looked at him doubtfully.

"Vitality is better than apathy, don't you think?" he asked her.

"You have a splendid attitude," said McLeod, "to see it like that."

"Might as well," said Shivers, looking at his watch.

"Let's talk about your research. What are you working on now?"

"It's quite fascinating," said Shivers. "I'm working on protein folding."

"What?"

"All protein molecules are heterogeneous unbranched chains of amino acids," Shivers said. "The reverse of this process is protein denaturation."

"I'm sorry," said McLeod. "I don't have the faintest idea what you're saying."

"I'll try to explain." Shivers talked on, and McLeod caught a word here, a phrase there—synthesis . . . primary solvent . . . covalent bonding . . . but had no idea what it all meant.

When he paused, McLeod asked him if this process would have any practical value.

"Not that I know of," said Shivers. "It's pure science. That's the best kind. That's what academic science should be. That's where the great advances in ideas come about. Let the commercial lab-O-ra-tories turn out the junk that makes money."

"Is that the kind of research Princeton chemists do— pure science?"

"It ought to be," said Shivers. "But not everyone agrees with me. Some of them are out to make money—they work on how to convert sunlight into hydrogen for fuel or on synthesizing a molecule. Ever since one of our professors did something that a pharmaceutical company paid millions for, things haven't been the same."

"Did he make millions himself? You can't blame people for wanting to do the same thing, can you?"

"Maybe not. But the university got most of that money. Of course, we never see it in this department. I don't mean to sound ill natured. I'm afraid I'm going to have to call a halt to this. One more question."

"If I have just one more question, I'd like to ask you

about the murder of a graduate student in the chemistry department. Did you know him?"

"I knew who he was," said Shivers.

"And why do you think he was murdered?"

"Why is anybody murdered?" Shivers stood up. "I said one more question, and that makes two. But I will say this about the recent event. I read the occasional murder mystery and it seems to me that a lab-O-ratory is an excellent place for a murder."

McLeod stood up, too. "Why?" she asked.

"Think about it. I'm sorry, but I have to call a halt, Ms. Dulaney. It's been very pleasant talking to you."

"I'll have to come back with a tape recorder and talk to you more about your work, Professor Shivers. And I have other questions. Thanks very much for seeing me so quickly this time. Can we set a date for next week for a follow-up?"

"Call me next week and I'll try to set something up."

McLeod left Shivers's office, somewhat shaken. Shivers was an interesting man, clearly smart, and there was a story there, but was she capable of writing it? She had not understood one word that he had said about protein folding. Chemistry was downright mystifying, a virtual code. Well, she would give it a whirl. She would consult Forrest Meriwether and try to read about protein folding before she went back to see Shivers. Even if she understood his work and wrote an article about him, would he prove any help in finding out about the murder of Owen West? She wouldn't learn much about it from Shivers, but he was still her only excuse for talking to anybody in the chemistry department. Why, oh, why couldn't the man who squealed on Greg Pierre have been a graduate student in English or history? Why chemistry?

As she thought about this standing outside Shivers's office, she decided to look around Frick while she was there. Walking down the hall, she saw laboratories with professors' names on them and then came to the chemistry library. She went in. It was one of those beautiful rooms you saw in unexpected places on the Princeton campus, with shelves and stacks of books, of course, but paneled walls and a big fireplace. Above the fireplace was a big plaque with these words—NON EST MORTVVS QUI SCIENTIAM VIVIFICAVIT. McLeod dredged up enough dregs of high school Latin to figure out a rough translation—*He's not dead who has made science live.* Well, I'm dead, then, she thought. I sure can't make it live. I can't even understand it.

Fourteen

MCLEOD CHEERED UP as she crossed Washington Road and headed slowly toward her office in Joseph Henry House. It was really getting warmer, she thought, and everything looked ready to burst into leaf and bloom. Thinking about the story on Shivers, she decided she would talk to some of his undergraduate students, get their comments on the class, and maybe get in touch with alumni who had taken the course. She could talk to other members of the chemistry faculty about Shivers—now that was a great idea, she thought. She wouldn't have to ask them about their work—that way lay madness—but just try to get quotes on what a great teacher he was and all that. And maybe she could find out from one of them something about Owen West. In fact, why not ask Owen West's professor about Shivers? She was so thrilled with this idea that she stopped stock still by the sculpture *Song of the Vowels* on Firestone plaza and congratulated herself.

What was his name, the professor in whose group Owen West had worked? Berman, that was it. Sandy Berman. She hurried toward her office so she could call Forrest Meriwether and Professor Berman. Inside, she stopped

when she realized that Joseph Henry House was empty—
there was nobody in the Humanities Council office. Had
something extraordinary happened? Then she remembered
it was only eight o'clock, and nobody would be around for
forty five minutes. She went back out the door and walked
down Nassau Street to the kiosk at Palmer Square, where
she bought a *New York Times* and a Trenton *Times* and took
them to Small World on Witherspoon Street for a cup of
tea.

The Trenton paper revealed that Owen West had died
from a blow to the head. His parents had come to Princeton from Wyoming and in their photograph in the Trenton
paper they looked dour and unhappy, rather like the couple in the painting *American Gothic*. But who wouldn't
look unhappy if your son was murdered? McLeod scolded
herself.

Mr. West told the newspaper that you would think that
a first-rate university would have better security, would
protect its students from criminal attacks. "I told Owen he
ought to have a gun when he worked late at night in the
laboratory," he told the reporter, who must, McLeod
thought, have been fascinated with this Western attitude toward law and order. She noticed that the university's response was given by the vice president for public affairs,
her friend and landlord, George Bridges. "The university
offers its deepest sympathy to the family and friends of
Owen West," George had said. "This is a tragic event, un-
foreseen and irreparable, and we all mourn the loss of a
young and brilliant scholar." He had discreetly refused to
comment on Mr. West's remark about the gun.

Very good, George, thought McLeod. She had not seen
him last night—he had stayed late at the office and she had
gone to bed early to get ready for her dawn interview with
Earl Shivers—so she had not heard about any of this.

When she turned to other news in *The New York Times*,
she noticed a story about the Massachusetts Institute of
Technology dismissing an immunology researcher because
he had fabricated data.

Scientific fraud! McLeod's heart leaped. Maybe scientific fraud was involved in the murder of Owen West. She gathered up her newspapers, bused her tea mug, and hurried back to her office. By this time, Frieda and the other secretaries were in the office.

"McLeod, isn't it wonderful? 'Spring is here, so blow your job—Now's the time to trust to your wanderlust . . .'"

"Where did you find that quotation, Frieda? It is a quotation, I trust."

"It's from a Rodgers and Hart song," said Frieda. "I love the line '. . . blow your job.'"

"Careful, Frieda," said McLeod. "You'll have us all out on our ears. But spring *is* here, isn't it? The magnolias are about to burst into bloom in the Woodrow Wilson plaza."

Gathering her mail from her pigeonhole, she went up the stairs. She called Forrest Meriwether at home and caught him before he left for Frist. When she asked him about protein folding, his answer was unintelligible to her, but he promised to send her an online link where she could read about the process.

Then she called Sandy Berman—his real name, she discovered after peering at the campus phone directory, was Sanford Berman. He sounded somewhat puzzled by her call, but agreed to see her.

"How soon could I come?" she asked.

"You might as well come now," he said. "The police won't let me in my lab."

Delighted, she took time to find her tape recorder, which she seldom used, and set out with it and a notebook in her big shoulder bag.

The same policeman was in front of Frick when she went back; he opened the door for her and waved her in with a grin. She found Berman in his office and they shook hands. He was tall and lean and had a hook nose and wavy black hair that flopped over his forehead. Unlike Shivers, the grand old man of the chemistry department, Berman was not dressed like the stereotypical professor. Instead of a tweed jacket and tie, he wore a black turtleneck. He smiled when he greeted her and waved at a straight chair by his desk. McLeod thought briefly that chemists really didn't seem to have very comfortable chairs for visitors, but smiled at Berman as she sat down.

"I'm doing an article about Earl Shivers," she said, "and I wanted to talk to you about him. You don't mind if I tape this, do you?"

Berman said he didn't mind, and she turned on the recorder and set it on his desk, which was bare except for a large paperweight made from an old Bunsen burner mounted on what looked like a granite slab. "I'm interested that Professor Shivers has taught the organic chemistry class so long."

"I think he's extremely proud of teaching that class," said Berman.

"Shouldn't he be?" asked McLeod.

"Oh, indeed he should, indeed he should," said Berman. "And he is." He smiled at McLeod.

"And I gather the students like him immensely, even though it's a very difficult course," she said.

"I guess they do," Berman said. "If students ever really like a professor. Sometimes I think that's an impossibility."

"Well, they must like Shivers. They play all those jokes on him," said McLeod.

"Does it demonstrate affection if you throw a pie in somebody's face? Or shoot water pistols at him?"

"It demonstrates something—you're saying there's a hostile edge to the horseplay?"

"Isn't that always true? Shivers looks like your quintessential Ivy League professor, but underneath, he has a wild streak. Of course, none of that matters. Teaching science is not a popularity contest. Does it matter whether the man who teaches organic chemistry is well loved or not?"

"In a sense I'm sure you're right, but to me the practical jokes say a lot. I think it's very interesting. It's a colorful tradition."

"It's a tradition, all right," Berman said. "And traditions have a way of going on and on at Princeton until they become downright unseemly and have to be—well, abolished. Like the nude Olympics."

"You mean you think Professor Shivers should not teach organic chemistry anymore?"

"As a matter of fact, off the record, I do think just that. A number of us have felt that way for some time, but somehow Shivers prevails, and the charade continues."

"You make it a little difficult to write an article about his teaching," McLeod said.

"Oh, don't quote me, whatever you do. And the student newspaper has written about him and the alumni magazine. But that proves my point—that teaching should not be a matter of personality. Shivers is a fine scientist—he's done good work on protein folding. And he has taught other courses and taught them well. It just worries me a little that orgo has become such a circus."

"It's not a circus the whole semester, is it? Isn't it just the last day? But tell me a little more about protein folding."

Berman discussed protein folding and the amino acid sequence, and McLeod could only hope that she could transcribe what he said when she played the tape back. It was like a foreign language.

When Berman stopped talking, she picked up the tape recorder, turned it off, and put it in her bag. Nothing he had said, McLeod thought, would be much use to her for an article about Shivers. But now to her real agenda. "Professor Berman, Owen West was in your group, wasn't he?"

Berman nodded. "He was indeed." He frowned, shook his head, and sighed. He clasped his hands on his desk top. "It's a terrible thing—an attack on a man in a chemistry lab . . . A fatal attack . . . Such a young man. I don't know what to make of it." He was clearly distraught, McLeod thought. "It's just terrible," he went on. "I had to talk to his parents last night."

"That must have been grim," McLeod said. "And graduate students are very close to their professors, aren't they?"

"Yes, it's a close relationship."

"Tell me, what was Owen West like?"

"He was a very well-trained researcher," Berman said.

"What was he like *personally*?" McLeod asked. Scientists were brainy, she thought, but they could be quite dense.

"Oh, he was a rough-and-ready cowboy from Wyoming. Wore cowboy boots and that sort of thing."

"Did he seem like the kind of person to be murdered?"

"What kind of person gets murdered?" Berman asked quietly.

"I guess I'm putting it badly," said McLeod. "Did he seem to be violent or the kind of person who would make enemies and die a violent death? Or was he a victim? Maybe it was a stupid question. Tell me more about what he was like?"

"I never thought of him as either violent or a victim," Berman said. "He had some personality problems—most of us do, I guess."

"What kind of personality problems did Owen West have?"

"He was harsh in his judgments sometimes, and hard to get along with occasionally. But I never dreamed he would be murdered."

"You had trouble getting along with him?" said McLeod. "I thought it was a rule of life for graduate students to get along with the professor. Isn't that the way it works?"

"You must have been a graduate student," said Berman, smiling broadly.

"I have a son who just finished his Ph.D.," she said.

"So you know something about it. It's true; that's the way it works usually, but Owen West was difficult, even with me, one of the most difficult students I ever had. And the other graduate students were always getting upset with him."

"Why? What did he do?"

"All sorts of things. He belittled people's work. He seemed to delight in making the younger ones feel insecure, and he tried to rattle the ones who were ahead of him. I shouldn't be telling you all this. I didn't say anything about this to the police."

"I appreciate your confidence. I really want to see the murder solved."

"Why are you so interested? Do you have a passion for abstract justice?"

"Not at all. A student of mine is under suspicion."

"Really?"

"Yes," and she told him about Greg Pierre.

"If he's innocent, surely he will be cleared soon," said Berman. "And you say he's a good student—I can understand your concern."

"I really want to see him out from under the cloud of suspicion. I'm sure he's innocent. He's had a hard time. But back to Owen West. He was difficult to work with, but did he do good work?"

"He did very good work."

"What kind of chemistry was he working on?"

"He was synthesizing molecules. We all are."

"Why do you synthesize a molecule?"

"It's an extremely important process. All the wonders that organic chemists have performed—artificial dyes, antibiotics, explosives, perfumes, pesticides—have been done by synthesizing molecules in natural products."

"How do you synthesize molecules?"

"It's a long and complicated process, involving breaking and connecting bonds between atoms—carbon, hydrogen, nitrogen, and oxygen atoms. You have to heat or cool the reaction mixtures, filter precipitates, remove solvents, extract solids, and much more. A synthetic chemist has to find suitable conditions and the right reactants for a certain transformation. It's almost like cooking. Most compounds are very complex and require many steps to obtain the final product. You may need a catalyst. You get intermediate compounds. It takes many different processes. And if one process doesn't work, you have to f:ind another."

"I'm afraid I don't understand the science—but maybe I will someday. You said you never dreamed Owen West would be murdered. But he was hard to get along with. Could he have angered another graduate student in your group? Driven him to violence, perhaps?"

"The police asked me if I knew anybody who would want to kill him, and I said I certainly did not. But I'll tell you—off the record, of course—that I've wondered about one of the other students."

"Which one?"

"I had better not mention names," Berman said. "It's all a nasty business." He stared out the window at the white-columned Woodrow Wilson School of Public and International Affairs.

"Maybe you have to mention names," McLeod said quietly. "So innocent people can be cleared."

Berman looked at her. "You're thinking of your student—maybe I'll have to name names. No, I won't. Sorry." He drummed his fingers on his desk. "You must forget what I said about another graduate student. I'm sure it's totally irrelevant. Even to clear your writing student."

"Let me switch to an entirely different topic," said McLeod with some regret. "Is it possible that scientific fraud was involved in the murder?"

"In *my* laboratory?"

"Of course not," said McLeod hastily. "I'm sorry. But would it be possible for scientific fraud to go on at Princeton? I read in the paper today about that case—"

"Oh, yes, the MIT case. Let me tell you, scientific fraud is virtually impossible to carry out," said Berman. "In chemistry, you have to keep all your data, describe exactly how you did your research, and other scientists have to be able to replicate the results. If they can't get the same result you did, then the fraud is exposed. Immediately. Science is cold blooded. The process works very fast."

"But that story in the newspaper this morning . . ." McLeod said.

"Cases of fraud are so rare that they always make big news. The press sensationalizes them."

McLeod's disappointment must have been clearly visible, for Berman smiled for the third time, this time in sympathy, and told her not to worry. "There are always lots of motives in laboratories. I'm surprised there aren't more murders."

"What kinds of motives?"

"There are all kinds of pressures—pressures for funds, for publication. You have to be first in this game. The first man that publishes a method for synthesizing a cancer cure can make millions. The man who was working on the same thing and finishes up just after the first man—that second man gets nothing. So competition is very real." Berman looked very thoughtful and sad as he spoke.

"I see. Being first is everything." McLeod closed her notebook and stood up. "Thanks so much," she said. "I really appreciate your talking to me."

"No problem," said Berman. "Good luck with your article on Shivers. Don't let me discourage you too much."

"I won't," said McLeod. "Thanks."

Fifteen

❦

AS MCLEOD LEFT Frick for the second time that day, she smiled at the policeman at the door.

"Hurry back," he said amiably.

"I will," she said. She knew she'd be back. This murder was becoming intensely interesting to her. She wished she knew more about the science, but she would persevere, even though she didn't understand what people were talking about half the time. She would finesse the science, as Chuck Hammersmith had said. And she would find out about the other graduate students in Berman's group.

She looked at her watch, saw it was almost lunchtime, and hurried to her office, where she sank down in her desk chair. Mercy, she was tired. She had gotten up early, interviewed Shivers at seven o'clock, then interviewed Berman. Two interviews in one morning. No wonder she was exhausted. And hungry. She would like a really decent lunch—not a sandwich.

She looked at her calendar: no lunch scheduled, but two student conferences that afternoon. The class met the next day and she had not planned one single thing. She'd better get down to it. She decided she'd go to Lahiere's—it was fancy but you could get a good lunch without spending too much money; she didn't mind eating by herself in the bar. She could have a glass of sherry while she waited for her lunch. Bliss, she thought. Then she would come back to the office and work like a fiend.

ATTRACTIVE AS THIS plan was, she didn't follow it. Once outside, she started toward Lahiere's, then turned around and came back. Sherry would be nice, but it would not do to reek of alcohol during a conference with a student. She went to the café in Chancellor Green and meekly bought a tuna fish sandwich and a bottle of tomato juice, which she took back to her office.

As she munched on her sandwich, she thought about her morning. Shivers had been interesting, one of those grand old professors who were ornaments of Princeton. Berman was younger and had seemed more forthcoming. They were interesting, but she must find out about Berman's graduate students. How could she do it? The only thing she could think of was a cumbersome route. She would interview one of Earl Shivers's graduate students, ask him for anecdotes about Shivers for her article, of course, and then she would ask the Shivers graduate student about the students in Berman's group.

Who were Shivers's graduate students? Surely she could find out the name of one of them. She really couldn't do anything except meet her students for conferences and plan tomorrow's class, but she would get started on this lead the minute she could.

Meanwhile, what was she to do with her class tomorrow? They were supposed to talk more about their final papers, she remembered. But what smaller projects had she planned for the second part of the semester? She flipped through her course notebook and saw that next week she had a visiting speaker, dear old Tow Sack from Tallahassee. His real name was Jim Burlap and he had worked for the *Star of Florida* for years and years. He was going to be in New York next week and McLeod had asked him to visit her class again. He had done it once before and, with his thick Southern drawl and vast storehouse of funny stories, had been a huge hit. So tomorrow she would prep them for Tow Sack's visit, talk about final papers, and assign a short paper to be completed for next week. What kind of paper? She looked in her notebook and mulled over the possibilities. They had already interviewed and written about each other, their roommates, a professor, and a person from a background totally different from their own.

She couldn't concentrate on the list of projects she had in her notebook. Why not make her students write a piece about a person in science—a student or a professor, whatever. Science writing was important. And difficult. Look at the difficult time she had had with her interviews with chemists, she thought; her students should have the same experiences she had had since they were nearly all English or history majors. She would think about it overnight, she told herself, and decide in the morning.

AS SOON AS her conferences were over, she decided to go back to Frick. She had remembered that many professors had assistants, who knew everything. Surely Shivers had an assistant—and McLeod could get the names of graduate students from her. She pulled on her jacket and hurried down the stairs and out the door. The same policeman was guarding the doors at Frick.

"What took you so long?" he asked her.

"I'm just slow," she said, and sailed through the door.

She went to the chemistry departmental office and asked who Shivers's assistant was.

She turned out to be a delightful little woman named Binky Tate who occupied a cubbyhole near Shivers's office. McLeod introduced herself and explained that she was doing an article about Earl Shivers and wanted to talk to some of his graduate students. Binky, who had a nice smile and curly hair, cheerfully wrote out five names with e-mail addresses on a sheet of paper and handed it to McLeod.

"Thanks," said McLeod, "and I want to talk to you about him, too, when it's convenient for you."

Binky grinned. "It's always convenient. I love to talk about my boss."

"I'll call to make an appointment," said McLeod.

"Fine. You can probably find the students in the lab-O-ratory," she said, pronouncing it the way her boss did.

"Good."

"I'll show you the way," Binky said, getting up.

"Oh, no, I can find it."

"Whatever," said Binky. She winked.

Odd little woman, thought McLeod as she hurried out with list in hand. Striding down the corridor, she saw a door barred by yellow police tape. Beside it stood a uniformed member of the campus Public Safety Office. McLeod was looking at the sign outside the door that said, BERMAN LAB, when Lieutenant Nick Perry came out of the door, nodded to the Public Safety man, and spotted McLeod.

"What are you doing here? Do you haunt every murder scene?"

"Hello, Nick," she said. "I'm here on business. I'm doing a story about Earl Shivers and I'm going to talk to some of his graduate students. How's the investigation going?"

"Slowly," he said. "Slowly but, I hope, surely."

"My student is cleared, I hope."

"Nobody's cleared at this point." He sounded tired and, McLeod realized, looked tired.

"I hope you solve it soon," she said.

"I do, too. I'd like to see you when I get some time."

"Me, too. Call."

"I will," he said.

"Good," she said, and went on her way, regretting only that she hadn't asked Nick about what had killed Owen West.

Around a corner in the corridor she came to a door with a sign beside it that said SHIVERS LAB and went in to see three people scattered around the large room, filled with work counters laden with mysterious equipment. McLeod looked at her list, read off the first name, "Jeff Jones," and looked around inquiringly.

"That's me," said a young man nearest the door. When McLeod smiled at him, he came over to her and she introduced herself. "Jeff, I'm writing an article about Earl Shivers and I want to talk to lots of people about him. I wonder if you could spare me a few minutes."

"Sure," he said. "What do you want to know?"

"Is there a place we can sit down?" she asked him.

Jeff looked around in a puzzled way. "I guess we can sit over here—where people write up their lab books." He led her over to a table with two chairs and they sat down. McLeod got out her notebook and smiled at Jeff.

"I just wondered what Shivers is like with graduate students. Do they play jokes on him the way undergraduates do?"

"No, we don't. This is serious business, what we're doing."

"But he's a good supervisor?"

"He is. His graduate students choose him, you know. Some advisors want to get all the credit for what you do or what you publish, but Earl's not like that. He's made his own reputation and so he's secure, not anxious. He's a good man. Would you like to talk to somebody else about him? Matt and Lisa are in his group, too."

"Sure," said McLeod. Jeff summoned the other two, and they came over. She noted that Jeff gave Lisa his chair and stood up beside Matt.

McLeod introduced herself again, explained her mission, and turned to Lisa. "I had forgotten there were women graduate students in chemistry," she said. "How nice to know you. Are there any difficulties for women in this chemistry department?"

"Not many. There are two women professors, you know," said Lisa. "One male professor told me when I started, 'No tears. I won't tolerate tears.' So I haven't cried once." All three roared with laughter—they had obviously heard about this before. "But most of them are fine with me."

"And Shivers? How is he with your femininity?"

"He's actually the one who said, 'No tears,' but he's from another generation. And he's gotten better. He's fine with me, too, now."

"That speaks well for him," said McLeod, "and for you, Lisa. You must have reassured him." They chatted a few more minutes, and as Jeff and Matt eased away, McLeod asked Lisa if she had known Owen West.

"Oh, yes, the Prince of Darkness we called him."

"Really?" McLeod felt a thrill of excitement. "Why?"

"I don't know. He was like, just mysterious and sullen. I certainly didn't know him very well, but that was my impression."

"Who else is in Sandy Berman's group?" McLeod asked.

"I don't know all of them. My friend, Melissa, is in his group. Melissa Martin. Hey, guys, who's in Berman's group—besides Melissa?"

Jeff didn't hear her, but Matt came over and gave McLeod two other names. She wrote them all down, got Melissa's phone number and e-mail from Lisa, thanked Lisa and Matt profusely, and left.

She felt as she left Frick that she had accomplished wonders. She had actually gathered a fair amount of material for an article on Shivers, and she had found a teeny bit more about Owen West—Prince of Darkness, indeed—and had the names of three graduate students who had worked with West.

She stopped by her office to call Melissa Martin, got voice mail, and left her home phone number and asked her to call that evening. Then she hurried home.

Sixteen

MCLEOD WAS SO late getting home that Wednesday that George got home about the same time she did—an unheard-of state of affairs.

"How did you get away so early—when there's an unsolved murder on campus?" she asked him.

"Things look so bad they couldn't be any worse. And I must say Chuck Hammersmith handles the media like a dream. I couldn't think of anything constructive I could do myself. When Tom left, I thought, if the president can leave, I can, too. Before I could get away, though, your friend Nick Perry came by the office. He said he had just seen you in Frick and wanted to know if you were meddling in the investigation. I told him not that I knew of. But what were you doing in Frick?"

"It makes me furious that you two would talk about me that way. As I told him, I'm doing a story on Earl Shivers, and I was in Frick to talk to some of his graduate students. I have learned nothing about the murder, nothing at all." (Well, she hadn't learned anything, really, now had she? she asked herself. Berman had said Owen West was bad tempered, and Lisa had called him the Prince of Darkness. That was hardly important information. It was no more than he could find out if he would just talk to people the way she did. She did not feel the least bit guilty, she told herself, and it probably was not important anyway.)

Just then the telephone rang and George went to the kitchen to answer it. "It's for you," he said, coming back to the living room.

"Thanks." Picking up the phone in the kitchen, McLeod found it was Lisa's friend, Melissa Martin. McLeod said she would like to talk to her, and Melissa asked, what about? McLeod said she was doing a story about a chemistry professor and was trying to talk to a broad range of people who might know him. Melissa had no time the next morning, but said she could see McLeod that night, if she liked.

McLeod said that would be fine and she would come to Melissa's home. She lived in an apartment in the new buildings for graduate students off Alexander Road. It was now after six o'clock and they agreed that McLeod would come at seven-thirty.

"I had thought we would go out to dinner," said George when she told him her plan.

"This won't take long. Can't we go at eight? Dine fashionably late?"

"I might as well cook here if we have that much time," said George. "Let's have another drink and then I'll go to the store."

"I can't have another drink before I go interview somebody."

"Who is this you're going to interview?"

"Just another graduate student," she said, keeping it to herself that it was not another of Shivers's students, but one of Berman's.

"Well, have a glass of water while I have another drink and I'll think about what to make for supper. I saw a recipe in *Gourmet* for a chuck roast that sounded wonderful. But it takes two hours."

"That's about right," said McLeod. "I love it that you read *Gourmet*."

"It was in the dentist's office," said George. "Okay, I'll go to the store right now. I'll be back before you leave."

WHEN MCLEOD LEFT, George was in the kitchen whistling as he chopped onions and garlic for his chuck roast. She found Melissa's apartment easily—she had given good directions, as a good scientist should—and found Melissa, who looked not at all like the tall, forceful woman she had expected. For Melissa was tiny, pretty, and extremely feminine, with blond hair that was carefully styled and not gathered into a ponytail like the hair of every other female on campus. She wore a silk shirt and the universal jeans, but her jeans were immaculate, and she wore gold earrings and lots of eyeliner.

They made small talk for a while. "So you teach writing—how interesting," and, "So you're a woman in the sciences—how interesting."

"I'm still not clear why you want to talk to me," Melissa said. "You're doing an article on Shivers. I scarcely know him."

"It's good of you to see me. I'll be frank—I am doing a story on Shivers—that's true. But I'm also very interested in the murder of Owen West and I wanted to talk to somebody who knew him."

"Why are you so interested in the murder?"

McLeod liked her directness. "Because one of my students seems to be a suspect and I want to find out who really did the murder so he can be cleared," she said.

"Won't the police . . . ?" asked Melissa, and hesitated.

"They're very good. Lieutenant Perry, who's in charge of the investigation, is actually a friend of mine. He's good. But he looks for hard evidence, and sometimes he doesn't talk to people enough. I've heard rumors that Owen West was hard to get along with. Did the police ask you about anything like that?"

"No, as a matter of fact, they didn't," said Melissa. "They did talk to everybody who works in our lab, but they were interested in where we were on Sunday night and stuff like that. They didn't ask me anything about Owen as a person, just did I know anybody who had a reason to kill him."

"What did you say when they asked you that?"

"I said no, I didn't. But that was Monday, and two days later, I have been thinking about Owen and you're right— he was hard to get along with."

"Of course, that's not a reason to kill somebody—just because he's hard to get along with," said McLeod judiciously.

"No, of course not," said Melissa.

Still, thought McLeod, it was interesting that everybody said the same thing. "How was he hard to get along with?" she asked.

"He was very competitive, for one thing. And for another, he was self-righteous. He believed it was his duty to tell everybody what they are doing wrong. That can be seriously annoying."

"I can imagine," said McLeod.

"We called him the Prince of Darkness."

McLeod smiled. "Did he ever tell you what you were doing wrong, Melissa?"

"He tried. He actually stole my lab notebook. Well, he took it and studied it and then told me the work I was doing competed with what he was doing."

"Did you have an argument about it?"

"Nah," said Melissa. "I just told him to bug off. He said that Sandy agreed with him. I told him that had to be a lie. And I pointed out that I'd been here before he was and was well into the work I was going to do. I said if he bothered me any more, I'd go not only to Sandy, but to the dean of the graduate school. I never heard another word from him. Literally, he never spoke to me again, but he never bothered me."

"I'm impressed," said McLeod. "You look so little and so feminine . . ."

Melissa laughed, and raised her arms as though pumping her muscles. "I'm tough," she said. "No, seriously, he was a bully. And bullies always back down. If people would just remember that. I tried to tell Sam . . ." She stopped.

"Sam?" said McLeod.

"Sam Chen."

"Is he in Berman's group, too?"

"Yes, he is."

"Did he and Owen West quarrel?"

"I hesitate to tell you any more," said Melissa. "Talk to Sam yourself."

"I certainly will. Can you give me the names of the other students in the group?"

"Yes. There's five of us—Owen, me, Sam Chen, Carey Srodek, and Scott Murphy."

"And their phone numbers?"

"Their voice mail and e-mail are in the campus directory. I don't know them offhand."

"Of course, I forgot about the directory. Thanks so much," said McLeod.

"And then there's his girlfriend."

"His girlfriend?"

"Owen West's girlfriend. He treated her abominably, I thought. She was a fool to put up with it."

"Who is she? Have the police talked to her?"

"She's Megan Snowden. I don't know whether the police talked to her or not," said Melissa.

"Is she a graduate student, too?"

"Yes, she is."

"Is she in chemistry?"

"No, she's in English."

"I wonder how they met," said McLeod. "English now seems a universe away from chemistry."

"I think they met when they both lived at the Graduate College their first year. But the universe apart was just one of the things Owen was always on to her about."

"What do you mean?"

"He was always telling her that people in the humanities weren't as smart as people in science."

"That's grounds for breaking up, but not grounds for murder," said McLeod.

"I know that," said Melissa. "But there was more. He yelled at her about the way she dressed and the way she cooked and the way she snored. Everything she did was wrong, according to him. And he ran around with other girls, too."

"Why did she stay with him?"

"God knows," said Melissa.

"Did the police talk to her?"

"I don't know. They must have. She and Owen lived together on Edwards Place. A nice apartment—they had all of us over a couple of times. Maybe the apartment was why they stayed together. Maybe she didn't want to have to find another place to live. Oh, I don't know. Why does anybody stay with anybody? But they do."

"I guess I'll try and talk to her, too," said McLeod.

"Good luck," said Melissa. "I've seen her twice since Owen died. She came over to Frick on Monday to see if it was true. She couldn't believe that Owen was dead. 'Without telling her,' she said. I think she thought he had committed suicide."

"Oh, dear. Oh, dear," said McLeod. "It is so sad. But I want to clear my boy."

"How did he get to be a suspect? Did he have some connection to Owen or chemistry or what?" asked Melissa.

McLeod told her about Greg Pierre. Melissa agreed everyone should work toward finding the real murderer, if for no other reason than to clear Greg.

McLeod thanked her fervently, and went home to dinner. The chuck roast was delicious.

She was exhausted after her full day of talking to people, and tumbled into bed as soon as she had finished the dishes. She felt doing the dishes was the least she could do since George had cooked. She would finish preparing her class tomorrow morning, she vowed.

Seventeen

❦

WHEN MCLEOD'S CLASS gathered in the seminar room on Thursday afternoon, things took an unexpected turn. Greg Pierre was the first student to arrive, and McLeod welcomed him and asked if he had heard from the police again.

"Yeah, they asked me to come down for a 'chat' yesterday. But I didn't have to stay long. I think they were just checking up to see if I'd say the same thing I'd said before."

"Did you?"

"I sure did. That's one lesson I've learned—tell the truth to the police."

"That's a lesson for politicians to learn. It's always the cover-up that gets them in trouble. Have you caught up on all your classwork?"

"Does anybody ever catch up at Princeton? I'm okay, I guess. But it's time for track and field and I run the fifteen-hundred-meter and the three-thousand-meter and I was out a week and it was spring break and the team was training in Florida."

"Good gracious! That's awful. You won't be thrown off the team, will you?"

"Not yet. Coach Lilly is a really good guy. And actually Princeton gives its runners more room than other schools do. I think it's going to be all right. I'm going to run in a meet this weekend. So I'm braced."

"Good luck!" said McLeod, as Olivia Merchant came in. She stopped dead still when she saw Greg, and said, "What happened to you? Are you all right?"

McLeod had somehow forgotten that the class's last sight of Greg had been his departure two weeks ago with a sergeant from the Borough Police Force.

Greg hesitated before he answered. "I went to jail, and the teacher got me out."

"I didn't get you out. It was Isabel," said McLeod.

"Who's Isabel?" demanded Olivia. Olivia, like Greg, was one of the best writers in the class. She was also very intense, and she focused like a searchlight on Greg. "Come on. What happened?"

Clark Powell came in, followed by a couple of other students. They all stared at Greg. "Congratulations, man," said Clark. "How'd you, like, shake your police escort?"

"Yeah, good to have you back among us. We thought we'd never see you again," said another student.

Greg seemed uneasy at all the attention. He tried to shrug off the questions, but the others were determined. "I was charged with a crime in Wyoming," he said finally. "I wasn't guilty and I got cleared. And I'm back. That's all."

"That's *all*?" said Olivia. "What do you mean that's *all*? What was the crime and how did you get cleared?"

McLeod wrapped on the table with her pencil. "It's quite a story," she said. "Maybe Greg will let one of you interview him, or maybe he wants to write about his adventures himself. Let him alone now and let's get started. Time is flying, or as my Aunt Maggie used to say, *'Tempus fugit,'* or as she sometimes said, *'Tempus is fugiting.'* She believed everybody ought to study Latin, but she fractured her Latin." She knew she was babbling, but she was regretting that she had mentioned interviewing Greg. And of course he didn't want to talk about his experiences—it wasn't generally known among students that he had used a false identity to get into Princeton.

Olivia's arm was upraised and she flapped her hand wildly. "Greg, can I interview you about all this?"

Clark Powell spoke up: "I'd like to talk to you about it, Greg. I could be your ghost writer."

Other students were muttering the same sort of thing.

McLeod rapped on the table again. "Class," she began, but Greg drowned her out. "I don't want to talk about it. I don't want to write about it. I don't want any of you to talk about it. I just want to forget it and get on with school and track and that's all. Some of you fucking preppies don't have any idea what it's all about." He stood up and took his backpack off the back of his chair.

"Don't go, Greg," McLeod said, standing up, too. "We'll leave you alone. I shouldn't have said anything about interviewing you. I'm sorry, very sorry. Forgive me. Give us all another chance. Don't go . . ." Her voice trailed off. "Good," she said, as Greg hung his backpack on his chair. He said nothing, but sat down again.

"Yeah, we're sorry," Clark Powell said.

"We're on your side, though, whatever . . ." said Olivia.

"Thanks," said Greg. He didn't look up.

"Okay," said McLeod, "Let's get started. I want to tell you about next week's class. A friend of mine, a legendary reporter from the *Star of Florida*, will be with us. His name is Jim Burlap. He'll tell you about his life of writing about people, mostly politicians, mostly Floridians, but I think you'll enjoy him."

She described Jim's work, said she would post some of his old stories on Blackboard, the program that teachers used to relay things to students, and urged them to be prepared with questions for Burlap. "And now it's time to begin thinking about the big paper, the ten-thousand-word piece for the end of the semester. You can write about anything you want to as long as you write about a person or people. This is not the time to write theory or history—unless it's a very personalized history—or even about events, unless you focus on a person or two or three persons involved in those events. You will be able to show all you've learned about interviewing people and researching people and making people come alive as you write about them . . ."

They asked her questions. Did it have to be somebody connected with the university? No, McLeod said, of course not. Could they take a story they had done earlier and expand it? Yes, but it might be better to tackle a fresh subject, unless there was a compelling reason to do the other one over. Did it really have to be 10,000 words? No, it didn't, she told them. That would be forty pages; twenty pages would be fine, but it could run as long as forty pages.

"Like one of those old *New Yorker* pieces?" said one of the students.

"That would be very good indeed, if you could turn out one of those," McLeod said.

Groans went up.

Finally, she got around to an assignment for the next week. "I want everybody to write about somebody in the sciences," she said. "I think this is one of the most difficult kinds of writing. I'm involved in a project of this kind myself; that's why I thought it would be a challenge for you. And science writers are greatly in demand. They make tons of money. I've posted some examples of science writing by Richard Preston and Michael Lemonick and other people on the Web site. Read those for starters, but remember the emphasis in this class is writing about people. Are any of you science majors?"

Nobody was.

"Are any of you taking science courses?"

They all were taking, or had taken, science courses, since two science and technology courses and a laboratory were required of all students at Princeton. Thus, McLeod's students were familiar with geosciences, ecology, evolutionary biology, and/or chemistry. One student was enrolled in Physics for Poets.

"I'm taking tons of science," Clark Powell said. "This semester it's organic chemistry."

"I thought you were interested in the theater," said

McLeod, who had furnished him with some costumes for a Theatre Intime production.

"I like theater, but I'm a premed so I have to take organic chemistry and a million other science courses."

"Oh, I want to talk to you," McLeod said. "About Earl Shivers."

"Sure," said Clark.

"This assignment will be easier for all of you than I thought," McLeod said to the class. "You all know somebody in science. So go to it. Talk to them about their work and write about it. I'll be very interested in your papers. They don't have to be long—say, a thousand words, or even less. But give it a whirl."

Greg Pierre was the first student to leave, and after he was gone, some of the others crowded around and demanded to know why he wouldn't talk about his experience.

"Look," said McLeod, "it's not easy for him. I could cut my tongue out for saying maybe you could interview him. He's had a tough, tough time, and now he's under . . ." She stopped herself before she revealed that Greg had been interviewed about the murder in Frick. "He's under a lot of stress," she said. "Be kind."

Most of them nodded and left. Olivia and Clark stayed to complain loudly that their deep desire to learn all of Greg's story was being thwarted.

McLeod left them in the seminar room and went to her office upstairs. She wanted to track down some more articles to post on the class's Web site. As soon as she could get that done, she would turn her attention back to clearing Greg.

But meanwhile, she could leave messages for Sam Chen and the other graduate students in Berman's group. Students all used cell phones but she didn't have those numbers. She would send them e-mails—either the e-mail or the telephone message ought to produce a response. But what excuse could she give for asking a lot of questions about Owen West? The truth, she decided. The truth was always best, and everybody seemed to be sympathetic to her desire to clear her student.

And there was Megan Snowden to be talked to. *Cherchez la femme* and all that. Sex was so often at the heart of a murder—yes, it was best to talk to Megan Snowden as soon as she could. She sent her an e-mail, and before she could leave her a phone message, Sam Chen called her.

"I got your a e-mail and your message. They sounded like it was something urgent," he said.

"It is," she said, and explained that she wanted to talk to him about Owen West. "Where can I meet you?"

"I can come to your office," he said.

"Great," she said, and told him how to find her. "I'll meet you downstairs. I want to be sure the door's open— it's getting late."

Eighteen

※

MCLEOD SAT ON a chair in the front hall of Joseph Henry House to wait for Sam Chen, who appeared almost immediately. McLeod got up to greet him. He was an attractive young man with tiny rimless spectacles and a nice grin. He was also extremely neat, wearing a spanking clean turtleneck and immaculate windbreaker.

"We can talk down here—my cubbyhole of an office is up on the third floor," she said, leading him to the sun parlor. "This is very nice of you to come over here," she said as they sat down.

"It's hard to find a place in Frick to talk," he said. "And you said you wanted to find out more about Owen West. Why?"

"A reasonable question," said McLeod. "Greg Pierre is a student in my writing class and he's under suspicion for the murder of Owen West, so I'm trying to find out more about West and maybe find out who killed him."

"Who is Greg Pierre?"

"As I said, he's a student in my writing class. He's very talented."

"And you feel like it's your responsibility to clear him? Why?"

"I feel like it's somewhat my responsibility," said McLeod. "Greg is my student, and I guess I'm a mother hen where my students are concerned. I suppose the police will find out who did it sooner or later, but if I can help things along, I think I should. So can you tell me anything useful about Owen West?"

"I don't understand," said Sam Chen. "Why do you think your student is innocent if the police think he did it?"

"I just can't see him as a murderer." When Chen looked dubious, she added, "And my instincts are usually sound."

"Why do the police suspect this student of yours?" Chen asked.

McLeod was exasperated. Was this man hostile, or just dense? But she must not lose her temper, she told herself. She had to win him over. Since she didn't want to tell him about Greg's false identity—by some miracle, that hadn't been in the papers yet—she said, "Owen West got Greg Pierre in trouble with the authorities in Wyoming. It all got straightened out, but the police seem to think Greg has the only motive for killing West."

"The police don't think that," said Sam.

"What do you mean?"

"They don't think your student is the only one with a motive for killing Owen West."

"Who else has a motive?" asked McLeod.

"They think I do."

"You? You mean they think you killed him. Are you serious?"

"I wouldn't joke about something like this, believe me."

"Why do they think that?"

"I'll tell you. I suppose I shouldn't help you at all. It's to my advantage if your student isn't cleared, isn't it? But I need to talk to somebody."

It was her white hair, McLeod thought for the thousandth time. The unlikeliest people poured out their secrets to her. Thank God, she thought, and waited for Sam Chen to tell her his story. However, he did not pour it out. It came, a sentence at a time, in response to questions.

"Why do they think you might have killed Owen West?"

"They have a couple of reasons. You didn't know him, did you?"

"No, I didn't. What was he like? Was he a congenial colleague? Did he get along with you and Melissa and Carey and Scott?"

"You have to get along with the people in your group," said Sam. "But Melissa started calling him the Prince of Darkness, and it caught on."

"Tell me what *you* thought of Owen West," said McLeod. "You, yourself."

"I thought he was a fucking asshole," said Sam, surprising McLeod that language like that could come from such a calm, disciplined-looking person.

"He was a real shit, if you'll pardon the expression."

McLeod shook her head dismissively. "I hear worse than that every day. But why do the police suspect you?" When Sam didn't answer her, she went on. "It's not just because you didn't like him, is it?"

"That's part of it," said Sam.

"What else?" she asked.

"They think I might have had a real grudge against him."

"Why?"

"We had words in the lab one day."

"What kind of words?" asked McLeod, wishing that Sam were more loquacious. It was slow work, pulling everything out of him a word at a time.

"He was naturally untidy," said Sam. "He would make a big mess in the lab and never clean it up. He intruded on other people's space. My space. He was not a good scientist."

"Did this bother the other people in your group?"

"It bothered me the most—I'm neat. But it bothered everybody else, too."

"That's not enough to make somebody kill him, though, is it?"

"If it goes on long enough," said Sam. "You couldn't work in the lab with him. Scott threatened to hit him one time. I heard him. I was hoping Berman would throw West out, but Berman is too easygoing. One time, I asked West to be more careful. It made him furious."

"Is that all? Did anything else happen? I mean, you feel so strongly about him . . ."

"He called me a Chink shit," said Sam.

"That's awful," said McLeod. "It's unconscionable." She thought a minute. "But is it cause for murder?"

"No, of course not, but everybody heard him. And everybody knows I had no use for him. I guess somebody must have told the police about it."

"Did they ask you about it?"

"Not at first," said Sam. "They just asked me where I was on Sunday night."

"And where were you on Sunday night?" McLeod asked out of simple curiosity.

"That's the problem," said Sam. "I was alone. I live in a small apartment in town. I went to the lab for a while Sunday afternoon. Owen was there when I left, and then I went to the movie at the Garden."

"What was the movie?"

"*March of the Penguins*," said Sam.

"I hear it's marvelous," said McLeod. "Did you like it?"

"I thought it was kind of boring—all those crazy birds trekking around all over Antarctica."

"Did anybody see you there?"

"Nobody I know," said Sam.

"What time was the movie over? What did you do then?"

"I got out about seven o'clock, I picked up some noodles at the Chinese place, got some beer, and took it all home and watched television for a little. I went to bed early—I wanted to get to the lab early before Owen got there on Monday—he usually comes in late."

"You didn't see anybody you knew at the Chinese place?"

Sam shook his head.

"And did you get any telephone calls after you got home?"

"No."

McLeod stared at him. She felt sympathetic, but what could you say to a man who's quarreled publicly with a man who is later murdered at a time for which he has no alibi? Good luck—that was about all you could say. "Did the police question you again?"

"Yes. And this time they asked me how I got along with West. They knew about the time we had words in the lab."

"One exchange of harsh words doesn't mean a murder—they know that. I can see why you're worried, though. Still we have to believe that justice will triumph, that the police will find the real murderer."

"But you don't believe that yourself. You're out to prove another man is innocent."

"Yes, I'd like to clear my student. I think the police will eventually find out who the true murderer is, but I'm just hoping to speed things up. If I—or anybody—could find out who the real murderer is, that would clear my student and—I presume—clear you, too. So help me all you can, won't you? Let's get to the bottom of this. What else do you know about Owen West? I've talked to a few people and I get the distinct impression that he was a nasty piece of work, a racist busybody who annoyed everyone with whom he came in contact. But whom did he annoy most? Think. You knew him for two years."

"So you don't think I killed him?"

"No, I don't," said McLeod.

"I'm glad you believe me."

"But listen to me. You have to help me find out more."

"I can't think of anything. I knew him for two years. but I saw as little of him as I could. I'll try to think about it, though."

"What about Melissa? She told me she had a run-in with him in the lab," said McLeod.

"That was typical of West. But Melissa's tough. She scared him."

"What about Cary and Scott? I haven't talked to either one of them yet."

"I don't know much about them, to tell you the truth," said Sam.

"Look, if we're going to get to the bottom of this, you have to help me. Tell me everything you know about Owen West and his relations with other people. Think."

"I will. I will. I want to help you."

"Great. Let me give you my telephone numbers and my e-mail," she said. "Call me anytime."

"Thank you, Ms. Dulaney."

"Thank you, Mr. Chen. Sam."

He left, and McLeod put on her coat and walked home. She realized when she came in the front door she was exhausted. It had been another long day—the class had been tense with the clash between Greg and the others, and then the long talk with Sam Chen had been unsatisfactory. She was glad that George wasn't home. She would find something to eat and go to bed early. Tomorrow was another day.

Nineteen

❧

ON FRIDAY MORNING, McLeod woke up early, put on her warm flannel bathrobe, and padded downstairs in her fleece-lined slippers. (She never wore either of these garments at home in Tallahassee, but was very glad to have them when she was in Princeton.) George wasn't up, so she brought in the newspapers. She made coffee for George and tea for herself and settled down at the dining room table. She found nothing new on the murder in the Trenton paper and no mention of it in *The New York Times*. This was not a case of no news is good news, she thought.

George came down, showered, shaved, and dressed for the office. She handed him the papers, and went in search of a notebook and pencil.

"Thanks for making coffee," said George when she came back. He was eating cereal with a banana cut up on it. "You went to bed early last night."

"I was worn out," she said. "Bone-tired. I was asleep by eight-thirty."

"Okay now?" he asked.

"Oh, yes. I'm resilient."

"How was your class yesterday?"

"Strange," she said, and told him about the students' eagerness to "interview" Greg Pierre and his angry reaction.

"I guess he's had enough questioning," said George.

"And he's getting more from the police. I wish this murder hadn't happened—"

"That's an understatement," said George, "of how the university feels."

"I'm sure," said McLeod. "Have you talked to Nick Perry?"

"Not since Wednesday. Have you?"

"I haven't. I'd like to. But I dare not call him when he's in the midst of a case. Oh, did anybody call me last night after I was in bed?"

"Yes. You had a call from a man with a funny name. I wrote it down over here . . ." He got up and found the scrap of paper and handed it to her.

"Carey Srodek," she read. Another one of Sandy Berman's graduate students. He had left another number, she noticed.

"Thanks," she said, and put the paper in her bathrobe pocket.

"Whatever happened to that sweater you were knitting for me?" George asked. "You were working away on it before the break, but I haven't seen it lately."

"I screwed it up. The pattern is very complex. I've got to get it straightened out before I can go on with it. Things have been so hectic around here I haven't thought about it. I'm glad you reminded me."

"Good. As I said, nobody ever knitted a sweater for me before. I was looking forward to my very own handknit sweater . . ."

"I promise," said McLeod.

They chatted a few more minutes until George got ready to leave. "I'll be home for dinner tonight. Let's eat in. Friday night is a bad night to eat out in Princeton."

"Right," said McLeod, and decided she was supposed to

cook that night. Oh, well, she said to herself, I'll think of something.

She opened the notebook and made a list:

Carey Srodek
Scott Murphy
Megan Snowden

She hesitated after writing down the last name. She should have talked to this woman before now. After all, there had to be some reason why everybody said, *Cherchez la femme* when there was a crime.

After chewing on the pencil for a while, she added "grocery store" to the list, and went upstairs to shower and dress.

IT WAS A beautiful spring day and McLeod enjoyed walking up Mercer Street and on Nassau Street to the campus. It was so great to see the little new green leaves coming out. She passed what she thought of as the "anthrax mailbox" and wondered for the thousandth time who had mailed the lethal letters. Once in her office, she called Carey Srodek.

"Sam and Melissa both told me about you," he said.

McLeod did not know whether to be pleased or otherwise by this, but arranged to meet him at Frist student center for coffee at ten. "You can tell who I am," she said. "I have white hair, and I have on"—she looked down—"a pink sweater."

"I have white hair, too," he said. "Very white, and I'll have on a blue jacket." He hung up.

A white-haired graduate student? She wondered how could that be? Some old geezer who was changing careers? She called Megan Snowden, Owen West's girlfriend, found her at home, and said, "I'm McLeod Dulaney, and I'm teaching a writing course this semester."

"Of course," said Megan Snowden. "I've heard about you."

It was nice to talk to someone who was not in the sciences, but in the English department, thought McLeod, where she was not totally unknown. "I'd like very much to talk to you," she said. "Could you have lunch with me today, or should I come to your place?"

"What did you want to talk to me about, Ms. Dulaney?"

"I'm sorry to barge in at a time like this, but I wanted to talk to you about Owen West."

A long silence followed. "Why?" Megan finally asked.

"I'm interested in why he—why he was killed. I'd like to find the person who did it and I thought you perhaps would be willing to tell me more about him than anybody else."

Another long silence, during which McLeod began to feel like a fool and a meddler. Why did she do this? She waited.

"All right," said Megan finally. "Yes. I'd like to talk. You're not connected to the police?"

"Heavens, no. Shall I come over to your place this afternoon? You live on Edwards, don't you?"

"That's right. When would you like to come?"

"About three?"

"Fine, I'll be here." She gave McLeod the address.

"I look forward to meeting you," McLeod said and hung up. She checked her e-mail and handled other messages.

WHEN IT WAS time to walk down to Frist, she decided it was such a nice day she would have a Coke instead of coffee or tea when she got there. She was humming happily when she spotted Carey Srodek at the colonnade in front of Frist; he was not an old geezer. but an extremely blond young man—who smiled widely as she approached.

"Ms. Dulaney? I'm Carey Srodek."

"That's me," she said.

"I thought it must be you, even though I couldn't see the pink sweater," he said, still smiling.

They shook hands, and she smiled back; she liked him already. "Thanks for coming," she said. He followed her inside and down the stairs to where the food and drink were sold.

"Café Vivian?" he said, motioning toward the small, darkish room that served as a coffeehouse. "Shall we go there?"

"You know, I really like to sit back by one of those south-facing windows. Is that all right with you?" She was glad when Carey nodded.

"I like sunshine, too," he said.

He got his coffee and she got her Coke and they settled down at a window table. "I like the view of Guyot Hall," she said and then got down to business. "If you've talked to Sam and Melissa, you know what my mission is," she said. "What can you tell me about Owen West?"

"Well, they said you're trying to find out who killed him. Is that right? Are you playing detective, or what? What's in it for you?"

McLeod decided maybe she didn't like Carey Srodek as much as she had thought she did. "I have a student who's a suspect, and I wanted to clear him— find the real murderer so my student would be off the hook. Now I've gotten caught up in the whole thing and I want to know more. There's nothing in it for me, except to clear my student. And of course, clear any other innocent suspect."

"Like me, or Sam Chen?" he said.

"Are you a suspect?"

"I think we all are," said Carey Srodek. "The police are questioning us all more than once."

"What do they ask you?"

"A lot about when I last saw Owen West, if I knew anybody who wanted to kill him, where I was on Sunday night, that kind of thing."

"Just for the record, where were you on Sunday night?"

"I was with friends."

"And they can confirm that you were with them."

"Of course they can." He took a sip of coffee, then another. "No, that's not true. I was with them awhile," he said. "I guess they'd tell the police I was with them the whole evening if I asked them to, but I wasn't. So I guess, well, I guess I don't have an alibi, really. You can see how I crumple and go back to the truth."

"That's great," said McLeod, who was liking him wholeheartedly again. "To change the subject slightly, how did you get along with Owen West?"

"He was okay, but he could be very annoying—he stole my laptop."

"Stole your computer? That's awful," said McLeod.

"Well, he picked it up in the lab and took it home. He wanted to find out more about what I was doing. He always wanted to know what everybody in the lab was doing. He brought my laptop back but he should never have taken it in the first place. He couldn't take a joke, either. I used to tease him about his snooping around other people's work, and it made him furious. But still, I used to say that I didn't regard him as the Prince of Darkness the way Sam and Melissa and Scott did. When he was alive, I knew I had to get along with him, and so I suppressed all my anger at him. Now that he's dead, I have to admit he was a terrible person. I don't even think he was a very good scientist. And he didn't pull his weight when we worked on something together. But lots of people are like that. As I say, when he was alive, I could get along with him."

"You know, those are the kindest words I've heard about him yet," said McLeod.

Carey smiled again. "If I get murdered, I hope somebody says something better about me than, 'I could get along with him.'"

"I expect they will," said McLeod. "I know he and Sam had words once. Did Scott and Melissa quarrel with him?"

"Oh, Melissa had one blowout with him right when he first came, but after that they had a truce. He and Scott were always snarling at each other. But I'll tell you who you ought to talk to is Wesley Bryant."

"Wesley Bryant?" said McLeod. "Who's he?"

"It's a she," said Carey.

"Who is she?" (*Cherchez les femmes*, thought McLeod.)

"She's a postdoc," said Carey.

"Postdoc?"

"A postdoctoral fellow. You know. She's doing research in Professor Berman's lab."

"And I should talk to her?" asked McLeod.

"I think you should," Carey said. "Owen was really interested in her computer. I don't think he ever took it anywhere, but I know he was doing something with it one day. I saw him."

"Thank you very much. I shall certainly talk to Wesley Bryant. I suppose I can find her in the directory? Tell me about postdocs."

"Well, they have their Ph.D.'s and usually they take a postdoc position because they didn't get a teaching job. They do research—they aren't allowed to stay long— while they look for a permanent job."

"I see. So you think she had a grudge against Owen West?"

"I didn't say that. I said you should talk to her. Of course, you should talk to Scott Murphy, too."

"I shall try and talk to everybody who knew Owen West. I have an appointment with Megan Snowden. Do you know her?"

"That's Owen's girlfriend. I met her a couple of times. She's in English, I think."

"So I understand. But back to Owen West. Can you tell me anything else about him?"

"He liked to play chess," said Carey.

"Really?"

"And he drank beer."

"Don't all graduate students?"

"I guess so. I do."

"How did he and Berman get along?"

"Berman's an affable sort. His lab is a good place to work. He lets you alone. But even Berman got annoyed with Owen from time to time."

"Over what?"

"Well, he didn't think the quality of Owen's work was so hot, I guess."

"But he wasn't threatened by Owen in any way, was he?"

"Not that I know of."

"And you didn't feel threatened by him either?"

"No. I guess it just wasn't my turn yet."

McLeod could think of no way to push the conversation any further and they parted.

Twenty

IT WAS EVEN warmer when McLeod set out to see Megan Snowden. She detoured to buy some tulips to take with her and then made her way down University Place to Edwards Place. Megan and Owen West had lived in an apartment on the third floor of an old house owned by the university.

Megan answered the door. She seemed very young and fragile to McLeod. She had light brown hair, very fine and long, which was swept up away from her face and caught at the back of her head with a huge clasp. She wore the ubiquitous jeans and a white T-shirt and over it a large man's plaid flannel shirt with the tails hanging out.

"Come in," she said. "Everything's a mess. I'm sorry."

"It looks fine to me," said McLeod, handing her the tulips. As far as student apartments went, it seemed to her to be immaculate. The furniture was the usual collection of graduate students' hand-me-downs—a used sofa that sagged only a little and was covered with a blue and white quilt, heaped with needlepoint pillows, and a worn leather chair—and Ikea bookshelves. There were fresh flowers already on the coffee table and interesting-looking pottery here and there among the books on the shelves—all in all, a welcoming room.

"Thank you for the flowers," Megan said.

"I see you have some others. They're beautiful roses," McLeod said.

"Thanks. Melissa Martin brought them around to me. I thought that was very sweet of her. Would you like a cup of tea? Or coffee? Or anything?"

"I'd love a cup of tea. I hate for you to bother, though."

"It's no bother," said Megan. "I'd like a cup myself."

McLeod followed her into the kitchen and watched as Megan first took care of the tulips, placing them in a blue pitcher and adding water. She filled an electric kettle and got out two mugs and opened a cabinet door to show a welter of boxes of tea bags.

"Would you like herbal tea? Earl Grey? English breakfast?"

"English breakfast."

"Me, too," said Megan, drumming her fingers on the countertop while she waited for the water to boil.

McLeod looked around the small kitchen with its cabinets painted pale blue and a drop leaf table with a blue cloth on it. The chairs at the table had needlepoint seat covers. It was a nice room—neat but not obsessively neat. "This must be a terrible time for you," she said. "I do appreciate your letting me come."

"I'm very glad to meet you. I've heard wonderful things about your writing class. I wish I had taken it—applied for it, at least—but now I've finished my course work and I'm working on my dissertation."

"I've had graduate students take the class from time to time. I don't have any this semester, though. "What are you writing your dissertation on? I know literary theory is big at Princeton."

"Not as big as it was a few years ago. I'm not doing theory. I'm working in the Cotsen collection—you know, the big collection of children's literature in the library—and I'm annotating the texts of some British children's books from the eighteenth and nineteenth century. I'm trying to give their context—the social and political meanings."

"What fun!"

"It is, I guess," Megan said. Then she said, "At last," as she poured the water in the mugs. She handed McLeod one and asked if she wanted sugar or milk.

"Nothing, thank you."

Back in the living room, they sat on the sofa, which was surprisingly comfortable, and sipped tea, eyeing each other over the rims of their mugs.

"Megan, tell me about Owen. Did anybody hate him?"

Megan looked down at her mug. "I don't know. But I guess somebody got mad enough at him to kill him, didn't they? Unless it was an accident. I just don't know."

McLeod waited, and after a few seconds, Megan went on. "I know he irritated people sometimes. He was from out West, you know, and he had a sort of rough-and-ready way. Oh, he could be courtly with women. He was with me, actually." She blinked away tears from her eyes, and McLeod handed her a tissue from her purse. "He was charismatic." She paused. "When he wanted to be."

McLeod remembered what Melissa had said about the way Owen yelled at Megan and wondered what was going on. Of course, after someone died, you did tend to idealize them, but still . . . "He was easy to live with, then?" she asked.

Megan looked at her. "Nobody's easy to live with," she said. "You know, in a relationship it's not give-and-take, it's give, give, give."

McLeod ached for this young woman. "I think he was lucky to find you, Megan. And this apartment—it's wonderful. You both must have enjoyed living here."

"I love blue, and he complained that everything was blue. But that was just a blip, I think."

"And his work—did you understand what he was doing in chemistry?"

"Not really. He tried to explain it to me, but it's too arcane for me."

"And did he understand your work with children's books?"

"He made enormous fun of me and what he called 'kiddie-lit,'" said Megan. "People don't take children's books seriously enough. Children's books are fun to read, and they actually reveal so much about the society at the time."

"Of course," said McLeod. "But Owen was supportive—he understood the time it took for you to do your research and writing, didn't he?"

"He was as supportive as any scientist would be of literary studies, I think," said Megan carefully. She finished drinking her tea and put the mug down on the old toy chest that served as a coffee table. "Actually, I think he thought it was better work for a woman than science."

"Really? Then what did he think about Melissa Martin?"

"He thought she was an uppity sort of woman. I told you he was from out West—and sometimes I think the feminist movement hasn't reached the Great Plains yet."

"But they got along, didn't they?"

"I guess so. I like Melissa a lot."

"And what about Professor Berman. Did they get along?"

"Owen thought he was too easygoing, but he was glad he was in Berman's lab. Berman isn't as demanding as some of the others."

"And Sam Chen? Were they friends?"

"I don't think so. I'm afraid Owen had a racist streak that bubbled out sometimes. And he thought Sam was a neatness freak."

"And Carey Srodek?"

"He hated him."

"Why?"

"I never knew exactly. Oh, we invited Carey when we had the other graduate students in his group over, but Carey only came once."

"What was the matter with Carey?"

"As I said, I don't think I ever knew."

"And Scott Murphy? I haven't met him yet. Were he and Owen friendly?"

"Not especially," said Megan. "I'm afraid I'm not being very helpful, am I? I hadn't really thought in an organized way about who could have killed Owen. I guess I should. I'll try to make myself mull over all these people. Maybe I can remember something."

"Did you know Wesley Bryant? She's the postdoc who worked in Sandy Berman's lab."

"I met her once, I think. No, I don't know her. Now I do remember this: Owen had great contempt for her. And he said he was going to make her squirm. And I said why did he want to do that? And he said she deserved it."

"Did he say any more about it than that?"

"Not that I can remember. Something about lab notes. Oh, I don't know. Maybe I'll remember it."

"Fine," said McLeod. "Let me ask you something entirely different. I'm doing an article about Earl Shivers. Do you know him?"

"I've met him. He's a real sweetie. He does needlepoint, you know."

"What! Needlepoint? Are you sure?"

"I'm very sure. He and I had a long talk about it. He started doing it when he was convalescing one time. I think he must be very good at it."

"For heaven's sake. I'm so glad you told me about this. It opens up a whole new side of him. I'll have to find out more and add it to my article. Speaking of needlepoint, did you do all these needlepoint pillows?"

"Most of them. My mother did one or two."

"And the seat covers in the kitchen?"

"Yes. Owen thought it was a ridiculous hobby, but I told him I had to do something with the right side of my brain after all the reading and writing I do."

"They're all beautiful. Thank you again for telling me about Shivers and needlepoint."

"Good, I'm glad I told you something useful, even if it wasn't about Owen. But what do you think about all this? You've talked to a lot of people. Do you have any idea who could have done it?"

"No, I don't. Can I ask you something else? Please

don't be offended. But where were you on Sunday night? I've started asking everybody that."

"I was here. Owen went to the lab—we had been out for a long walk earlier that day and I was tired. I did a little needlepoint and then I went to bed early. When I got up the next morning, Owen had not come home."

"That was unusual, wasn't it, for him not to come home?" asked McLeod, who was remembering what Melissa had said about Owen and his two-timing.

"Occasionally he would work all night, but he would call when that happened. I was worried this time, so I called the lab and somebody told me he was dead. I thought they meant it was an accident, or maybe even suicide. I didn't believe he was dead. I went over there. And it was true. Melissa was at the lab and she walked back home with me. I told her she didn't have to, but she did."

"She is a nice young woman, isn't she?"

"Yes, she is."

"Does Owen have family near here?"

"They're all in Wyoming. His parents came East, but they went back yesterday. They are furious with the university."

"So I gathered from the newspaper. But you talked to them?"

"Oh, yes, I had met them before. But you know, Owen and I weren't engaged, or anything. As far as his parents were concerned, I was just a passing girlfriend."

"Are you staying alone, Megan?"

"Yes, I am, but I'm fine." she said. "As fine as I could be under the circumstances. I actually did some work this morning. Life goes on, doesn't it?"

"It does," said McLeod. "I think you're wonderful. Thank you so much for talking to me. And think about all these people that Owen knew. Who was really, really angry with him?"

"I will think about it," said Megan. "I promise."

"And here are my telephone numbers—home and office—if you think of something." McLeod jotted them down on a page from her notebook, tore it out, and handed it Megan.

"Thanks," said Megan, absently stuffing it into her jeans pocket.

Twenty-one

※

ON THE WAY back to her office, McLeod thought about Megan—that nice young woman—and Owen West, who sounded more repulsive the more she learned about him. Melissa Martin had seen Megan as the victim in her relationship with Owen, but interestingly, Megan did not view herself that way. She seemed to take Owen as he was, warts and all, and seemed satisfied with him that way. A good way to live, thought McLeod.

At the office, she called Wesley Bryant, the postdoc, and asked if she could talk to her about Owen West.

"What about him?" asked Wesley Bryant. "Are you a detective?"

"No, I'm teaching here this semester and one of my students is, I think, unjustly implicated in his murder. I want to clear him if I can."

"I hardly knew Owen West," said Bryant.

"But you knew him, and know the lab, and every little bit of information helps."

"Oh, all right," Bryant said ungraciously. She finally agreed to see McLeod on Saturday. "We still can't get in the lab—not until Monday. We'll have to meet somewhere else."

McLeod suggested they meet for lunch at noon at the Annex. Bryant agreed. McLeod hung up and checked her computer in vain for a message from Scott Murphy. She sent him another e-mail, and was putting on her coat to go home when the phone rang. It was Scott.

"I can come to your office," he said.

"Let's meet at Small World," she suggested.

"Or the bar at the Annex," he said. "I'm ready for a beer. It's Friday."

"Sure," she said. "I'll be right there."

She gave her desk a final sweep, brushing papers into a file drawer, put on her coat, turned out the light, and went downstairs. "Good night, Frieda," she called as she went past the office door on the first floor.

"Shakespeare said night is 'death's second self,'" Frieda caroled cheerfully as McLeod made her way toward Joseph Henry House's front door. "It's in a sonnet," McLeod heard Frieda shout as she went out.

"Good heavens! How gloomy," McLeod said to herself. It was just a step across Nassau Street to the Annex, and she was soon seated at a table in the bar. She waited, and waited some more, and told the waitress several times that she'd wait for her friend to get there before she ordered. Finally, she asked for a Diet Coke, and sipped it while she waited some more.

After some time she watched a lone young man stand by the outer door and look around the bar. She held up a hand and waved at him tentatively.

The young man came over. "McLeod Dulaney?"

"Scott Murphy?" she asked.

"That's me," he said. He took off his jacket and hung it over the back of the chair across from her and then slid into the chair. "Sorry I'm late," he said.

McLeod looked at him. He was tall and dark, with black hair and a black mustache. He wore a hooded sweatshirt that had a picture of a bear on it. He had an air of bravado about him that she hadn't seen often on a college campus.

"That's all right," she said, although she was irritated at being kept waiting.

"How long have you been here?" he asked. "My mom called just as I was leaving and I thought I'd better talk to her. I couldn't tell her a beautiful woman was waiting for me." He grinned, pleased with himself.

What a jerk, thought McLeod. His mother was probably younger and prettier than she was. But she merely smiled at Scott, as the waitress came up to take his order.

"So, you want to talk to me about the Cowhand, do you?" said Scott, giving her his full attention.

"Is that what you called him? Some of the others called him the Prince of Darkness."

"Oh, he wasn't that bad," said Scott. "They just didn't understand Owen. That's the problem." The waitress brought his beer; he poured it into a glass and took a huge swallow that emptied half the glass's content.

"I'd love to hear your view of him," said McLeod. "Tell me what he was *really* like."

"Oh, you know, he was a good ole boy. He was from Wyoming and proud of it. He was kind of a swinger."

"What do you mean—a swinger?"

"Well, he had this nice little girl shacked up on Edwards Place but that didn't keep him from meeting other women."

"And you approve of that?" asked McLeod, feeling like a stern old woman.

"I *admire* it," said Scott. "You have to give him credit for gall."

"That's one way of looking at it." McLeod took a sip of Diet Coke. "What about Owen in the lab? Was he good to work with?"

"He was all right," said Scott.

"He wasn't too messy for you?"

"What? Oh, messy. You've been talking to Sam Chen. I'll admit Owen could be messy—he spilled an oil bath one time and the floor got slippery and Sam raised hell about it. He slipped in the oil and he felt he'd lost face or something. Sam made a mountain out of a molehill, and that made Owen furious, and he made a volcano out of a mountain."

McLeod admired Scott's turn of speech, but she wanted more information. "Sam said you and Owen almost came to blows one time," she said.

Scott shrugged. "I wouldn't put it that way. I really wouldn't." He finished off the beer and looked around for the waitress.

"How would you put it? I mean, you were annoyed with him, I understand."

"He was annoyed with me, too, I guess."

"What was it about?"

"You're persistent, aren't you?"

"I am," said McLeod sternly.

"It was about space. He kept spreading out in the lab, taking up more and more space. Finally, I had hardly room enough to work in. So we talked it over, and worked it out. Simple." Scott was still looking around for a waitress, who finally appeared. He ordered another beer, and turned back to McLeod. "That's all it was. Nothing to kill a man about." He smiled kindly at McLeod.

McLeod knew that Scott Murphy wasn't telling her the truth, not the whole truth, certainly. What was he *not* telling? she wondered. She asked him where he was from—an easy personal question was always good to throw out when an interview wasn't going well. McLeod had learned in years of newspaper work.

"I'm from California, God's country," he said. "And I'm going back there as soon as I get my Ph.D. I swear to God I'm not going to stay on this godforsaken East Coast."

"I can understand that," said McLeod, "although fall is kind of nice in Princeton."

"Yeah," said Scott, as another beer appeared. He took it and poured it into a glass and drained the liquid quickly. And then he opened up. "I didn't mind Owen in the lab so much," he said. "And that's the truth. But the real truth is that I hated him. You know what he did? He stole my girl. And like I said, he *had* a girl. But that wasn't enough for him. He stole my girl."

"Was he that cute?" asked McLeod. "I mean, I haven't heard anything that made him sound like Casanova."

"He had charm when he wanted to turn it on," said Scott.

"You mean he stole your girl while he was living with Megan?"

"No." Scott roared it out. "*No*. He stole Megan. Megan was my girl until Owen came along."

"And he had another girl back then, too?" asked McLeod.

"Sure, a nice girl. But that wasn't good enough for him. He had to have *my* girl."

"Megan is certainly an attractive young woman," said McLeod. Poor Megan, she thought. Neither one of these young men was her idea of a Prince Charming. Having to choose between Scott and Owen—well, it would be a lose-lose proposition in her opinion. Scott had certainly gotten drunk fast, but perhaps, she thought, he had been drinking before he came.

She tried to think of something encouraging to say, but all she could manage was: "I tell my children that the sweetheart you lose is the sweetheart you don't want to keep."

"Yeah," said Scott morosely. "Keep telling them that."

"Can you tell me anything else about Owen West?" she asked.

"Nope," he said. "I need another beer."

It was hopeless. She wasn't even going to ask him where he was on Sunday night. She got up to leave, pulling out five dollars to leave for her Diet Coke and laying it on the table. "Thanks so much. You've been very helpful," she said.

Twenty-two

❧

WHEN SHE GOT home, George was already there. "I left early," he said. "I've changed my mind. Let's go out to dinner. Maybe the Lawrenceville Inn?"

"Lovely," said McLeod, who was so exhausted that she could only slump into a dining room chair.

"I'll call and make sure we can get in," said George.

"Fine," she said.

"They can take us if we come right this minute," George said when he hung up the phone. "Are you ready? Can you go now?"

For a minute she hated George Bridges. All she wanted to do was take off her shoes, put her feet up, and rest. But she pulled herself together. "Sure," she said.

Without going upstairs to change her clothes or even wash her face, she followed him out to his car and rode silently to Lawrenceville.

"What's the matter with you?" George asked when they were seated at a table in the front room of the old farmhouse that had been turned into a first-class restaurant.

"I'm just dead tired, that's all," she said. "I can't sparkle."

"Okay," said George. "You don't have to sparkle. I'll carry on both sides of the conversation. You just sit there and doze off."

McLeod was too tired to laugh, but she had to smile, as George asked questions and then answered them. "And what did you think of the movie *Walk the Line*?" he asked, and then turned his head to answer himself, "Well, I've always been a fan of Johnny Cash and I thought it was wonderful," he replied.

"Have you seen it? Really, I mean?" she asked.

"Not yet," said George, "but I know I'd like it."

With such stratagems they got through dinner and went home.

AFTER A GOOD night's sleep and a good breakfast, McLeod was ready and able to face Wesley Bryant at lunch. At noon, she was back at the Annex, sitting on the little bench by the door to the stairs to Nassau Street.

Two men came in and found tables, and then a dumpy woman entered and stood by the door looking around. McLeod got up. "Are you Wesley Bryant?" she asked.

"I am," said the woman. "You must be McLeod Dulaney."

"I am," said McLeod. "Thanks for coming."

"I suppose it would have been churlish not to," said Wesley Bryant.

McLeod smiled at her, pleased that Wesley seemed have a sense of humor, or irony, or something. They were shown to a table for two by the wall and sat down. Wesley Bryant was in her thirties, McLeod guessed, and overweight. Her brown hair was badly cut and her clothes were nondescript. Don't be so judgmental, McLeod told herself, this woman may not be a fashion plate but she is bound to be smart, smarter than you are.

Bryant picked up the menu, looked at it, and laid it down. "I know what I want, a cheeseburger," she said. "Now what is this all about?"

"I'll have the chef's salad. As I told you, I want to help my student—"

"Why is your student a suspect?"

"It's a long story, but I think he's innocent. I'm trying to talk to everybody who knew Owen West, hoping that if I can get enough facts, I'll have something to take to the police."

"Fair enough," said Wesley Bryant. "What do you think I can tell you?"

"Tell me everything you know about Owen West."

"I don't know what to say . . ."

"You know what?" asked McLeod. "Hold on a minute. First, tell me a little bit about yourself. Where are you from?"

"I'm originally from North Carolina—the western part."

"Sure, the mountains," said McLeod. "I used to go to Montreat when I was in high school."

"That's the Presbyterian center," said Bryant. "I went to Lake Junaluska myself."

"So you were a Methodist."

"That's right, I *was* a Methodist. My father named me for John Wesley. I had to be a Methodist, but I'm not anymore. I'm not anything."

"I thought I heard a faint Southern accent," said McLeod.

"It's not like yours," said Wesley.

"I guess not. But I still live in the South—in Tallahassee. I'm just up here for the semester. But what town did you grow up in? Asheville?"

"Close," said Wesley. "It was Waynesville. And I don't want to live down there ever again."

"I like it up here," said McLeod, "but I still spend most of my time 'down there,' as you say. Lots of Southerners feel the way you do, though. Where did you go to school?"

"I went to the state college in Asheville."

"Did you major in chemistry?"

"I did. I knew I wanted to do chemistry. My father was a pharmacist and he encouraged me. I went to graduate

school at Duke and got my Ph.D. I had a one-year instruc-
torship at Penn, but they didn't offer me a tenure-track job.
My adviser at Duke helped me get this postdoc position
but I can't stay here more than two years." She sighed. "It's
a dog's life."

"It certainly is. My son just got his Ph.D. at Yale and
he's thrilled at the prospect of a one-year appointment in
California."

"Things do work out. I'm very optimistic. I just had an
article accepted by *Science*. That will be a real help in getting a job."

"Congratulations!" said McLeod. "Publication is important, isn't it?"

"Publication is *everything*," said Wesley.

THEIR FOOD ARRIVED, and Wesley bit into her cheeseburger with enthusiasm. McLeod ate a little salad and then
said, "Back to Owen West. Did you ever work with him at
all? Did you socialize with him? Was he a good guy? Did
you like him?"

"Okay," said Wesley, wiping her mouth. "I did not work
with him. We both worked in Berman's lab but I have my
own project and my own space. Well, I sort of have my
own space. Owen West took up so much space it's ridiculous. Maybe I'll have enough room to work in now—I hate
to sound like I'm glad he's dead—I'm not glad he's dead—
I'm just glad he won't be in the lab anymore."

Would one scientist kill another scientist to get more lab
space? McLeod wondered to herself.

"As for socializing, we didn't," Bryant was saying. "I
don't know whether he was a good guy or not, and I didn't
particularly like him. But I didn't feel strongly about him."

"Carey Srodek said I should be sure and talk to you,"
said McLeod, and waited. Wesley ate french fries and said
nothing. McLeod persisted. "Why would he say that?"

"I have no idea."

Megan had said that Owen was going to "make Wesley

squirm." What had he meant? McLeod wondered. How to phrase a question? "Owen was never rude to you?"

"No," said Wesley.

"Never threatened you?"

"No," said Wesley.

"Can you think of anything you ever did that could have made Owen mad?"

"No, I can't."

"Did you get the sense that the other graduate students did not like Owen? They called him the Prince of Darkness."

"I didn't know that. I guess I didn't pay much attention to the graduate students."

"Do you work very closely with Sanford Berman?"

"He's my supervisor. We're all working on synthesizing molecules, but I have my own project. It's really measuring the properties of molecules."

How on earth could you measure the properties of molecules, wondered McLeod, but let it pass, as Wesley continued, "I guess I'm more driven than any of them. I have to get something done and something published so I can get a teaching job. The graduate students want to do something that they can get published and get their Ph.D.'s. Berman doesn't seem to be very ambitious. He has tenure. And he doesn't seem to need more money. I don't know how it will all end."

"I'm sure it will all end happily for everyone," said McLeod. "This is the important question. Can you think of anybody who might have had a reason to kill Owen West?"

"Nobody but your student. You said Owen did him an injustice. Isn't that a reason?"

"I don't think he killed him. I really don't."

"Every student should have a teacher as protective as you are," said Wesley.

"Where were you Sunday night?" McLeod asked quickly.

"Good heavens! You mean you suspect me?"

"I ask everybody that. If I can remember. No, I don't suspect you. You seem very detached from it all. Actually, I don't have a likely suspect. It seems a motiveless crime. I'm beginning to think a mad vagrant did it. Can anybody get into Frick any time? I mean could they before the murder?"

"Pretty much. At night and on the weekends, you are supposed to swipe your ID in the door, but somebody is always leaving one open or you could go in right behind somebody else. I think it's pretty much open to the world."

"See," said McLeod, "it's probably just a tramp and I've wasted everybody's time, including my own."

"You're a writer. Maybe you can write something about it," said Wesley.

"We'll see. But where were you on Sunday night? I'm just curious."

"Sunday night? I was in my apartment watching television."

"Anybody with you?"

"Not a soul."

"Did you get a telephone call?"

"Not that I remember," said Wesley.

"Nobody has an alibi," McLeod said sadly. "Not really. Look, let me ask you a question about something besides the murder. Do you know Earl Shivers? I'm writing an article about him and I'm interested in what anybody can tell me about him."

"You don't think he's a suspect, do you?"

"No, I don't. Do you know him?"

"I've met him. And I know his work on proteins. That's all."

"Well, thanks a lot for coming. I really appreciate it. And thanks for answering all my nosy questions. I wish you luck with your work."

"Thanks for the lunch. And I wish you luck with your detecting."

"Thanks," said McLeod. "I don't think I'm actually 'detecting.' I just want this thing to be solved so Greg Pierre is out from under the cloud of suspicion. Looks like I need luck, I must say. And I don't think the police are getting anywhere, either."

"Maybe it was suicide."

"Can someone give himself a fatal blow to the head?"

McLeod paid the check and they went upstairs and said goodbye on the sidewalk. McLeod had never felt so frustrated in her life. She was up against a stone wall.

Twenty-three

MCLEOD WENT TO her office and e-mailed Carey Srodek, asking him to call her. She had to find a chink in the stone wall—she wanted to ask him a question but thought it was better not to send it by e-mail. Besides talking to Carey Srodek, she wanted to ask Megan what Owen had meant when he said he was going to "fix" Wesley Bryant.

Then she remembered Greg's track meet. She called home and, when George didn't answer, left a message telling him she was going to the meet and urging him to join her there if he could.

As she set off down the hill toward Jadwin Gym, she was glad she had remembered the meet. It was chilly, but warmer than she had expected. It was nice to be walking down Washington Road and on her way to watch an athletic event for a change—instead of interviewing potential murderers.

Inside Jadwin, she followed the small crowd to the balcony and easily found a seat in the front row and looked at the spectators. There were lots of parental-looking spectators and some high school kids. She particularly admired one teenager wearing a T-shirt with the legend, TO THOSE ABOUT TO RUN, WE SALUTE YOU.

Then she tried to figure out what was going on. She was about to ask the man behind her if he knew what event was next, when George slid in beside her.

"Hello!" she said. "I'm glad to see you. How did you get here so quickly?"

"I just missed you. I could hear the phone ringing when I was unlocking the front door, but by the time I got there, you had finished your message and hung up. I thought it was a good idea to come to the track meet, so I drove down here."

"I never thought about driving!" said McLeod. "I walked. I hope I can get a ride home with you. I don't want to have to plow up that hill on foot."

"Sure. But why this sudden interest in Princeton track and field?"

"I have a student running."

"Oh, I should have known. Greg-Pierre-slash-Bob-Billings. Of course. Now I understand. You know, he's the luckiest man who ever lived. Here he just spent a week in jail for forgery, theft by deception, wrongful impersonation, and falsifying records. And Coach Lilly is letting him run in a track meet."

"Well, the university dropped those charges, and Greg is reinstated."

"True, but he missed out on all that training," said George.

"I think Coach Lilly likes him. And he's a great runner, I understand."

"That's right. I still say he's lucky."

"It's about time he had some luck," said McLeod. "But what's going on here? I can't figure it out. And I don't see Greg."

"I got a program." George glanced at it and looked across the gym. "They're doing the pole vaulting over there on the other side. See them? The long jump is going on right down there in the middle of the track. And the next event is the sixty-meter dash."

"When do they run the mile?"

"It comes after the men's sixty-meter dash and the women's sixty-meter dash, and the sixty-meter hurdles."

"Greg is going to run the mile."

"It won't be long."

McLeod looked at the program and saw that it was the Princeton Invitational Track Meet, with competitors from a wide range of colleges including Columbia, Washington and Lee, Muhlenberg, Kutztown, Delaware, Franklin and Marshall, and Montclair State.

The students who won the dashes were incredibly fast runners, McLeod thought. She decided the women were better at the hurdles than the men, slower maybe, but they knocked over no hurdles, while the men had them falling like dominoes.

"There's Greg!" she said.

And there he was in Princeton's black tank top with black shorts. He looked taller and thinner and older than he did in class. Finally, it was time for the mile race, which George said would be five laps around the oval track in Jadwin.

Three Princeton runners were in the first heat, and McLeod watched as they lined up with several others at the starting point. They knelt, poised, and a gun cracked. They were off. Greg loped easily around the track in second place for several rounds, and in the final lap sped up and passed the front runner and finished yards ahead. In the finals, he did the same thing, started off well but made no effort to take the lead until the final lap, when he spurted up and easily won.

"A mile is a long way to run," McLeod said.

"They have much longer races than one mile, you know. They'll have a three-thousand-meter race today, but in the championships they have a five-thousand-meter and sometimes a ten-thousand-meter."

"Mercy. How long does it take to run ten thousand meters?"

"It's twenty-five laps. About thirty minutes."

"A marathon," said McLeod.

"Not quite. A marathon is twenty-six miles and takes hours."

"I see," said McLeod, who knew quite well that a marathon was twenty-six miles, but it made George happy to be sitting in the gym explaining the fundamentals of track and field to her. So it made her happy to sit in the gallery and learn about track and field.

"Let's go down and congratulate Greg," McLeod said.

"You can go," George said. "I'll wait for you here."

She went down on the main floor of the gym and made her way to where Greg was standing alone by the track, apparently the only athlete not surrounded by relatives and girlfriends.

"Congratulations!" she said.

"Ms. Dulaney!" he said. "You came to the track meet." He seemed dazed by her presence. "Thanks. Thanks."

"I'll see you next week," McLeod said.

"Sure," said Greg. "Sure."

"He's nice," McLeod told George as they walked toward his car.

"He's a great runner," George said. "How was your lunch?"

"Fruitless. And I don't mean I didn't have any fruit to eat. I didn't get a thing out of Wesley Bryant. Except she's from Waynesville, North Carolina. She says she scarcely knew Owen West."

"You've talked to everybody around. Who do you think did the murder?"

"I haven't a clue. I really don't. I can't get a handle on it. I'm completely at sea. A couple of people have said a chemistry lab is always full of motives for murder, but I don't see it. I wish I knew what Nick Perry thought."

"As a matter of fact, I wish I knew what Nick Perry thought, too. This unsolved murder isn't doing Princeton any good, you know. We've weathered violent episodes before, even the murder of the president and the deaths of professors, but this is different somehow. And West's father won't shut up. He keeps going to the media to complain that Princeton doesn't protect its students. He was on the O'Reilly show yesterday."

"Let's ask Nick to dinner tonight," said McLeod. "I know he doesn't socialize much when he's working on a murder case, but this is Saturday night and nothing seems to be going on. Shall we try?"

"Good idea. Should we ask anybody else? Maybe I could get Polly." (Polly Griffin, who worked at the university's art museum, was a sometime girlfriend of George's.)

"Sure," said McLeod. "Fine." She liked Polly Griffin, but, although she thought Nick might be more forthcoming if nobody else was there, hesitated to say so for fear George would think she was jealous.

"Maybe Nick would be more comfortable if it's just us," George said, to her relief. "Will you call him? I'll cook. Let's stop by the grocery store."

"I'll call him right now," McLeod said, fumbling for her cell phone.

She left a message at the police department in Borough Hall, and they headed to Nassau Street Seafood for something to cook for dinner. George opted for Chilean sea bass (very expensive) and got smoked trout for hors d'oeuvres.

"Too much fish?" he asked.

"Never," said McLeod. She suggested they get the market's very good roasted beets and twice-baked potatoes— "just to make things easier," she said—and she picked out fresh lettuce for salad. Then they went next door to Chez Alice for fruit tarts for dessert and a selection of cheeses.

"Wow!" said McLeod as they headed to the car. "Even if Nick can't come, we'll have a nice supper."

"If I don't screw up the sea bass," said George.

"You won't." Her cell phone rang. It was Nick, saying he would like very much to come for dinner, and just the three of them was fine with him.

Twenty-four

THEY BUSTLED ABOUT smartly, getting ready for dinner. George went through his cookbooks looking for the very best recipe for sea bass. McLeod tidied the parlor and the dining room and decided to make lentil soup for a first course, a move of which George approved.

Then George groaned over his cookbooks. He was rejecting, he said, "Sea Bass Coated with Pine Nuts" and "Steamed Sea Bass Fillets with Fresh Thyme and Leek Sauce." "What I really want to do is this 'Baked Sea Bass with Eggplant and Ginger,'" he said. "But it calls for not only eggplant, but cubed tomatoes, fresh gingerroot, and coriander, none of which we have."

"If you really want to do that one, I'll go get all the stuff. I want to get some flowers anyway."

"That would be great," said George. "And maybe you better not make the soup. If I have to fool with the sea bass, I can do that when you talk to Nick while you eat smoked trout in the parlor. It might be difficult for me to do the sea bass while we're eating soup."

"Anything you say. We have plenty to eat, without the soup. I'll go ahead and make it, though, and we'll have it for tomorrow, if we need it." She started out. "I guess it's turning colder, isn't it? I'd better get a coat."

"Wait a minute, McLeod," said George. "This recipe is perfect. You make it ahead of time. And then when it's time to eat, you put it in a hot oven for just ten minutes. It can cook while we eat the soup."

"Whatever you say."

"I do like your docile mode."

"Thanks. I think it's appropriate when you're doing your heavy-duty cooking. Do we need anything else?"

"Just a medium eggplant, a couple of fresh tomatoes, gingerroot, and some fresh coriander."

"Aye, aye, sir."

WHEN THE DOORBELL rang a few hours later, McLeod glanced around and felt proud. The parlor looked lovely with the fire blazing away and tulips in a pitcher that had belonged to George's mother. She went out to the front door in the little hall and welcomed Lieutenant Nick Perry, chief of detectives for the Princeton Borough Department of Police.

Nick grinned, handed McLeod a bottle of champagne, took off the Greek fisherman's cap he wore on his bald head, and slid out of his raincoat.

"Is it going to rain?" McLeod asked him.

"I don't think so. It was so much warmer today I wore it instead of a heavy jacket."

George came out of the kitchen and greeted Nick. "Good to see you," he said. "Glad you could come."

"Me, too," said Nick. "I feel guilty taking time off, but I feel like this is the first minute I have been off the job since the murder was reported. I need to get away."

They showed him into the parlor, and Nick sighed with satisfaction as he sat down on the sofa. George immediately handed him a glass of scotch on the rocks.

"George, man, thank you," Nick said.

McLeod had brought her knitting downstairs, and she took George's sweater and began to work on it. George brought her a glass of sherry and put a plate of smoked trout and small pieces of toast on the coffee table. Then he disappeared.

"How is the murder investigation going?" McLeod asked. "You don't still suspect my student, do you? That's my main concern."

"We suspect everybody. With the Princeton Borough Police, every person is guilty until proved innocent."

"Not really, Nick?"

"You know what I mean. Nobody is exempt from investigation. Just trying to find out who had a motive or means or opportunity in this case is a major undertaking."

"I can understand," said McLeod. "But it's hard to imagine a motive for killing a graduate student in a chemistry lab, isn't it? What are the most common motives—sex, money, revenge. A poor geek in a lab doesn't seem to arouse those motives."

"Don't be so sure. Your student had revenge for a motive, if anybody ever did. Graduate students aren't such geeks that they don't have sex. As for money . . ."

McLeod waited eagerly for the rest of this sentence, but Nick shrugged and said, "Well, I guess they don't have any money, do they?"

"What have you found out?"

"I've found out that Frick Lab, the building, is a sieve. It has a dozen entrances and exits. Practically anybody can walk in and go in one of the labs. I've found out that Owen West's father is a loudmouthed nuisance."

"I know George is irritated with the way he blames the university for poor security that caused his son's death," McLeod said.

"And he blames the police of Princeton Borough for not solving his son's murder in what he calls 'a timely fashion.'"

"And what else have you learned?"

"That Tom Blackburn blames us for not solving the murder 'in a timely fashion.'"

"Nick, I didn't know that. He hasn't complained publicly about it, has he? I mean, it hasn't been in the papers, has it? George hasn't mentioned it to me. But he is so super-discreet—he never tells me anything about what goes on at the university."

"It hasn't been in the papers yet, but I dread to pick up the paper every day. Blackburn has called the chief and the mayor and even suggests we get help from the state."

"That's awful. Does George know? He must."

"I suppose he does. That's one reason I was glad to come over here for dinner. There are lots of reasons why I'm glad to be invited, but that's a good reason for taking time off to come here. I thought I could talk to George about it."

"I'm sure you can. More scotch?" Nick accepted a re-fill, and McLeod went on with her questions. "Nick, what was used to kill Owen West? I haven't seen anything in the papers, except that it was a 'blow to the head.'"

"We don't know what the instrument was," Nick said. "We've searched Frick inch by inch and almost the whole campus inch by inch. We've called in help from the Township and West Windsor and Lawrenceville to work on the search. We've gone through the garbage bags from Frick and from the outdoor garbage cans near there. It could be anywhere. It was probably a hammer of some kind. The chemistry people say there are always all kinds of tools lying around a lab that you could hit somebody with and kill them."

"Could a woman do it?"

"I don't see why not. Women work out these days. They're strong."

McLeod had a brief mental picture of tiny, blond Melissa Martin hefting a hammer and killing Owen West.

"But what have you found out about the murder?" Nick was saying, as she brought her attention back to him.

"What do you mean?" said McLeod. "Why would I find out anything?"

"Come on, McLeod. I saw you at Frick myself, and whenever I talk to somebody connected with the murder, they say. 'Oh, yes McLeod Dulaney asked me about that.'"

"I don't believe it. It's true I'm doing an article about

Earl Shivers, but he's not involved in the murder. Or is he?"

"As I said, everybody is involved as far as I'm concerned, until they've shown me they're not involved. But you've been talking to a lot of other people in the chemistry department."

"I've interviewed some people about Shivers," said McLeod. "And one of those people was Sandy Berman, in whose lab Owen West worked. And then I did talk to some other graduate students in his group—I am interested in clearing Greg Pierre, you know."

"Who did you talk to?"

"Everybody I can think of. Berman, as I said. And the other graduate students in Berman's group—Carey Srodek, Melissa Martin, Scott Murphy, and Sam Chen. And Owen's girlfriend, Megan Snowden."

"Well, what did you find out? Have you cleared your student?"

"I haven't talked to anybody that I'm sure committed the murder, if that's what you mean. Oh, Melissa Martin had a brief run-in with Owen at one point, but I don't think it amounted to much. Owen borrowed—or stole— Melissa's lab books. Owen called Sam Chen a Chink shit, and Sam bitterly resented West. Who wouldn't? Carey Srodek said Owen took his computer. Scott Murphy told me that Owen West stole his girlfriend. Just stuff like that. I haven't come across anything really telling, but none of them liked Owen. They called him the Prince of Darkness. They thought he was nosy and interfering and officious. He stole things—notebooks, computers, girlfriends."

Nick seemed interested. "You do have a way of finding out things," he said.

McLeod took the praise with a grain of salt. She realized that she, as usual, had told Nick more about what she had done than he had told her about what he knew. In fact, he had told her nothing, except that they had not found the murder weapon yet.

"Soup's on!" George came in the parlor to summon them to the dining room.

"Why didn't you call me?" she asked him. "I would have helped with the last-minute stuff."

"Don't worry. I did it."

The soup was fine, but it was soon eclipsed by the sea bass, which was, as she had expected it to be, another of George's culinary triumphs.

"I hope you add this to your permanent repertory," McLeod told him. "And I want to look at that recipe. Maybe I can handle it—and dazzle the folks back home in Tallahassee. Would it work for pompano?"

"I won't say it's exactly easy," said George, looking smug. "No, I have to admit it's easy. Anyone could handle it."

"Even me," said McLeod.

After dinner, when they sat in the parlor with coffee, Nick brought up President Blackburn's complaints, and asked George what could be done.

"I knew Tom called Chief Ives, but I thought it was just to explain how important it was to the university to get the murder investigation wrapped up."

"He didn't need to tell us that," said Nick. "It's important to us to get it cleared up, too."

"And I didn't know he called the mayor. I would guess that, again, he just wanted to explain how important it was to the university to get the thing tied up and out of the way."

"The voice of the president of the university carries enormous weight in this town," said Nick. "But this is a matter that we don't need to be told is important."

"I see what you're saying," said George. "I'm sure Tom hasn't meant to suggest that the Borough Police aren't doing all they can to solve this murder. And I'm sure he hasn't meant to impugn your ability to handle the case . . ."

McLeod decided it would be tactful for her to go back to the kitchen and let George and Nick talk alone. She could load the dishwasher while she was being discreet.

When she went back to the parlor, George and Nick had apparently finished their discussion of Tom Blackburn and were talking about the Philadelphia Flyers and the New

York Rangers—ice hockey teams—and hockey was a game about which she knew nothing.

"We forgot to serve the champagne Nick brought with dessert!" she said.

"Better late than never," said George, getting up.

"You don't have to open it now," said Nick. "Save it for another time."

"Oh, no," said George, who was back in seconds with three flutes and the champagne. They toasted a solution to the murder.

"Nick, I've been meaning to ask you," said McLeod. "Were the Borough Police ever involved in the anthrax investigation? Those anthrax-laden letters were mailed in that box on Nassau Street. Did you have anything to do with all that?"

"Not a thing. The FBI did it all, and they never even informed us about what was going on."

"Did they ever suspect anybody in Princeton of mailing those anthrax letters?"

"They thought about the possibility. But there was no evidence that anybody here was involved."

"It's a terrible thing to happen in Princeton, isn't it?" asked McLeod.

"It sure is," said Nick. "Not just that some mad scientist was using one of our mailboxes to send deadly substances to the United States Senate and to television people. That was bad enough but the little bit of anthrax powder that leaked out of the letters contaminated our regional post office. They still haven't finished detoxifying it and I don't know when it will reopen."

"But at least you don't have to solve that puzzle."

"That's right," said Nick.

Twenty-five

❧

AFTER NICK LEFT, McLeod and George were in the kitchen doing the last of the cleanup when the phone rang. McLeod looked at the clock as George answered—it was eleven. She wondered, as a shiver of fear went down her back, who would call that late?

"It's for you," George said, handing her the phone. McLeod was genuinely alarmed by the time she squeaked out a "hello."

But it wasn't—to her intense relief—Rosie or Harry. It was Carey Srodek. Only a graduate student would call that late, she thought.

"You wanted me to call you?" Srodek said.

"Yes, I did. Thanks for getting back to me," she said, as calmly as though it were ten o'clock in the morning. "I wanted to ask you why you urged me to talk to Wesley Bryant. I followed your suggestion and, as a matter of fact, had lunch with her today. But she seemed completely neutral about Owen West. Can you tell me more?"

"I'd rather she told you herself."

"I don't think she will. And this is a murder case."

"Let me think about it," said Carey. "I'll call you tomorrow. I'll call you Sunday afternoon."

"Why don't you come by here. I'll give you a simple supper, if you like."

"Come by where?" asked Carey.

"Oh, I'm sorry. Where I live. It's very close to the campus." She gave him the address on Edgehill. "About six o'clock."

"Thanks. I'll see you then."

"Who have you invited to dinner now?" George did not seem annoyed, just amused, thank heavens.

"It's Carey Srodek. One of Berman's graduate students. I don't know why I invited him. The words just came tumbling out. Will you be here? I hope it's all right."

"Of course it's all right. I will be here. What are you going to serve?"

"Something simple. There's tons of lentil soup left over."

"Maybe we can do better than that," George said. "I'm on a roll with that sea bass."

"Great."

"I don't know why I did it," she said again.

"You suffer from compulsive hospitality," George said. He patted her kindly on the shoulder.

She smiled at him. What else could she do?

THE NEXT MORNING, McLeod watched the clock as she waited for it to be nine so she could call Megan Snowden. The minutes crawled by while she ate her toast and drank her tea and read the newspapers. George came downstairs, found the *Times* crossword, and started to work on it.

"Do you ever do the Sunday crosswords?" he asked her.

"I never get the chance," she said.

"I have a copier upstairs. I can make a copy for you if you want to work on it. I just never thought about it before. I know you do the daily ones."

"No, that's all right. I can't ever finish the Sunday one. It's too big."

George was soon lost in the puzzle and McLeod went upstairs and got her knitting. At least she could work on his sweater. At last it was nine o'clock, and she called Megan and arranged to come to her house at eleven.

She knitted until it was time to grab a notebook and set out for Edwards Place. Megan opened the door of the apartment—she was wearing another large man's shirt, tails flapping, over a sweater and blue jeans.

"Come in," she said. "It's good to see you again. Will you have some tea?"

"No, thanks. It's nice to see you, too, Megan. How are you doing?"

"Sit down, McLeod." McLeod settled on the sofa with the needlepoint pillows and Megan sat on a wooden Windsor chair. "I'm doing pretty well, thank you," she said. "I have a lot of work to do, so that actually helps. What's going on? Do you know? Are the police making any progress?"

"I saw the detective in change, and according to him, it's still a mystery, to put it literally," said McLeod.

"Oh, dear," said Megan.

McLeod could think of nothing helpful to say, so she tried to look sympathetic. But I am sympathetic, she thought. Who wouldn't be? "Look, I hate to bring up something that may be painful," she said, "but I want to ask you about Scott Murphy."

Megan looked startled. She put her mug down on the table next to the Windsor chair. "What about Scott? What could be painful about Scott?"

How to put this? McLeod wondered. "He told me that you used to be his girlfriend and that Owen West stole you away. I thought that was interesting, to say the least, that it might be significant, I mean."

"Did you?" said Megan. She seemed less friendly. "Why?"

"It seemed to me that it gave Scott a motive for murder."

"Oh. I see. But I think Scott was exaggerating. Just being dramatic. That's the way he is."

"You mean you weren't his girlfriend?"

"In a way, I guess I was. Scott and I have known each other a long time. We were at Swarthmore together. We were just friends, really."

"Really?" asked McLeod. "Scott certainly didn't seem to see it that way."

"I guess we were more than friends. But there was no reason for him to get mad at Owen. Owen didn't steal me away, you know. It was a free-will choice."

"The history of crime is full of stories about men who killed other men because they had 'stolen' a woman," said McLeod.

"That's true," said Megan. "But that doesn't mean Scott Murphy killed Owen."

"I understand. But I'm trying to learn all I can about Owen, and anybody who might have been angry enough to kill him," said McLeod.

"I know you are, but I don't think Scott had reached that stage. I expect he's just worked himself into a frenzy thinking he was betrayed or something."

"Isn't it people in frenzies that kill people?"

Megan put her hands over her ears. "I don't want to hear any more about Scott. I've known him for years. And actually, our mothers were friends a long time ago. We met in college but we had each heard about the other. I feel very tender about him."

McLeod began to feel guilty. How do I get myself in positions like this? she asked herself. Here I am torturing a bereaved young woman. But she couldn't stop. "You know the first time I talked to you, you told me a little bit about Owen and Wesley Bryant, the postdoc. Have you remembered anything else about her? For instance, how was Owen going to make her squirm?"

"I have thought about that since I talked to you. It had something to with her lab books. And the work she was doing on her own. I never paid much attention. I guess I should have listened more carefully when he talked about the people in the lab and their work." Her face crumpled, and tears began to roll down her cheeks.

"Oh, Megan, that's all right. Don't worry about it. I'm

sorry. I come in here asking all these questions, and I must seem very hostile to you. I'm truly sorry."

Megan wiped her eyes. "It's all right. I know you're trying to help. Well, help attain the greater good, or something. But it is hard. You ask all the questions that make me think of Owen's dark side. Yes, he had a dark side. Don't we all? But I want to think about his other side, his good side. He could be very generous and kind, and nobody cares about that anymore. Not you or the police. Or anybody. It's awful."

McLeod was about to resolve to give up all detective work forever and ever, so help her God, when Megan shook her head, as though to clear it, and looked at her steadily.

"Have you talked to Carey Srodek?" she asked.

"I did," said McLeod. "The same day I saw you the first time."

"I told you Owen hated him, but I couldn't remember why." She laughed bitterly. "Now I'm talking about Owen's dark side myself. But I guess we have to, don't we? Owen hated him because Carey accused him of being a snoop—can you imagine? And Carey made fun of him. Carey does have an unusual sense of humor, and it hit Owen the wrong way. Owen called him the Albino."

"Albino? Oh, because of that blond, blond hair."

"That's right," said Megan.

"Did he ever threaten to make Carey squirm, the way he did Wesley Bryant?" McLeod asked.

"I don't remember it if he did. No, Wesley didn't make Owen mad the way Carey did. I asked you if you talked to Carey, because I wondered what you thought of him."

"I liked him, but I thought he was odd. He said things that were a little bit weird. But that's all I can say. And weird's not necessarily bad."

"But it's not a guarantee of goodness," said Megan sharply. "I've wondered if he didn't kill Owen. I really have. You made me start thinking about who could have murdered him, and I've decided Carey could have done it. What do you think?"

"I think anybody in that lab could have killed Owen," McLeod said. "Feelings certainly ran high, didn't they?"

"Yes, it makes me glad I'm in English, doing kiddie-lit, and not chemistry."

"It's been my experience that feelings can run high everywhere," said McLeod. "Rare books departments and seminaries and, I suppose, convents."

They were both silent. "Don't you want some tea?" asked Megan.

"Yes, thanks." While Megan made the tea, McLeod sat in the living room and brooded. It was interesting that Megan had focused on Carey Srodek as the murderer, instead of Scott Murphy. Scott's motive for murder would seem to be much stronger than Carey's, which was nonexistent, as far as she could tell. And Carey Srodek seemed to her, from brief encounters with both of them, to be a much more stable person than Scott Murphy.

Then a possible motive for Carey occurred to her: self-defense. Owen West had hated Carey Srodek. She could imagine a scene where Carey interrupted Owen in the laboratory on Sunday night and began teasing him. Maybe Owen had attacked Carey, and Carey had reacted automatically and slammed Owen on the head in self-defense. He probably had not intended to kill Owen, just stop him from coming after him. But then when he saw that Owen was dead, he had panicked and left the body in the lab and taken the weapon with him and disposed of it.

This version of events made a lot of sense, McLeod thought.

Megan resisted the self-defense idea, because she did not think that Owen was a man who would become violent. But McLeod had no problem with the idea of Owen West and violence. She liked her theory and resolved to go straight home and call Nick Perry and tell him she knew who the murderer was.

Twenty-six

"WE HAVE A murderer coming to dinner," she told George when she got home and found him in the dining room still working on the crossword puzzle.

"What do you mean?"

She told him what Megan had said and explained her new theory with pride. "I trust Megan's intuition," she said. "She knew Owen West better than anyone else did, and if she thinks it might be Carey Srodek who killed him, I have to take her seriously."

"Did she offer any reason for Carey to kill Owen West?"

"Just that Owen hated Carey. She seems to think that if Owen hated him, then he was no good and, ergo, must be the murderer. The flaw in her reasoning is that Carey seems to have no motive. I mean being hated isn't a motive, is it? So that's when I thought of self-defense." McLeod sat down at the table and smiled proudly.

"It's possibly the flimsiest reason for murder I've ever heard," said George.

"You mean self-defense?"

"Self-defense can be a credible motive, but you're making the whole thing up out of nothing. You're fantasizing. Besides, if it was self-defense, he would have reported the murder and told the police what happened. Nobody is going to convict him if it was self-defense."

"Sensible people get rattled," said McLeod.

George sighed. "Anyway, I think we're not in mortal danger if this desperate graduate student comes to dinner."

"I didn't think we were. If my theory's correct, he wouldn't attack us unless we attacked him first."

"I'm sure that's true," said George.

"We can ask him questions and maybe find out how he really felt about Owen West."

"Poor man. What are you going to give him for dinner? Besides lentil soup, I mean."

"What would be good—hearty and filling for a poor graduate student?" mused McLeod.

"Steak."

"Why not? Shall I go get some?"

"I'll go," said George. "And I'll cook it."

"Great," said McLeod.

"I'll stop by the office while I'm out. But I won't be long," George said.

THE SOUP WAS back on the stove, ready to reheat. The table was set, the salad made, potatoes were in the oven, and the steak lay on the cutting board, warming to room temperature.

McLeod had a glass of sherry, and George had a martini.

"He's late," said George.

They each had a glass of water.

"He's very late," said George.

"He sure is," said McLeod. "It's seven o'clock and he was supposed to come at six. An hour late. Let's eat."

"Good," said George. "I hated to suggest it."

George cooked two steaks. The soup was better than it had been the night before. The potatoes, after two hours in the oven, were surprisingly good. They decided against dessert and had a brandy instead.

"I guess I should call him," McLeod said. "I should have called before we ate."

George, who was loading the dishwasher, said nothing.

McLeod called Carey's apartment. The phone rang several times before an answering machine clicked on.

"We missed you tonight," she said to the machine. "Did you forget? Please call me tomorrow." She turned to George. "Well, that's that."

"Don't worry," said George. "The steak was good."

"I shan't worry," said McLeod. "He's good at self-defense."

On Monday, McLeod sent Carey Srodek an e-mail, but received no answer. It was Tuesday afternoon before she knew why he hadn't come to dinner.

Twenty-seven

ON TUESDAY AFTERNOON, Nick Perry appeared in her office, trailed by Sergeant Popper.

"Hello!" she said, happy to see Nick. "This is a surprise. Sit down. I'll find two chairs."

Nick looked grim—not at all like the jovial man who had come to dinner Saturday night. "We need to ask you some questions," he said, unsmiling.

"All right," she said. "Would you rather go downstairs to the sun parlor? Or a conference room?" she asked. "It's more comfortable. And there's more privacy."

"That would be better," said Nick.

"Let's go," she said, stood up, and led them downstairs. Somebody was in the sun parlor, so McLeod led them to an empty seminar room, where they sat around the big table.

"What is it? What's going on?" McLeod asked.

"What did you want to talk to Carey Srodek about?" said Nick.

"What?"

"What did you want to talk to Carey Srodek about?"

"What are you getting at?"

"Why did you keep calling Carey Srodek?"

"You don't have to yell at me. He was supposed to come to dinner Sunday night and he didn't show. I called to see if he was all right."

"Why was he coming to dinner?"

"I wanted to talk to him," said McLeod. "Actually, I think he may be the murderer. I was so sure he was the murderer, I meant to call you Sunday afternoon, but George said I was fantasizing. Is that why you're asking questions? Is he the murderer?"

"Why did you think he was the murderer?" Nick asked.

"Megan Snowden told me something that made me think Carey just might have killed Owen West in self-defense. You must have come to the same conclusion. Did you?"

"So you invited this man you thought might be a murderer to dinner?"

"That's right," said McLeod.

"Why?"

"Actually, I had invited him to dinner before I decided he was the murderer. Then George thought I was foolish and my theory of self-defense was weak, and he said he was sure we were in no danger from Carey. But Carey never came. What's he done now?"

"Why did you think he killed Owen West?"

"Megan thought he did it. Megan was Owen West's girlfriend—"

"I know," said Perry.

"She said Owen hated Carey. She thought that made Carey a suspect. I really didn't see why Carey would kill a man just because the other man didn't like him. But then I thought about it and decided Megan's intuition had to count for something. I thought that Owen might have tried to kill Carey. And then Carey killed Owen in self-defense."

Nick ignored her idea completely. "Tell me when you saw Carey Srodek last," he said.

"I only saw him once. It was Friday. Last Friday morning. We had coffee at Frist."

"Why did you meet him for coffee?" Nick asked.

"I was trying to find out about Owen West. I talked to all the graduate students in his group. I told you that."

"And what did he tell you? Refresh my memory."

"He told me that Owen West had 'borrowed' or stolen his computer but brought it back. He said Owen wanted to know what everybody in the lab was working on. He said Owen was thin-skinned. I think that's about all."

"And that was the last time you talked to him?"

"I talked to him on the phone Saturday night after you left. I had e-mailed him and tried to get in touch with him. He finally called me back at eleven o'clock on Saturday night."

"Why were you anxious to get in touch with him?"

"I wanted to find out more about the lab. I wanted to talk to him again—maybe ask him why Owen hated him. So I invited him to supper Sunday night. And then I wanted to see him again to decide if he could kill a man in self-defense and then hide it from everybody."

"What were you calling him about Sunday night?"

"That was because he didn't show up for supper. We went ahead and ate without him, but not until about nine o'clock, I guess, I decided I had better call and see if he was all right. Do you know what happened to him? I haven't heard from him at all. What do you think of my self-defense theory?"

"I'll tell you this. Carey Srodek did not kill Owen West in self-defense. There was no sign of any struggle in the lab when West was murdered."

"Carey could have cleaned it up."

"McLeod! I've never seen you be so unreasonable. You're acting like some ditsy amateur detective in a mystery story."

"Why does everybody think I'm crazy?" asked McLeod. "It's an interesting idea that I have—isn't it?"

"It's completely invalid," said Nick. "And I'll tell you why. Carey Srodek was murdered in his apartment sometime Sunday. When you called him, he was already dead."

McLeod gasped. Her hand flew to her mouth, and her eyes stared at Nick Perry. "That's terrible. I'm so sorry.

Oh, Nick. Would it have helped if George or I had gone to his apartment when he didn't show up?"

"No, McLeod. I think it was too late then."

"Who did it? Do you know?" she asked him.

"No," said Nick. "I don't. We just found out about it. And I get over there and find a piece of paper lying on his desk with your name and telephone number on it. We check his machine for phone messages and there you are, on the machine. I don't think you're responsible for his death, but I knew we had to talk to you. As soon as the forensic people from the state got there, Popper and I left and came here. And I'd like to know more about you and your wild theory. Tell me again what made you think he killed West in the first place?"

"As I said, Megan Snowden put the idea in my head."

"Why did she think he killed West?"

"She said Owen hated Carey Srodek. She seemed to think that was reason enough for him to kill Owen. She said Carey ridiculed Owen. And I thought, well, maybe Carey went by the lab that Sunday and started teasing Owen and Owen attacked him. Carey defended himself and killed Owen. That was my theory, anyway."

"You didn't mention this theory Saturday night," Nick said.

"I didn't have this theory then. I didn't think of it until Sunday—that's when I talked to Megan again."

"Again? You had talked to her before?"

"Yes, on Tuesday, the same day I talked to Carey Srodek."

"You do stay busy, don't you?" said Nick. "Where were you on Sunday?"

"I was at home until I walked around to Edwards Place to see Megan at eleven o'clock. Then I was home the rest of the day."

"Was George there the whole time?"

"George was there all day, except for the time he went to the grocery store. And I think he popped by the office while he was out."

"What time did he leave?"

"It was about twelve-thirty or one, I guess. And he was back by two." She stopped and looked at Nick. "when was Carey killed?"

"Early Sunday afternoon," said Nick.

"You don't think I rushed over to where ever he lives and killed him while George was out, do you?"

"We have to ask these questions. You know that," he said. "All right, let's go over this again." And he asked all the questions at least one more time. And then he asked her if they could tape a statement. That took another hour and it was after five when the two policemen stood up.

"Thank you very much, Ms. Dulaney," said Nick.

"You're welcome, Lieutenant Perry," she said.

"Don't leave town," said Nick.

"Don't worry. I won't."

She was exhausted. So that's what a thorough going-over from the police was like, she thought. And she was a friend of the policeman—what must it be like for someone to whom the police were actually hostile?

Twenty-eight

MCLEOD SLOWLY STARTED back upstairs. When she heard Frieda call her from the office, she turned and went to the doorway of the Humanities Council Office.

"Two policemen were looking for you. Did they find you?" Frieda asked.

"Of course they did. If two policemen can't find me in Joseph Henry House, then they're not very good at their job."

"I guess you're right. Is everything all right?"

"Everything's fine, Frieda. Thanks."

"'When constabulary duty's to be done, A policeman's lot is not a happy one,'" intoned Frieda.

"That's from *The Pirates of Penzance*," McLeod said.

"Correct!" said Frieda.

"That's the first time I recognized any of your quotations."

"Somebody said that anything done for the first time is either wrong, or a dangerous precedent, but I can't remember who it was that said it."

A pity, thought McLeod, since that was a pretty good quote. She went back upstairs and sat down at her desk.

She thought about Greg Pierre. What was he doing last Sunday afternoon? She hoped this time he had a solid alibi. And Sandy Berman? Wesley Bryant? Melissa? Sam Chen? Scott Murphy? Could any of them have killed Owen West and then murdered Carey Srodek? Or Megan Snowden— was she as blameless as she had always seemed? Was it a sure thing that one person had killed both young men?

This was a horror, she thought. An awful situation. Unbelievable. She put her head on her arms on her desk and wept.

Frieda found her like that when she came upstairs. "I have it," she announced exultantly. "It was Francis M. Cornford."

McLeod raised her head and looked at Frieda, bewildered. "What was Francis M. Cornford?"

"The chap that said you should never do anything for the first time," said Frieda. She seemed to really look at McLeod for the first time. "Is something wrong?"

"Yes, something's wrong," McLeod said. She could hear herself sobbing, "There's been another murder!"

"What! Are you sure? Who was it?"

"It's another chemistry graduate student," said McLeod.

"Was it in Frick, too?"

"No, it was at his apartment."

"McLeod, the police, the ones that were just here—they weren't after you on account of the murder?"

"They don't think I did it—at least, I hope they don't. No, they don't. But I had been trying to reach the student. My telephone number was on his desk and my voice on his answering machine. And they wanted to talk to me about when I saw him last—that kind of thing."

"I see," said Frieda. "This must be terrible for you. Are you all right? Can I get you a cup of tea? Anything?"

"No, thanks, Frieda, I'll be all right. It was a shock when they told me about it. And they were here a long time. I was worn out by the time they left. But I'm okay now."

"Was he—the student that got murdered—was he in your class?"

"Oh, no, I hardly knew him. It's too complicated to explain, Frieda, but I wanted to ask him some questions—that's all."

"I see," said Frieda, who clearly did not "see." "Let me know if there's anything I can do. Please. I'm going home now, but I hate to leave you here alone."

"It's all right. I'm going home, too. Thanks, Frieda."

She went downstairs with Frieda and got her coat from the rack and went out the front door when Frieda did. The wind was blowing the budding trees on the quadrangle in front of Nassau Hall.

"It's going to rain," Frieda said. "Do you have an umbrella?"

"No, I don't, but I don't have far to walk." On the way home, she felt infinitely weary, infinitely depressed. She was worried about Greg Pierre again, and she was annoyed with herself because she had forgotten to ask Nick Perry who found Carey Srodek's body, and when. And how he had been killed.

The rain began to fall by the time she passed the anthrax mailbox. It's raining and I don't have an umbrella, or even a hat, she thought, and I'm getting old. I'm lonely, she thought. And I know George won't be home tonight—a second murder would certainly keep him at the office. She should call somebody and ask them over tonight, but who? There was her old friend Fiona, whose husband taught at Princeton Seminary, but the two of them were away for the semester in Capetown, of all places. Maybe Celestine Silver? She was much older than McLeod, but still lively and working on a book about women flower painters. She hadn't seen Celestine for weeks. As she climbed the steps to the front door, which, she was thankful, was sheltered by the porch roof, she got out her key. She vowed to call Celestine as soon as she was inside.

She took the mail out of the box on the porch, glanced through it when she finally got inside, and went upstairs to towel her hair and brush it. It wasn't all that wet, she was happy to see; she went back downstairs and picked up the phone. Celestine Silver did not answer. Well, that settled that, thought McLeod. She was on her own. She went to the kitchen and opened the refrigerator. Not much was in there. She and George had eaten at home last night and pretty well cleaned up the leftovers, all but a big chunk of steak left over from Sunday night when Carey Srodek was supposed to come to dinner and never showed up. Well, she wasn't about to eat a murdered man's steak.

She had just decided to make herself an omelet when the phone rang. It was George. He was indeed going to be home late. "Have you heard about Carey Srodek?" he asked her.

"Yes. Nick and Popper came by to see me. My name and number were on Carey's desk and my message was on his machine, so they wanted to talk to me."

"So now you're a suspect?"

"I hope not. Do you know who found Carey?"

"He didn't show up at the lab yesterday or today, and the other graduate students began to worry. One of them went over to where he lives on Wiggins Street and went in his apartment—it wasn't even locked—and there he was."

"Which graduate student was it?"

"I'm not sure. It was a woman—let's see, Melissa Martin."

"She's cute," said McLeod. "And nice, too."

"You go ahead and eat," George said. "I'll grab something when I get there."

"I was going to have an egg," she said. "There's that leftover steak—you can have that."

"No, thanks," George said. "I'll have some eggs, too."

McLeod hung up the phone, took the steak out of the refrigerator, and put it in the garbage. A pity, she thought. Then the phone rang again.

She hoped it wasn't George saying he'd changed his mind about the steak. It wasn't. It was Megan Snowden.

"I hate to bother you," she said, "but I want to tell you about something I found yesterday."

"You're not bothering me," said McLeod. "What is it?"

"I'd like to show it to you," said Megan.

"Shall I come around?" she asked.

"Would you mind?" asked Megan.

"Not at all," said McLeod. "I'll be there in a jiffy."

She looked at the clock. It was after six. She scribbled a note for George, spread peanut butter on a slice of bread, ate it swiftly, drank a half glass of milk, and put her coat back on. She found her rain hat and ran through the rain to the garage; she drove to Edwards Place, sure there would be a parking place this time of day.

Twenty-nine

❧

MEGAN OPENED THE door of the apartment as soon as McLeod knocked. "I hope I didn't disturb you," she said. "I hated to bother you at home."

"It's perfectly all right," said McLeod. "That's why I gave you my telephone numbers. I'm glad you called."

"Would you like some tea?"

"No, thanks, I don't believe so," said McLeod, marveling that Megan was always so *nice,* her apartment always so clean, and she always looked so neat, even though she always wore a man's shirt, untucked, with shirttails flying, and jeans. "What did you find?" She sat down on the sofa with the blue and white quilt and adjusted the needlepoint pillows behind her back.

"I don't know what it means, exactly, but I think it means something," said Megan, who sat down in the chair opposite. "I was going through some of Owen's things. His folks asked me to handle his clothes—and everything else that was here, too. They said they had photographs of him at home and letters from him, and some of his books, and they looked around the apartment and they didn't see anything they wanted to remember him by. I didn't want to go through his things. But I figured I had to. Still, I couldn't bring myself to just pack up his clothes and get rid of them. I mean, there hasn't even been a funeral, for heaven's sake. But I started going through his books and papers."

She stopped, pulled a Kleenex from her pocket, and blew her nose. McLeod waited.

"He didn't have much here. He kept his chemistry books at the university. He had a few other books—he liked to read about the old West—and those are here. And he kept some business stuff here, of course—checkbook, receipts, title to his car and automobile insurance, and income tax papers, stuff like that. It was all in a file drawer in a little desk. I have a much bigger desk in the room we used for a study, but I do all of my work here and, of course, he worked in the lab."

Get on with it, McLeod was thinking. She gritted her teeth, but managed to smile encouragingly.

"And I found this stuff. Wait! Let me get it." Megan got up and disappeared for a minute, returning with a manila folder in her hand. "Would you look at it? Tell me what you think of it." She handed the folder to McLeod and sat back down in her chair, and back stiff, eyes wide, watched McLeod with great expectation.

McLeod opened the folder and at first did not know what to make of the contents. There were pages and pages of photocopies of what looked like gibberish to McLeod. As she stared at them, it occurred to her that they were scientific notes or calculations of some sort. Flipping over the data sheets, she found drafts of three letters Owen had written. Two were handwritten and very brief.

The first read simply:

Dear Wesley:
    I'm enclosing a copy of the letter I intend to mail to the editor of *Science* unless you follow the suggestions I made the other day.
                                        Your friend,

A second handwritten letter was equally brief. It was addressed to Sanford Berman and said that he was enclosing a copy of a letter he had written and felt it was his duty to mail. He apologized for any inconvenience this might cause his professor, but he was sure that he had no choice to do otherwise.

The third letter was much longer and had been keyboarded on a computer. It was addressed to the editor of *Science*, which even McLeod had a firm enough grasp of science to know was a premier scientific journal. In it, Owen apologized for bringing up a difficult subject but wrote that he felt it was his duty to inform *Science* that the work described in an article by Wesley Bryant and recently accepted for publication in *Science* was questionable, to say the least. "After I was unable to replicate Bryant's work involving the protein kinase assay of the molecules synthesized in Professor Berman's lab," Owen West had written, "I studied her lab notebooks and determined that her entire project was a fake from beginning to end." There was more detail, which was too technical to mean anything to McLeod, but the main thrust of the letter was clear.

"This is terrible!" McLeod said. "Did you know about this?"

"I had no idea," said Megan.

"Did he mail the letters? Are these just copies?"

"I don't know," said Megan.

"This is really dynamite," said McLeod. "But I don't understand. Professor Berman told me himself that it was impossible to carry out a fraud in a chemistry laboratory. He said it would be instantly caught."

Megan shook her head, bewildered. "But Owen says clearly that . . ." she broke off

"Is Owen's computer here?" McLeod asked. "We could look and maybe find out what he did with the letters. If he has printouts. he may have already mailed them."

"His computer's at the lab."

"Oh, dear," said McLeod hopelessly.

"What should I do with these things?"

"Maybe you should get his computer from the lab," said

McLeod. She was thinking that if Owen had sent the letters to Wesley Bryant or Sandy Berman, then either one of
them might be very eager to get ahold of Owen's hard
drive.

"I see what you mean," said Megan. "And I suppose I—
or Owen's parents—should get the computer. But I don't
want it here if it's got that explosive stuff on it."

"I see your point. I hope no one knows about these hard
copies."

"What should I do with them? What do you think?"

"I think you should give them to the police," said
McLeod.

Megan's looked aghast, "Oh, no, I hate to do that."

"I know," said McLeod. "But you—"

Megan interrupted. "It's not just Wesley and Sandy—
that's bad enough, but I think people will misunderstand
Owen."

"But you really must show them to the police, Megan.
They may be the answer to who murdered Owen."

"I know, I know," said Megan. "That's why I called you.
But I hate to get anybody in trouble. And besides, they
looked—the police went through Owen's papers right after
he—after he was killed."

Megan really was *too* nice, McLeod thought, too nice
for her own good. It was all very well not to want to incriminate someone you knew, but when it was a case of
murder, especially the murder of your own fiancé, you
should be ready to speak up.

"They didn't realize what this folder was, I guess," said
McLeod. "It was just in the file drawer with all his finan-
cial records, wasn't it?"

"That's right."

"Megan, I don't see any way to avoid showing it to
them," said McLeod.

"Shouldn't we at least give Wesley Bryant a chance to
explain everything? I mean, she's a woman."

And a Southern woman at that, McLeod thought.
Should they tell Wesley about the letters? No. Wesley was
so happy to have published an article, and she would be

devastated to find out—if she didn't know already—that Owen, or anybody, was going to denounce her work as a fake. And she would be devastated again if the police knew about the letters. Just to know the letters existed would be bad enough, and if she really had faked her work, then it would be worse than hard to bear—it would mean the end of things for her if they were public knowledge.

She longed to talk to Nick, but she knew he must be incredibly busy with this new murder. The new murder—she and Megan had not even mentioned it.

"Megan, have you heard about Carey Srodek?"

"No. What about Carey Srodek?"

"His body was found today. In his apartment. He was murdered. Sunday afternoon."

Megan gasped. "I had no idea," she said. "I haven't seen anybody today. Haven't been out of the house."

"I worry about you, spending so much time alone," said McLeod. "At a time like this."

"This was unusual. I have friends, and they've been wonderful. They come over and they bring food and stuff. No, it was just today that I was all alone. I would have thought Melissa Martin might have told me about Carey, but I haven't heard from her."

"I don't know how much everybody knows," said McLeod. "The police came to see me immediately because a piece of paper with my name and telephone number was on Carey's desk, and my voice was on his answering machine."

"Are you a suspect?" Megan asked. Her eyes were as big as salad plates.

"I hope not. But speaking of suspects. You used to think Carey might have murdered Owen. But since Carey's been killed, too, it looks like he can't have been the murderer."

"I guess you're right," said Megan. "I had already forgotten I ever thought Carey did it." She was quiet, and McLeod waited. "And now it really looks like Bryant may have done it, doesn't it?" Megan said thoughtfully.

"It sure does," said McLeod. "She had a motive, if any-

body did. By the way, where were you Sunday afternoon?
I saw you at eleven."

"I was here the rest of the day. Scott came by for a little while."

"Scott Murphy?"

"That's right. Do you think I might need an alibi?"

"I'm a nut," said McLeod. "I'm in the habit of asking all
these questions, and I can't stop. I wonder where my student was on Sunday afternoon. He's the reason I got so interested in this murder in the chemistry lab in the first
place."

"Yes, I know," said Megan. She stood up. "Do you want
a cup of tea? Or a glass of wine? How about some wine? I
feel like I need a drink."

"I'd love a glass of wine," McLeod said.

"I have a bottle of red," Megan said, and made for the
kitchen.

McLeod followed. "Can I help? I can open a bottle of
wine."

"So can I," said Megan, who proceeded to demonstrate
her capability forthwith, then poured wine into two plain
wineglasses. They clicked glasses and Megan said, "To
Owen."

"To Owen," said McLeod politely, and followed Megan
back to the living room.

"To Owen," repeated Megan. "Poor Owen." She took
another swallow of wine, and set her glass down. "You
know, I have to say this. I don't think Owen was a blackmailer. I know you think that. I know that's what it looks
like. But I don't think he was doing that for money. I'm
sure he thought it was a matter of principle. Or something."
The last phrase made her sound not sure at all it was a matter of principle.

"You could be right," said McLeod. "I don't know
enough about what happens in the scientific world to have
an opinion. I can't possibly make a judgment about what
he did or was going to do."

She finished her glass of wine, and felt a little giddy. "I
should call Lieutenant Perry," she said.

"Please don't call him right away. Have some more wine."

"No, thanks, better not," said McLeod, remembering her scanty dinner and realizing she couldn't drink any more alcohol and drive home.

"I still think we should consult Wesley," said Megan. "Don't you?"

"Not really," said McLeod.

"Let's sleep on it," said Megan.

"Good idea," said McLeod.

Thirty

AS SHE DROVE home, McLeod thought about the papers
Megan had found. What on earth did they all mean? Was
Wesley Bryant a woman who would fake lab results? It
seemed unlikely, but then McLeod learned that almost anybody is capable of almost anything.

Wesley had been so excited about publication. And
publication was apparently crucial to her future as a scientist. Was this possibility of a real step forward on her career path going to evaporate? What would happen to her if
it turned out she had fabricated the results of a scientific
enterprise?

And it appeared that Owen West had really been a con-
temptible person, blackmailing a colleague. It was over-
whelming. And she wanted to know more.

Whom could she ask about the publication of scientific
papers and charges of fraud? Sandy Berman? No, he might
be involved himself, she thought.

What about Earl Shivers? No, she didn't really know
him well enough, she thought, and then remembered that
she needed to interview him again. She wanted to ask him
about his needlepoint, for one thing. Did he really do

needlepoint? If she was interviewing him, she could throw in some questions about a few other matters. She would call him in the morning, she resolved.

Thank goodness it had stopped raining, she thought as she pulled into the garage. She wouldn't get drenched on her way into the house. Once inside, she decided to call Forrest Meriwether. Graduate students stayed up late, and he was bound to know more than she did about scientific publication.

Before she called him, she made herself another peanut butter sandwich and ate it. Forrest answered the phone immediately.

McLeod identified herself and asked if she could come to see him. "I want to ask some questions," she said.

"You always want to ask questions," said Forrest. "But sure, come on over. Or I'll come to your place, if you like."

"No, I'd like to see your digs at the Graduate College," said McLeod. "I'll be right over. How do I find you?"

Forrest gave her his room number and told her what entry to look for and how to find it.

"Be there in a jiffy," said McLeod, who had not yet taken off her coat. She licked her fingers, and set out once more. It was a short drive over to the Graduate College, down Mercer Street and on Springdale Road and up the drive to the tall, imposing Cleveland Tower, which stood beside the sprawling Graduate College residence halls. The tower crowned the hilltop overlooking the golf course that stretched out to the south. In all the time I've spent at Princeton, she thought, I've never heard the carillon that's on top of Cleveland Tower. I must come over for a concert sometime. Sometime—another time. Following Forrest's instructions, she entered the quadrangle of Thomson College and felt as though she had come into another world. It was dark, and Ralph Adams Cram's Gothic buildings cast sinister shadows, as she hurried down the walk by the building on her left. She found Forrest's entry, and then his door easily enough.

"Come in," he said, opening the door as soon as she knocked. "I tried frantically to clean up this place as soon as you called. Then I realized it was hopeless. You have to take me as I am—a poor graduate student." Forrest, face shining with his customary smile, beckoned her in and shut the door.

"Actually, I think it looks rather neat," said McLeod. "And I shall report to your mother that it was immaculate."

"Thanks. What do you want to ask me? It must be important to bring you out at this time of night."

"Of course it's important," said McLeod. "All my questions are important."

"Yes?"

"Yes. This is about the chemistry department. You know about Owen West—well, his girlfriend, Megan, found papers in his desk that she couldn't understand. He seemed to be blackmailing Wesley Bryant, the postdoc. There was a letter in his folder addressed to Wesley, and it said he had checked her data and couldn't replicate her work. And he was going to notify the editors of *Science* magazine.

"Whew!" Forrest stared at her. "That's big-time stuff."

"Is it really? I thought it might be. But there's one curious thing. He wrote a letter to Sandy Berman, too. I didn't understand that."

"Oh, that's simple," Forrest said. "His name would be on the article, too. He had to be listed as a coauthor. She's working in his lab. But he probably didn't know the details of her work. Just put his name on it. That's routine."

"Then could Owen blackmail him, too?"

"I shouldn't think so. Berman's a tenured professor. It wouldn't be pleasant for him if he and his postdoc were accused of fraud. Still I think he could weather it. Of course, he wouldn't want it to happen. I think it would be suicide for a graduate student to try to blackmail his own professor."

"Had you heard anything about this?"

"No, nothing," said Forrest. "I had heard Bryant had had an article accepted, but no hint of anything fishy about it. Then what do I know? I'm just a first-year grad student."

"You obviously know more than I do," said McLeod. "I

wish I could show you the whole file Owen had. I guess I could take you over to Megan's apartment or something, but there were all these xeroxes—sheets of paper with formulas and things written on them. I couldn't figure out what they were."

"They could be photocopies of her lab notes."

"That's what they are!" said McLeod. "I wondered." They sat in silence for a few seconds, then she asked, "What would it mean for her future if Owen mailed these letters?"

"If she couldn't prove the charges were false, it would mean she had no future. Not in science. None at all. She couldn't get a job cleaning the sinks in any laboratory."

"But if she could prove the charges were false?"

"Once the charges are made, she's in jeopardy. She would have to prove her results could be replicated. And other people would have to replicate them. The best-case scenario is pretty bad. All her life, people would say, 'Wasn't there some hanky-panky about those experiments she did at Princeton?'"

Princeton! thought McLeod. If this came out, it would mean more problems for George. Poor George. She stood up. "Well, thanks, Forrest. You've been great."

"Sorry to have bad news. I guess it's bad news. But that's the way it is."

"Anyway, I got to see your nice, neat digs. Thanks again." Then she had a thought. "I never asked you about Earl Shivers. I'm going to do an article about him."

"He teaches orgo. I know that."

"Is that all you know?"

"He's the grand old man of the department, I guess. But in my humble opinion, he's a has-been."

"A has-been?"

"He hasn't done anything new or published anything new in years."

"What about the protein folding?"

"He hasn't published anything on it."

"But what about his orgo classes? And the jokes the students play on him?" asked McLeod.

"Oh, that stuff. Teaching is one thing. Real scientific work is another thing."

"Isn't teaching the basis of the academic life?"

"I suppose it is," said Forrest. "But what interests me is all the ground-breaking work going on in chemistry. Shivers isn't doing any of that at all."

"He believes in pure, basic research, not research that will make some pharmaceutical company even more profitable. I know that much."

"Sure. That's what all academics who aren't on the cutting edge say."

McLeod was a little disappointed to hear Forrest talk like this. But it didn't devalue her article at all, she reassured herself. "I understand he does do needlepoint," she said.

Forrest roared with laughter. "I've heard about that," he said. "He does it at committee meetings. It drives everybody mad."

"I can see how it would," said McLeod. "Anyway, thanks for all your help, Forrest. I really appreciate it."

"Keep an eye on Berman. From what I hear, he's going to be the next one who's going to make big bucks."

"Really? Good. I like Berman. He's been nice to me. So you don't think this possible fraud will hurt him all that much?"

"I don't know. But somehow I don't think it will."

"Don't tell anybody about all this. Please, Forrest."

"I won't. I promise."

And then McLeod remembered Carey Srodek. What kind of life was she leading, that she would forget the murder of someone she knew? "Forrest," she said, "have you heard about Carey Srodek?"

"No, what about Carey Srodek?"

"His body was found today. He was killed in his apartment."

"McLeod, is someone eliminating all the chemistry graduate students? Don't tell my mom—she'll insist I withdraw."

McLeod said nothing.

"That's a bad joke," he said. "But it does make you think—two chemistry graduate students. And both in Berman's group. Do you think it's Berman?"

"I have no idea," said McLeod. "I've got to get home. I'm about to drop in my tracks. Keep in touch, Forrest. And be careful," she added.

Thirty-one

WHEN MCLEOD DRAGGED her weary bones into the house on Edgehill, George was in the kitchen, pouring scotch—lots of scotch—over ice cubes in a tall glass.

"What a day!" he said, and gulped his drink.

"You can say that again," said McLeod.

"You've eaten?" asked George.

"I guess so. I had two peanut butter sandwiches and a glass of milk and lots of red wine."

"Great nutrition. What happened to the omelet?"

"Megan called, and I went over."

"Still detecting? Did Megan have any insights about Srodek's murder?"

"She didn't even know about it."

"And you're just now getting home?"

"After I came home from Megan's, I went to see Forrest Meriwether, over at the Graduate College."

George wasn't listening. He was looking in the refrigerator. "What happened to that steak?" he asked.

"I threw it out. You said you didn't want it. And I certainly didn't want to eat a murder victim's steak."

"You're right. I don't really want it. I'll make an omelet.

Can I make it big enough for you to have some?" He took out the eggs and got down a mixing bowl.

"No, thanks. George, how was Carey Srodek killed?"

"Blow to the head," he said, breaking an egg into the bowl.

"Just like Owen West?"

"That's right." He broke another egg into the bowl.

Like breaking heads, McLeod thought, as she sat down in the kitchen's only chair and watched George crack open two more eggs and then beat them with a whisk. "You know, you can't really say there's a bright side to a murder, but I'm tempted. Since Carey Srodek has been killed, I think Greg Pierre should be cleared."

"Why?" asked George. He was melting butter in the iron skillet.

"Because Greg has no motive for killing Carey. They can't say that Carey had done anything that would make Greg seek revenge."

"You're clutching at straws," said George. He opened the refrigerator again and got out the cheddar, found the grater, and began to grate cheese into the eggs.

"Why do you say that?"

"The police seem to think—and I should think they're right—that the murders are connected. Both victims were chemistry graduate students, working in the same lab. The method is the same. Isn't it likely Owen West's murderer killed Srodek because Srodek knew something that might incriminate the murderer of Owen West?"

"So you're saying the murderer of both of them could be Greg—as well as anybody in the lab?"

"Don't you agree?"

"I guess so," said McLeod. "I mean, theoretically, I see the point. Well, I still want to clear Greg."

George again wasn't paying attention—he had poured the eggs and cheese into the skillet and watched the mixture with total concentration. She got up and opened the refrigerator and got out salad greens and quickly made George a salad while he finished cooking his omelet. When he had flipped it onto his plate, she brought his salad

and followed him into the dining room, where he sat down
to eat.

"Was the press terrible today?" she asked.

"Horrible," he said. "But at least this murder didn't
happen on campus, and they didn't find out about it until
this afternoon. Still they were in full cry by three o'clock.
They demanded to know what was going on in the
Princeton chemistry department. We trotted out Hank
Hollingsworth—"

"Oh, why Hollingsworth? Forrest Meriwether is in his
group."

"Hollingsworth is the department chair—that's why we
called on him. He held a press conference and assured
them all that everything was under control in Frick Lab,
that undergraduate classes are going on, and that research
continues in the labs. He was very reassuring. But it's a ca-
tastrophe. The trustees are concerned. Alumni will be
upset. The development office is afraid that this is going to
hinder fund-raising."

He took a bite of omelet. "I'll let you eat in peace,"
McLeod said. "I'm going upstairs. I'm exhausted."

SHE GOT READY for bed, turned the covers back, and
climbed in. But she sat up, her back against the headboard,
thinking for some time. Then she reached for her notebook
and wrote out a list of names, jotting down a few words
after each name. The result:

> Wesley Bryant—ask about letters (With Megan?)
> Scott Murphy—ask again about Megan
> Melissa Martin—ask about Carey Srodek. Did he have
>   a girlfriend?
> Sam Chen—ask anything
> Sandy Berman—ask about letters, Carey, etc.
> Greg Pierre—check on

That was quite a list, she told herself, after studying it
for some time. Six people to see. She was so tired she

wasn't going to set her alarm clock, but she hoped she would sleep well and wake up early.

Then she reached for the notebook again and added a name to the list:

Earl Shivers—ask about needlepoint

Shivers probably wasn't connected to the murder at all, but if for no other reason than her own curiosity, she had to ask him about his needlepoint. And she should try to finish that article, or at least start on it.

Then she turned out the light and settled down in bed.

Thirty-two

MCLEOD DID WAKE up early on Wednesday—but not because she had slept well. She had been restless and she had waked up, she was sure, a dozen times during the night. She blamed it on all that red wine she had drunk at Megan's apartment. Drinking after dinner was fatal, she told herself, and she was old enough to know better. Besides the wine, her incessant worrying about Greg Pierre—and Megan and Wesley Bryant—had kept her awake. What a life, she thought as she pulled herself out of the bed at six-thirty.

She took a shower and dressed and went downstairs, brought in the newspapers, made some tea and toast, and sat down in the dining room. *The New York Times* had a brief story about Carey Srodek; *The Times* of Trenton, as usual, had much lengthier coverage since it was a local story, but told her nothing she didn't already know. By the time George came downstairs, she had finished reading the papers, had made coffee for him, and had started on the Wednesday crossword, her favorite puzzle of the week. It was easy, but not too easy, and always had a little trick to it.

"Thanks for making coffee," George said when he brought his cereal and coffee to the table. He sat down and started on his Total. "What are your plans for the day?" he asked.

"Hazy," said McLeod.

"Who do you plan to interrogate today?"

"There are about half a dozen people I'd like to talk to today," she said. "But I don't know whether I'll be able to see anybody or not. I've got to wait until nine o'clock to call people. But I'll wander over to my office before then. I do have class tomorrow, after all."

"Good luck. Let me know if you find out anything crucial. We need to clean up this mess."

"I will."

In her office, McLeod looked at her class notebook and was reminded that Tow Sack Burlap, her old reporter friend from Tallahassee, was coming to talk to her class the next day. Thank heavens, she thought. Tow Sack had been a big hit when he had visited another class of hers a couple of years ago. He would entertain the class—and with any luck they would learn something from him, too.

She closed the class notebook and opened the notebook she had brought from home. Greg Pierre was the last name on that list but he was her first concern. She looked at her calendar and saw that he was due for a conference that afternoon at four. And Olivia Merchant was coming at three. That limited her afternoon somewhat, but she had the whole morning.

She called Megan. "I've slept on it, as you suggested," she said. "Shall I talk to Wesley? Or should we both talk to her? Or should you go to the police?"

"Oh, let's talk to Wesley," said Megan. "And please do come with me. I'm scared to go by myself."

"I don't think she's dangerous," said McLeod.

"I didn't mean *scared* scared," said Megan. "But I don't see how you have the nerve to go see people and ask questions like you do."

"Years of being a newspaper reporter have given me the skin of a rhinoceros. I'm impervious to insult. Okay. We'll go together—and take the letters. First, I think we should make another photocopy of them, and leave it somewhere."

Megan gasped. "You're right. And I never would have thought of it."

"I'll call her now and get back to you. Is anytime today all right with you?"

"Sure," said Megan.

"I'll let you know." She called Wesley at home and caught her. "Could I come by and see you again?" she asked. "It won't take long."

"I'm on my way to the lab," Wesley said. "Can you meet me there?"

Horrors, thought McLeod. She didn't want to tell her that Megan was coming, too, and they needed privacy. "The lab's a terrible place to talk," said McLeod. "Can I come by your place? Or we could meet at Small World . . ." Small World was bound to be crowded this time of day; it would be as awful as the lab. "Or come here. If you don't mind. It's not far from Frick. It's quiet and we can sit down in comfort. I'm in Joseph Henry House. Where the Humanities Council is." Silence from the other end of the line. "You know the yellow frame house between Chancellor Green and Nassau Street." It was like talking to someone on another planet, she thought, as no confirming noises came from the phone. People in science didn't know the Humanities Council from a hole in the ground. But wait—

"That yellow house facing the green in front of Nassau Hall?" said Wesley at last.

"That's it!" said McLeod.

"All right. I'll be there in a minute," said Wesley.

"Thanks very much. But you don't have to hurry. I'll meet you downstairs."

She hastily called Megan back and told her to hustle over with the letters. "We can Xerox them here," she said. "But we have to hurry."

"You know, I already Xeroxed them. I went across the street to the U-store and did it just now. I can leave the copies of the copies here."

"Oh, you brilliant girl!" said McLeod.

"I'm teachable," said Megan.

McLeod hung up, grabbed her notebook and a pencil, and went downstairs. Megan arrived first, clutching a tote bag. She had on jeans, but instead of her customary flopping man's shirt, she wore a light sweater and a quilted lime green jacket. Her hair, as usual, was neatly pulled back and caught with the huge tortoiseshell clasp.

"We can talk here in this sunroom," said McLeod, ushering Megan into it. "Why don't you wait here, and I'll wait by the door and bring her in."

She did not have to wait long. Wesley arrived looking harried.

"Thanks so much for stopping by. We can talk in here," McLeod said, leading her to the sunroom. "You know Megan Snowden, don't you?"

"Yes, I do," said Wesley, who looked somewhat surprised. "How are you, Megan?"

"I'm surviving," said Megan.

Beside her, Wesley looked even older and dumpier than she had on Saturday. She also looked puzzled.

"Megan and I have something to show you," said McLeod. "Before we turn it over to the police, as I think we should do. Anyway . . . take a look and tell us what you think." She looked at Megan. "You brought the folder, didn't you?"

"Oh, yes, I wasn't thinking," said Megan, who had been watching raptly. She reached into the tote, brought out the manila folder, and handed it to McLeod.

McLeod, in turn, handed it to Wesley. "Megan found these papers among Owen's things," she said. "I thought they should go to the police, but Megan wanted you to see them first."

Wesley looked at each of them in a puzzled way and then opened the folder. She flipped through the pages, and then she began to laugh. She laughed for a long time. Megan and McLeod stared at her, looked at each other, and turned back to watch Wesley. McLeod had dreaded Wesley's reaction. She had expected—what? Shock? Fear?

Rage? Contrition? Anything but laughter, hearty, unrestrained laughter.

At last Wesley stopped laughing, wiped her eyes, and looked at Megan and McLeod. "I'm sorry."

"Don't apologize," said McLeod. "Just tell us what's so funny."

"The whole thing," said Wesley. "Owen thought he was such an operator . . ." She broke off and looked ruefully at Megan. "I'm sorry," she said.

Megan shrugged, and Wesley continued.

"He tried to blackmail me," she said. "It's ludicrous."

"Something just occurred to me," said McLeod. "What made him think a postdoctoral fellow had money to pay blackmail?"

"Oh, he didn't want money," said Wesley.

Megan interrupted. "I told you yesterday I was sure he wasn't doing it for money," she said to McLeod. "As I said, it was a matter of principle, I'm sure."

Wesley looked at her. "It wasn't exactly a matter of principle," she said. "He didn't want money; he wanted to be listed as a coauthor on my article."

"Had he worked on the experiment at all?" McLeod asked.

"Not at all. He didn't know anything about it. That's why he stole my lab book—well, borrowed my lab book." She looked apologetically at Megan.

"I don't see how he could have determined that your results didn't add up . . ." McLeod's voice trailed away.

"My results do add up!" Wesley's message was loud and clear. "Make no mistake about it. I know what I'm doing. And I defy anybody to do what I did and not get the results I got."

"But what was Owen basing his charges on?" McLeod asked.

"I told you it was ludicrous. He wanted his name on an article in *Science*, and he made this wild try to scare me into making him a coauthor. It was ridiculous."

The other two women watched her silently. Megan was the first to speak. "I'm sorry," she said.

"You don't need to apologize," said Wesley. "You didn't do anything."

"I know. I was going to say I was sorry you had such a low opinion of Owen."

"I don't know what other kind of opinion I could have," Wesley said. "Now I'm sorry to hurt your feelings, Megan, but I have to be frank. This is too important to pussyfoot around."

"What did you do when Owen showed you these letters?" McLeod asked hastily.

"I thought he was mad," said Wesley. "I had never heard anything like it. There's always rivalry and competition in laboratories, but this beat anything I'd ever heard of. I didn't know what to make of it at first, but I told him he was crazy, that I hadn't fudged any of my data, that it was all straightforward, and that if he knew the first thing about scientific technique, he could replicate what I did. I told him he didn't scare me at all with his threats, that I wasn't going to make him a coauthor. No way."

"Weren't you frightened at the idea of charges of fraud?" asked McLeod. "Even if you knew there was no basis for them?"

"I have to say it wasn't a pleasant prospect. Of course not. I considered going to Berman about it, but then I thought about Owen—he's young, I told myself. Give him a chance to pull out of it. Just forget about it."

"What about Berman? Did Owen try to blackmail him?"

"I advised him not to try. I told him it would be fatal for a graduate student to try anything like that with his professor, whose goodwill is absolutely essential to him. I assume he took my advice."

"Have you heard from *Science*? Did Owen actually mail the letter to them?"

"I don't think he did," said Wesley. "I haven't heard anything from them about it."

"You didn't tell me any of this when I was asking you about Owen on Saturday," said McLeod.

"No, I didn't. I didn't kill Owen and I didn't think any

of this was relevant to the murder. The less said about it the better, is the way I felt. The police didn't ask me about it— they asked if I had ever been annoyed with Owen. I was very annoyed with Owen, but I didn't see any use in opening up this can of worms. Now you've opened it up. I should have known it would come out." She made a face, then smiled. "It is funny, isn't it? The nerve of him."

McLeod glanced at Megan. who looked as sad as though her world had ended. Wesley, however, seemed to be enjoying herself.

"I guess it's a good thing we didn't show them to the police. You seem very confident," McLeod said. "It appears that Megan's judgment was right."

"Yes. I'm glad you asked me about them instead of passing them on," said Wesley.

"I'm just sorry that Owen looks like such an oaf," said Megan. "I still wonder if there's some explanation for what he did."

"Everybody wants to be published, my dear," said Wesley. "It's understandable." She stood up. "Well, I must be going. Thank you for showing those ridiculous documents to me."

"Thank you for coming by," said McLeod, standing up, too, and walking with her to the door.

"And where's your office?" Wesley asked. "Upstairs?"

"Yes, up on the third floor. Would you like to see it?"

"Sure. Call it scientific curiosity."

"I understand about curiosity," said McLeod.

"I thought you would," Wesley said. There was a hint of malice in her voice that made McLeod wince. Oh, dear, she thought, she'd made an enemy. Nevertheless, she plodded up the stairs ahead of Wesley until they'd reached what she thought of as the garret with the cubicles for visiting writers. They could see Stephen Cohen, the foreign correspondent who was also teaching a class this semester, talking on the telephone in his cubicle. He nodded at them.

"So you don't have a private office," said Wesley.

"No, I don't. But this is my cubicle here, by the window. I have a great view of Chancellor Green. Sit down a minute. I have one chair besides my desk chair. And I don't think we'll disturb Stephen. I want to ask you about Carey Srodek. What was he like?"

"He was a very nice young man. A straight arrow. He didn't spread his stuff all over the lab. He never handled other people's lab books. He did sometimes tease people, I believe. I didn't know him well, of course. His death is terrible, simply unbelievable. I suppose it's connected to Owen's. What do you think?"

This was positively chatty for Wesley Bryant, and McLeod resolved to take advantage of this unusual loquacity. "I think they must be connected. Before Carey was killed, Megan thought he might have killed Owen. I thought that was kind of interesting, but I couldn't figure out what Carey's motive would be. How did Owen and Carey get along in the lab?"

"I really couldn't say. As I told you, I didn't spend all that much time with the graduate students." Wesley was the old Wesley again. She stood up. "Thanks for showing me your office."

She turned and started down the stairs.

McLeod followed her down and waved her out the front door before she joined Megan in the sunroom. "What do you think?" McLeod asked Megan.

Megan thought a minute before she spoke. "I don't know what to think. You know Wesley made it clear that Owen wasn't really blackmailing her. I think Owen had probably helped her with her experiments and he just wanted his fair share of the credit."

"I must say that explanation has never occurred to me," McLeod said.

"And yet I don't think Owen would blackmail her just to get his name on an article. I guess I think she's lying. I wanted to show her that stuff before we gave it to the police, but now I'm almost sorry we did."

"Do you? I thought she was quite persuasive. Oh, well, we've done our best. And as you say, the police must have seen those letters when they went through Owen's desk.

We can just let it go for a while, or we can tell Lieutenant Perry about them."

"Let's let it go for a while," said Megan.

"All right. I do wonder why she wanted to see my office."

"If she's the murderer, I'd say she was going to go after you next," said Megan, getting up. "Be careful. I guess I'd better go. Well, thanks, McLeod. I'll talk to you soon. You can keep these—I have the copies." She handed McLeod the folder and left.

McLeod took the papers upstairs, looked at her watch, and then at the list of names in her notebook. She had several hours before her conferences with students and she decided she would go over to Frick and talk to anybody she could find.

Thirty-three

EARL SHIVERS WASN'T in his office, and McLeod, realizing he taught his orgo class on Wednesday, popped in to see his assistant Binky Tate.

"Hello there," caroled Binky, obviously remembering her. "How's your article coming?"

"Slowly," said McLeod. "I came to take you up on your offer—you said you loved to talk about your boss."

"I do, I do. Sit down. Or would you like to go get some coffee? It's time for my break."

"Fine," said McLeod. "Where do you go for coffee?"

"We'd better go next door to Woody-Woo so I can let it all fall out."

"By all means."

Binky got up, took her down jacket from a hook and her billfold from the bottom drawer of her desk, and led the way across the plaza with its big pool and the abstract sculpture to the white-columned Robertson Hall, home of the Woodrow Wilson School of Public and International Affairs, known informally as Woody-Woo.

In the small café at the east end of the building, they got coffee and tea and sat down at a table.

"Let it all fall out," said McLeod, notebook on the table.

"Shivers is wonderful to work for," Binky began piously. "He is brilliant, industrious, patient, kind, thrifty, all those good things."

McLeod laughed. "Thanks. Now tell me what he's really like."

"He drives people hard, but he really is good to work for," said Binky. "I have to admit it."

"Does he really do needlepoint?"

Binky looked surprised. "He really does. Didn't you notice the pillow on the seat of my desk chair? He did that."

"I didn't notice it. It's fantastic. Not many men do needlepoint."

"There was that football player—Rosie Grier," said Binky.

"That's right. Tell me, do you think he really likes all those jokes the students play on him?"

"Don't quote me, but I think he hates it. Despises it. But he has to be a good sport. It's gone on all these years and there's no way to stop it, but he won't quit teaching orgo. You have to admire him."

"What's not to admire?" said McLeod agreeably.

"Right," said Binky.

"To change the subject, what do you think of the murders? Did you know Owen West or Carey Srodek?"

"I knew Owen West—he was always all over the place—but I did not know Carey Srodek. I tell you one thing. It's kind of interesting. We haven't had so much excitement around here since 2002 when the FBI was snooping around."

"In Frick? What was the FBI doing in Frick?"

"You know about the anthrax scare?" asked Binky.

"Well, sure—those letters with anthrax powder that went to the Senate and to networks in 2001. They were mailed from Princeton—from that mailbox on Nassau Street opposite University Place," said McLeod. "That's all I knew. I remember they suspected some man in the Washington area."

"That's right. But after they found out that the anthrax

letters were mailed from Princeton, they came swooping down. You know it was serious—the regional post office had to close for nearly five years while it was fumigated, or whatever they call it. A couple of postal workers who handled the letters were seriously ill. The FBI came to Frick and looked around and examined all our glove boxes.

"Glove boxes? What's that?" asked McLeod, who pictured cedar boxes lined with tissue paper containing white kid gloves.

Binky deleted that mental picture. "They're big, hermetically sealed boxes. You stick your hands in through two holes and your hands are in gloves. With the gloves, you can move stuff inside. The boxes can protect the material inside from contamination from the outside. Or they can protect the people outside from the stuff inside, like when they're working with anthrax or chemical weapon materials."

"I see," said McLeod. "Are there many of them in Frick?"

"Lots," said Binky. "Frick is a building full of dangers . . ." Her voice sounded like the voices people assume for Halloween when they play act as ghosts and witches. "You have to be very, very careful in Frick Lab."

"I've seen the signs in the corridors about emergency showers and emergency eyewash."

"Oh, yes. A chemist's lab is indeed fraught with peril." Binky's voice was back to normal and her eyes twinkled. She picked up her cup, gulped the last of her coffee, and put the cup down. She stood up. "I've got to get back to that wonderful job with my divine boss," she said. "Can I tell you about anything else?"

"You've been great," said McLeod. "Thanks."

BACK IN FRICK, McLeod headed upstairs and found Sandy Berman at his desk in his office.

He looked up when McLeod came in, but he said nothing.

"Can I talk to you a minute?" she asked.

"Sure." He looked at his watch. "I've got a few minutes."

"Did Owen West ever threaten you in any way?" she asked, as she sat down in Berman's uncomfortable guest chair.

"Threaten me? What do you mean? Is that psychobabble—do you mean did I feel threatened by him?"

"No, I meant it literally. Did he threaten you?"

"Do you mean physically threaten?"

"I don't mean a threat of violence, but did he try to blackmail you?"

"Blackmail me? What would he blackmail me for?"

"He apparently tried to blackmail somebody else, and I have some reason to believe he was going to try something on you. And I wondered if he did."

"Owen West, a blackmailer? I can't believe that."

"I saw the letters myself," she said.

"Look here, I have not led a blameless life, but so far as I know, I've done nothing that I could be blackmailed for. My life is not exactly an open book, but there's nothing I'd pay money to keep hidden." Berman, looking straight at McLeod, suddenly smiled. "At least that I can think of right now," he added.

"I'm glad he didn't try to get to you," she said. "It was just a worrying sort of idea I had, so I just wanted to know."

"And why did you just want to know?"

"I'm still trying to find out who killed Owen West—because of my student. I can't stop trying."

"Well, now another one of my graduate students has been killed," said Berman. "It's appalling. I want the murderer found, even if it is your pet student."

"Tell me about Carey Srodek."

"He was an exemplary student," said Berman. "Neat, precise, hardworking. His death is a tragic loss."

"I'm sorry. I met him once, and I can believe what you say."

"And I'll tell you right away that he never tried to blackmail me."

"You must have been worried when he didn't show up Monday or Tuesday."

"I have to confess I wasn't worried. I was annoyed. One of the other graduate students, Melissa Martin, was concerned. She had tried to call him on Monday and she left a message. When he didn't call her back and didn't show up Tuesday, she walked over to Wiggins Street and, well—found him."

"A terrible experience for her, wasn't it?"

"Yes it was."

"Do you think the same person killed Owen and Carey?"

"I have no idea whether we have a serial killer in Princeton, or whether my lab is the setting for a coincidence so unlikely as to be improbable."

"I see," said McLeod. "Let me ask you about something else."

"Please do," said Berman.

"You must be very proud of your postdoc," McLeod said.

Berman looked at her, eyebrows raised.

"I mean, having an article about the work you and she are doing accepted by *Science*."

"It's her work," said Berman. "Yes, I am very happy for her. It's a feather in her cap, all right. Now you'll have to excuse me, McLeod. I've got less pleasant things to do. I have to call Carey's mother."

"Is she coming?"

"No, she's a widow and not well. Her brother is coming later when the police release Carey's body."

"It's terrible for you. Thanks for taking the time to talk to me. I appreciate it."

Berman nodded and got up when she did. Outside his office, McLeod turned, not in the direction she had come, but the other way, and walked aimlessly down the corridor. When she saw a sign on the door, BERMAN LAB, she went in. Berman's three surviving graduate students and Wesley Bryant were all there, not working, but standing by one of the counters, talking.

She stopped at the door. She had forgotten about Wesley. She would have loved to talk to Sam Chen and Melissa Martin and Scott Murphy, but she could scarcely ask them questions about Wesley with Wesley in the room. But she could, she reasoned, at least ask them about Carey Srodek, and went in.

Wesley left the group as McLeod joined it. "Still sleuthing?" Scott Murphy said.

"I guess you can call it that," said McLeod. "Tell me about Carey Srodek. Do any of you have any idea who could have killed him?"

"We were just talking about the possibility that it was a burglar or tramp or somebody who did it," said Melissa, who looked, McLeod noted, as pretty as she had the night McLeod had seen her at home.

"Yeah," said Scott. "He didn't bother anybody here. We think he was just unlucky."

"Did he have a girlfriend?"

"He did. Her name was Stella," said Melissa. "I don't know her. I only saw her once or twice. I don't think I ever talked to her."

"But you think somebody around here—in the lab— had reason to murder Owen West?"

They looked at each other and then at McLeod. "Well, it's easier to understand why Owen might be knocked off," said Sam Chen. "Nobody liked him. But Carey was all right."

Melissa and Scott nodded.

"So you think it was somebody outside who killed Carey? This is a tough one, isn't it?" McLeod asked. "Thanks, guys. Let me know if you think of something." She glanced around the lab as she left—and noticed Wesley Bryant did not look up from her work.

I'm going to give up on this, she thought as she walked back toward Joseph Henry House. Nobody likes me. Some people hate me. I'm not helping Greg, and he's the one I care about.

Thirty-four

❧

BACK IN HER office, McLeod found an e-mail from Greg Pierre canceling his conference that afternoon. "Team has a workout this afternoon. Can I come tomorrow at eleven?" Disappointed, McLeod sent him confirmation of the change of time.

Checking her voice mail, she found a message from the director of the Humanities Council, her boss, asking if she could have lunch with her today. McLeod looked at her watch. After eleven—she hurriedly punched Victoria Sullivan's extension.

"I'd love to have lunch, Victoria," she said. "I hope I'm not calling you back too late."

"Not at all. Is Prospect at twelve all right with you? Come on down when you're ready."

What was this about? McLeod wondered. She did not know Victoria Sullivan as well as she had Ginger Kingsley, the director who had first hired her. Victoria was more distant, but obviously efficient. No one ever called her Vicky. It would be good to talk to her now, McLeod thought. She looked down at her clothes—black pants, black sweater, and brilliant red and pink silk scarf—nothing sensational, but nothing disgraceful either. She headed downstairs and popped into the ladies' room to actually comb her short white hair, something she had to admit she rarely did once she was dressed for the day.

When she went into the director's office, a big pleasant room on the first floor of Joseph Henry House, she saw that Victoria outclassed her in her gray pantsuit and maroon silk shirt. Oh, well. Victoria was a tall, slender woman with dark hair and a Ph.D. in German. And she looked terrific.

"I'm glad you could come on such short notice," Victoria said.

"I'm glad you asked me," McLeod said. "My social life is not exactly brimming over with luncheon engagements."

They took their coats from the hall rack and walked down to Prospect, chatting amiably. When they were settled in the Garden Room with prelunch glasses of wine, having ordered chef's salads, Victoria asked her how the semester was going.

"Very well," McLeod said. "It's a great group. Only one fly in the ointment—I have one student who's been having a hard time ever since just before break. He's a wonderful writer, and I feel very protective."

Victoria asked politely what the problem was, and McLeod sketched in Greg's entanglement with the law in Wyoming and the way the police seemed to think he was involved in the murder of Owen West.

"Or at least, they seemed for a while to think he was involved." She went into some detail about the police and Greg. "I'm not sure if he's in the clear now or not. I hope he is. But now there's been a second murder. I'll just feel better when they're solved and he's free of suspicion."

"I see," said Victoria. "That's why you've been talking to people about the murder."

"Yes, that's why." McLeod gulped some wine. "How did you know I was talking to people about the murder?"

"A couple of people mentioned it to me." Victoria sipped her own wine and looked at McLeod over the rim of her glass.

"They haven't been complaining, have they?"

"No, not exactly complaining." Victoria smiled. "I just thought I'd better talk to you about it, and I'm glad I did. I can see why you're concerned and want to do something. But go easy on faculty members. A professor at Princeton has very special status. Of course, I see your point, too, and I'd say keep up the good work, but keep me informed, will you? We don't want to disturb the chairman, do we?"

The chairman of the Humanities Council was a distinguished professor and a notoriously hands-off chairman, who was chiefly interested in his own research. "And that's an ideal situation, isn't it?" Victoria Sullivan had asked someone who questioned his attention to duty.

McLeod was happy to promise to report her activities to Victoria, but she realized she was being warned—warned politely and cheerfully, but warned. They finished their lunches engaged in agreeable gossip about various members of the staff and faculty.

SHE HAD JUST settled down at her desk again when she heard a female voice asking Steve Cohen, who surprisingly was still in his cubicle, where she could find McLeod Dulaney.

"Right over here," said Steve. "I'll show you." He appeared, ushering Melissa Martin, looking lovely as usual, before him into McLeod's cubicle.

"Thanks, Steve," McLeod said, smiling at Melissa.

Steve gazed at Melissa, looking downright foolish with admiration, almost panting. Melissa gave him a smile of gratitude, but turned her attention to McLeod. "I found you!" she said. Steve gave one last look of longing and went back to his cubicle.

"I want to talk to you," Melissa said.

"Great. What about? Here, sit down." McLeod was very conscious of the presence of Steve Cohen nearby. She could see him in her mind's eye, listening and waiting for another glimpse of Melissa. She lowered her voice to say,

"Let me have your coat. I don't have a coat rack but I can lay it over here on the filing cabinet."

"I wanted to talk to you," Melissa said again, when they were seated. "You know I told you to talk to Sam Chen when you came to see me at home that time."

"Yes. Why did you tell me that?"

"I didn't really think he was a murderer, but I knew Owen had insulted him and I thought that would give you an idea of how monstrous Owen could be. I didn't think Sam killed Owen, but now I'm worried because the police have hauled Sam off to Borough Hall for questioning."

"I just saw him in the lab," said McLeod.

"They came right after you left and took him away."

"Good heavens!" said McLeod. "Why? Did Carey insult Sam, too?"

"Of course not," said Melissa. "Carey wouldn't do anything like that. He did tease people, but I don't think he was ever, ever mean to Sam."

"What was Sam doing Sunday afternoon?"

"He was home alone."

"What were you doing Sunday afternoon?"

"Me? I was home alone, too. The police asked us all about that, and I don't think anybody in the lab had an alibi, if that's what you mean. They didn't take any other people down to the station."

"They must have a good reason to want to talk to Sam," McLeod said.

"I can't imagine what it would be," said Melissa. "Can you do anything?"

"Not a thing that anybody else couldn't do. If one of you has a bit of information that would help Sam or help the police in any way whatsoever, you must give it to them. You know that, don't you?"

"Yes, we do. But I understand you have some information you haven't given to the police."

"What do you mean, Melissa?"

"Scott was telling us about what Megan found out about Owen and Wesley Bryant. And she said she had told you."

"Scott Murphy?"

"That's right. He and Megan seem to be taking up where they left off when Owen entered the picture."

"I had gathered. But now you think I'm obstructing justice? Is that what you're saying?"

"Well, you and Megan . . ." Melissa hesitated.

"Do you think Wesley was fudging her data?"

"I don't know. I don't know. But I thought you really wanted to clear up this murder and everything," said Melissa. "Like for your student and everything. And it does look like Wesley might have had a motive. What I mean is, shouldn't the police talk to her—instead of harassing poor old Sam Chen."

"We don't know that they're harassing him," McLeod said mildly. "But I see what you're saying. At first, I was all for turning the papers over to the police as soon as Megan showed them to me, but Megan insisted that we talk to Wesley first. And when we did, I found Wesley rather convincing."

"What did she say?" Melissa interrupted.

"She laughed. Uproariously. She said Owen was trying to blackmail her into making him a coauthor."

Melissa laughed, too. "I see why she thought it was funny—in a way."

"You laugh, but you've made me think," said McLeod. "Another reason we didn't give them to the police was that Megan said the police went through Owen's desk after his murder and must have seen the letters and didn't think they were important."

"But they were blackmailing letters! Whether he wanted money or coauthorship, the police should have been interested."

"Well, there were all these pages and pages of copies of incomprehensible lab notes . . ." said McLeod. "But I agree. Okay, you've convinced me. We should show them to the police, although I think I better ask Megan first."

"Tell her, don't ask," advised Melissa.

"We'll see. Thanks for coming to talk to me. Now tell me, why are you so concerned about Sam Chen?"

"I'd be concerned about any fellow student. And Sam's a nice guy. I guess I want to be sure he gets a fair shake."

"Tell me about Scott Murphy. When I talked to him, he was drinking. He was really bitter that Owen had stolen his girlfriend, and now that Owen's out of the way, he seems to be seeing a good bit of Megan, even 'taking up where he left off,' as you put it. Do you think he could have been mad enough to kill Owen? Incidentally, Megan told me they were together Sunday afternoon. But he told you he didn't have an alibi?"

Melissa looked surprised. "He did. Maybe he did get mad and kill Owen. I hadn't really thought about it."

"It's a possibility, although he didn't strike me as a murderer when I talked to him. And I don't know how to find out more, do you?"

"Not really," said Melissa.

"And back to Wesley. Could she have faked her results? What do you think?"

"I don't know. I don't know," Melissa said. "A week ago, I would have said, 'Absolutely not,' but now, I don't know. Everything is so horrible and we're seeing the ugly sides of everybody—it's like turning up rocks and seeing the worms underneath, isn't it?"

"That's exactly what a murder investigation is like," McLeod said.

Melissa began to cry and McLeod did not have the heart to ask her if she, too, had had reason to kill Owen West.

McLeod, afraid that Steve would come and attack her for torturing Melissa, succeeded in calming her down and sending her on her way.

Thirty-five

WHILE SHE WAITED for Olivia Merchant to appear for her conference, McLeod cleaned up all her e-mail and voice messages, made plans for Tow Sack's appearance the next day, and thought about the murder case. Finally, she called the police department and asked to speak to Lieutenant Perry. Of course, he couldn't come to the phone, and she left a message. It wasn't long before he called her back.

"Come to dinner tonight," she said. "Whatever time you can make it. Just us." (She was terse to avoid wasting Nick's time.)

"I can probably come, but not before nine o'clock," he said.

"Fine," she said. "Dinner will be ready—come when you can."

"Terrific," he said.

Olivia appeared for her conference and was worried about her interview with a scientific person. McLeod read the troublesome passages—it was a piece on the work of a professor in the Department of Ecology and Evolutionary Biology who was writing a book on animal habitats.

McLeod helped her pick the best examples from the vast store of information she had gathered from the professor.

"He loves to talk about his work," Olivia said.

"That's good."

They both liked the part about the bowerbird, who builds a sort of "castle of love" to win a mate and decorates his creation with garlands of flowers.

"It's wonderful material, Olivia," McLeod said. "I look forward to reading it again when it's finished."

She got ready to go home, remembering to take with her the folder Megan had given her.

AT HOME, MCLEOD thought about dinner. What could she serve for Nick—and probably George, too? That reminded her that she had better get in touch with George. Gina put her right through, and George said yes, he would be home for dinner, and having Nick was a good idea. Should he ask Polly?

"Will Nick talk as freely if she's here? You brought that up on Saturday," she said.

"That's a good point. And you say Nick's going to be late, nine, or later? Okay, I'll be home before then. Are you cooking?"

"I'm cooking," she said firmly. "I thought my poor man's coq au vin would be good, but you're supposed to cook it a day ahead. I want to have something that's all ready when he gets there, or at least ready to pop in the oven. I don't want to have to spend time in the kitchen after he gets there. I'll think of something."

"I have complete confidence," George said.

She hung up and finally settled on chicken tetrazzini, a casserole that could be assembled ahead of time and required only thirty minutes in the oven. It wasn't earth-shattering haute cuisine, but it was good—simple and hearty. She wrote out her grocery list and set out to gather the ingredients for dinner.

Back at home, she boiled the chicken, cooked the spaghetti in the chicken broth, sautéed the mushrooms and

onion and garlic, made a tomato sauce, and combined it all
in George's big casserole. She washed arugula and sec-
tioned oranges for a salad that would also contain black
olives. For dessert, she'd have ice cream, if anybody
wanted any. And for a proper Southern flourish, she made
biscuits and had them ready on a cookie sheet to go in the
oven when the tetrazzini did. Then she set the table, and
went upstairs and took a hot shower, dressed again, this
time in a long wool caftan, and went downstairs carrying
her knitting bag. She knitted peacefully as she sat on the
sofa in the parlor with a fire in the fireplace and thought
about Megan and Scott and Wesley and Sam. What a tangle it all was, she was thinking, and then discovered a real
tangle. She had made a mistake in her knitting and would
have to rip out three rows.

IT WAS ALMOST ten o'clock before Nick arrived. George
had been home for some time and kept offering McLeod a
drink, but she had turned him down. "I want to have my
wits about me," she said. "I'll have one when Nick gets
here."

McLeod greeted Nick at the front door. She cut short
his apologies for his tardiness and rushed to the kitchen to
put the tetrazzini in the oven. When she joined Nick and
George in the parlor, George had built up the fire and
poured Nick a large scotch.

"This is great," said Nick. "You two are the only people
I know who'll put up with my hours like this. I really appreciate it." He sipped his scotch. "And while I'm being
grateful, George, let me thank you—you must have talked
to the president. Haven't heard a peep out of him since last
week."

"He's a reasonable man," George said. "And the focus
has shifted a little from the university since the second
murder occurred off campus."

"But it's still in my bailiwick," Nick said. "It seems
hopeless. We can't find the murder weapon, not even with

all the help we've had from police from Lawrenceville and Pennington and Hightstown."

"McLeod, you need a drink," George said. "Martini?"

"No, thanks, I'll have a glass of wine."

"I was gulping my scotch and didn't even notice you two didn't have anything," Nick said. "It may be that a detective is not fit for polite society, not when he's in the midst of a murder case. I apologize."

"Don't worry about it," McLeod said. "I'll get my wine and bring some chips. I forgot them."

"Sit down," said George. "I'll get everything. Talk to Nick—or listen to Nick. I'll be right back. Anything need doing in the kitchen?"

"Put the biscuits in the oven," said McLeod. "That's all." She turned to Nick and smiled. "You must be very frustrated."

"I am, and then some. Have you found out anything? I know you're still asking questions."

"Nick, I'm always asking questions. You know that. I found out one very interesting thing . . ." She stopped as George returned with a tray holding chips, his drink, and McLeod's wine.

"Red all right?" George asked her.

"Perfect."

"Am I interrupting?" George said. "I heard silence fall when I came in."

"Not at all," said McLeod. "I just paused for the drinks. Nick asked me if I had learned anything, and I was about to answer him. I did find out something very interesting that I think you ought to hear about, Nick. But first, I have a question for you: Why did you take Sam Chen down to the station?"

"McLeod, we're going to take all the people from that lab—the other two graduate students and the postdoc—down to the station, too. We don't have a situation room at Frick and we want to really talk to these people. We can talk to Berman—at least he has an office—but there's no place to talk to the others."

"If you need an on-site room," George said, "surely we can arrange that. Did you ask anyone about it?"

"Professor Hollingsworth was not disposed to be cooperative," Nick said.

"We can fix that. If we can't find space in Frick, we can certainly find a room nearby—in Green Hall, or Hoyt. I can guarantee you a situation room on campus," George said. "If I have to give up my office in Nassau Hall."

"Thanks," said Nick. "That would be a help. We've already talked to Chen and Wesley Bryant and Scott Murphy. We'll bring Melissa Martin in tomorrow, and then if we have a room on campus, I want to interview everyone in Frick Lab, the whole building. We have simply got to find out what's behind these murders. We never made much headway with the first one, and usually the second murder really provides a whole new perspective. But this one baffles me. Who would want to kill a graduate student? To tell you the truth, McLeod, and I know this is going to upset you, Pierre or Billings or whatever his name is, is still my favorite—simply because he has such a good motive." He paused only a second when McLeod began to object violently and went on, "But why Srodek? Why kill him, unless he knew something incriminating. That's what we're working on now."

"Well, at least, I'm glad to know Sam Chen wasn't singled out as a prime suspect," McLeod said.

"You're always upset about some student," Nick said. "He's not in your class, is he"

"No, he's a graduate student. I have had graduate students in the class, but he's not one of them. I'm like Melissa—he's a minority student and I feel like he's not as tough as some of us." McLeod stood up. "Let me check on dinner," she said, and hurried to the kitchen.

She tossed the salad and got out the butter, poured water in the glasses, and put the red wine bottle on the table. Then she removed the casserole from the oven, set it on a trivet on the dining table, and put the biscuits in a napkin-lined basket. It was all ready.

George and Nick came promptly when she called them, sat down, and proceeded to eat heartily.

After his third helping of chicken tetrazzini, Nick sighed and leaned back in his chair. "That was wonderful."

"It was very good indeed," said George. "I'm afraid I'll never again have a front room boarder like you."

McLeod smiled and gave him thumbs up. "Dessert, anyone? We have ice cream."

They refused ice cream, and George said he'd make coffee and bring it to them in the parlor.

"Now, McLeod, you said you had some information for me," Nick said when he had put a log on the fire and they had sat down.

"I do," said McLeod. "Let me show you something." She got up and returned with Megan's manila folder and handed it to Nick. He opened the folder and looked at the papers. He read the letters and stared—apparently uncomprehending—at the pages of lab notes.

He looked up at McLeod. "Where in hell did you get this?"

"You haven't seen it before?"

"No, I have not."

"Somebody in the police department saw it."

"Where was it? Where did you get it?"

"I got it from Megan Snowden."

Nick thought a minute. "Oh, yes. Owen West's girlfriend. It was in their apartment?"

"Megan says this was in Owen's desk. She found it after his parents asked her to handle the disposition of all his things in the apartment. Nick, she said that the police must have seen it when they went through his desk."

Nick cursed. He cursed with fluency, imagination, and at some length. He was still muttering curses when George brought in a tray with the coffee and cups. He took the cup of coffee absently and asked, "And how did these papers come to be in your possession, McLeod?"

"When Megan found the folder, she called me," McLeod said. "It was yesterday—heavens, it was only yesterday and it seems like weeks ago—right after I talked to you and Sergeant Popper. I told her she should give it to the police. That's when she told me that the police had seen it. She knew it was important. But she wanted to show it to Wesley Bryant before she turned it over to the police. She thought Wesley might have some explanation, and besides she didn't want it to go public because she knew that it made Owen look bad. She cares about Owen's reputation, so she at least wanted to delay revealing all this."

"So what happened?" asked Nick.

"Well, we talked to Wesley first thing this morning."

"And?"

"Wesley laughed. She thought it was the most ridiculous thing she'd ever seen. She said Owen wasn't blackmailing her for money. He wanted to be named a coauthor on an article she had had accepted for *Science* magazine. She insisted that she did not feel threatened by Owen West, that the whole thing was ludicrous. And she refused to make him a coauthor."

George reached over to take the folder from Nick and went through the papers. He looked taken aback, McLeod thought.

Nick was brooding. "I wish I had seen this before I interviewed Bryant again this afternoon," he said.

"I called you the first chance I had," McLeod said, and then she realized that that wasn't true, that it had taken Melissa Martin's scolding to push her into handing the papers over to the police. "Almost the first chance," she added, and realized she had to confess to Megan that she had given the papers to the police. Well, she could handle that part, she thought. It was undeniably the thing to do.

Nick looked at his watch. "Too late to call anybody now." He sounded regretful. "It's eleven o'clock. Well, I'll give Berman a call first thing tomorrow morning."

"And Wesley?" McLeod asked.

"Her, too. But I want to find out if she did falsify her data if I can. And I'll talk to Megan Snowden—that's for sure."

"Good luck," McLeod said.

"Any other little nuggets you're withholding from the police, my dear?" Nick asked her.

"Nothing that I can think of." She searched her memory and, in an effort to make a clean sweep of everything she knew, dredged up what she'd learned about Scott Murphy and Megan. "You knew they were together before Owen West entered the picture, didn't you?"

"Not really," Nick said.

"And now they seem to be together, or getting there, again," she added. "Now I've told you all this stuff. Tell me something: Does anybody have an alibi for either Sunday afternoon?"

"If they do, it's shaky at best."

"Megan told me she and Scott were together this past Sunday. But Scott told the people in the lab he didn't have an alibi," McLeod said.

"Hmmmm," said Nick. "I think it's time I left. I can't thank you enough for the food, McLeod, and for the information, of course, which you finally decided to share with the authorities."

"All's well that ends well," McLeod said vaguely. "I'm glad you could come to dinner. Let's do it again. We don't mind eating late, do we, George?"

"Of course not," George said gamely.

Thirty-six

❧

ON THURSDAY MORNING McLeod started preparing for her class that afternoon. She had mixed emotions when another e-mail from Greg Pierre canceled his conference appointment. In the South, her elderly relatives used to say, "It's a blessing . . . but it's a pity," when describing an event that had complex results. In this case, the cancellation was a blessing because she had to meet Tow Sack Burlap, who was scheduled to talk to her class, at the Dinky Station at eleven-fifteen, so an eleven o'clock conference would have been nearly impossible, but it was a pity because she really wanted to see Greg and find out how the second murder had affected him. Still, she reflected, he would surely be in class that afternoon.

Then Wesley Bryant called and wanted to come and talk to her. McLeod, intrigued, agreed. "Come on over," she said, "or would you rather I met you somewhere?"

Wesley said she'd be at Joseph Henry House shortly, and McLeod went downstairs to wait for her. Wesley arrived looking untidier than ever and almost panting. "I wanted to talk to you," she said. "Before I go to the police. I guess I'll go to the police. And Berman. I have to talk to

Berman. My life is over. There's no doubt about it. I don't know what I'll do."

"Come on, sit down on the sun porch. Would you like coffee, or tea? I wish I had some brandy. I think you need brandy, but I bet we don't have any here. Coffee?"

"Thanks," said Wesley. "I'd love a cup of coffee—milk, no sugar, please. I'll come with you and help."

"Sit down," McLeod said firmly. "I'll be right back. I don't need help. Really I don't." She got a mug of coffee from the pot in the little kitchenette and poured a dash of milk into it. After a second's hesitation—she didn't want to take the time to make tea—she poured a mugful for herself and carried them both into the sun parlor.

Wesley grabbed hers. "Thanks," she said, and swallowed. Then she began to weep. Tears streamed down her cheeks and she sobbed and gulped for air and continued to weep.

McLeod waited, at a loss for something to say. "I'm so sorry, Wesley, whatever it is. Can you tell me about it?"

Wesley only sobbed louder and tried to wipe her nose with her sleeve.

"Be right back," said McLeod as she dashed out the door. She popped into the Humanities Council Office and asked Frieda—who had never failed her yet—for Kleenex. Frieda obliged with a neat plastic-wrapped package of tissues. McLeod hastily tore the package open and hurried back to the sun porch. Wesley now lay facedown on the rattan sofa and continued to weep. Her coffee mug lay on the floor, coffee spilling on the tile. Never mind spilled coffee, thought McLeod, tucking the tissues close to Wesley's hand. She raced back to Victoria Sullivan's office. "Victoria! Do you have any brandy?" she asked as soon as she saw through her open door that Victoria was at her desk. "It's an emergency."

Victoria, to do her credit, did not turn a hair. "I don't have brandy," she said, getting up, "but I have this," and she pulled a bottle of single malt scotch from the bottom drawer of a file cabinet. "Can I help?"

"I don't think so," McLeod said over her shoulder as she

fled back to the sun porch, admiring Victoria. No wonder nobody calls her Vicky, she thought; she's too impressive.

Wesley was sitting up when McLeod got back to the sun porch, and scrubbing at her face with a tissue. McLeod picked up the empty coffee mug from the floor, poured it half full of scotch, and handed it to Wesley. "Here, drink this. It can't hurt."

Wesley looked up at McLeod the way a small child looks at his mother when he's handed something to drink. She took a swallow of scotch, coughed, and took another. "I really need some water," she said.

"I'll get some," said McLeod, rushed to the kitchenette, and returned with water.

Wesley took a sip, poured a little of the water in the mug of scotch, and drank some more. She gave a massive sigh and looked again at McLeod. Finally, she spoke. "You know, I did fudge my data," she said, and paused.

McLeod sat down in a rattan chair facing the sofa. She could hardly say she was surprised. She had wanted to believe Wesley was telling the truth yesterday morning. Wesley was a woman and a Southerner and science needed more women, more successful women, and she had been thrilled at Wesley's imminent publication. And so she had wanted to believe Wesley, believe that Owen West's charge was so ridiculous it was worthy only of laughter. She had tried to believe it, but she had never really succeeded.

"Not much," Wesley was saying. "I didn't cheat much. It wasn't blatant, but it wasn't quite right. I couldn't get it exactly right. And I thought it was so close I'd never be caught. And that stupid clunk of an ignorant cowboy! He caught me. If he'd concentrated on his own work, this would never have happened. But no, he had to meddle in my affairs and try to replicate my experiments . . ." Wesley rambled on.

McLeod worked at processing what Wesley was saying. Wesley had lied. She had faked her results. And Owen West had caught her. But something didn't make sense. A small, maybe 40-watt, lightbulb of worry went off above McLeod's head. "Why did he want to put his name on an article he knew was based on faulty data?" she asked Wesley.

Wesley gaped. "I forgot I told you that's what he wanted," she said. "I was not telling the truth then. That's the trouble with telling lies, isn't it? You can't ever remember what you've said." Wesley wiped her eyes again, sniffed, and took another swallow of scotch.

"What did he want?" McLeod asked.

"Coauthorship was the last thing he wanted. He wanted money. That's what he said. I think he just wanted to cause trouble. Didn't want me, a woman, to get published before he did, even though I'm years older than he was, a better scientist than he was, a better person, really. But I shouldn't say that, should I?" She sniffed again.

"What are you going to do now?" McLeod asked.

"I don't have a clue."

McLeod wondered if she should offer her more scotch. Or more coffee. Instead, she just waited.

"The police called at the crack of dawn this morning and they want to talk to me again," Wesley said. "They must know about Owen West's threats, don't you think? And I'm going to tell them the truth. And tell Berman. And e-mail *Science* and withdraw my article." She lost control again. "My article! My article!" she wailed.

McLeod reached for Wesley's mug. It wasn't empty, but she poured a bit more scotch in, and waited.

"I'm going to kill myself," Wesley said. "I swear I am. I can't go on living after this. I'll lose my postdoc position. I'll never get another job. I'll have to go back to Waynesville, North Carolina, and be a dental hygienist and work for my father." She was sobbing again.

McLeod was afraid to offer her any more whiskey—it was only ten o'clock in the morning—but what to do with her?

"Listen!" she said. "Tell me one thing. Did you kill Owen West to stop him from blowing the whistle? Tell the truth. As they used to say to us in the South, 'Tell the truth and shame the devil.'"

Wesley pulled out two more tissues and mopped her

swollen face. "No, I did not. I swear I did not. I didn't know what I was going to do about that crazy, horrible, evil, no-good, awful monster Owen West, but I wasn't going to kill him. I thought I'd just wait and see if he really had talked to Berman, or written to *Science*, and see what happened next." She paused. "I must say I was relieved when he was found dead in the laboratory. But I did not kill him." She stared at McLeod, and repeated: *"I did not kill him."*

Wesley Bryant had a wide emotional range, McLeod thought, and remembering the wild laughter of twenty-four hours ago, possibly great dramatic ability. But here she was, and McLeod felt guilty in a way because she was the one who had told the police about West's threats. "What can I do to help you?" she asked.

"Can you go with me when I talk to the police? I guess that's what I came over here to ask you. I'm sorry I'm such a mess. I don't often go to pieces like this. I guess I never have."

"Everybody should go to pieces every now and then," McLeod said. "Then you can put yourself back together, maybe in a new shape."

"You're very encouraging," said Wesley, managing a smile. "Will you go with me?"

"I'm sorry, I can't. I have my class this afternoon, and I have a guest speaker coming from out of town. I have to meet him at the Dinky and take him to lunch and then my class starts at one-thirty."

"I see." Wesley looked so downcast that McLeod was afraid she was going to start crying again.

"Look, it will be all right. I know Nick Perry, the head of detectives for the Borough, and he's a very nice man."

"That's the one I was going to see."

"When are you supposed to go there?" McLeod asked.

"I was supposed to be there now," Wesley said. "I came here instead. Do you think they're out looking for me?"

"I shouldn't think so. I could call Lieutenant Perry, if you like, and tell him you're on your way. Or would you feel better if you had a lawyer go with you? I know a lawyer in town . . ."

"No, that's one more person who would have to know about this," said Wesley. "Of course, if things get worse, like I'm accused of murder, then I'll have to get a lawyer. But I think I'll wait. I wish I had a friend, though. I'm sorry you can't do it."

"I am, too," said McLeod. "But you can handle this, Wesley. You know, I bet it will all work out. As my Aunt Maggie says, 'The darkest hour is before the dawn.' So probably the worst is over."

"No, I don't think the worst is over," said Wesley. She stood up, brushed her pants, and shook her head. "Thanks for holding my hand—coffee, whiskey, whatever. I really appreciate it. Here I go. I wonder if I should call a tumbrel."

McLeod had to admire her.

Thirty-seven

MCLEOD WENT INTO the ladies' room and splashed cold water on her face and dried it off. Frieda met her at the door as she was coming out and said, "'Bells in your parlors, wild cats in your kitchens, Saints in your injuries, devils being offended . . .'"

"Where is that from, Frieda? It certainly describes my morning so far," McLeod said.

"*Othello*," said Frieda. "Isn't it marvelous? That was one upset lady you had on your hands. I could hear her screeching in my office.

"I'm sure you could. I expect they could hear her in Nassau Hall."

"What's her problem?"

"She has to talk to the police," McLeod said. "Poor woman."

"Poor woman," agreed Frieda, and went into the ladies' room.

McLeod went back to the sun porch, picked up the mugs and the bottle of scotch, put the mugs in the kitchenette, and took the scotch to Victoria Sullivan's office. "Thanks so much," she said. "It was very useful."

"Everything under control?" asked Victoria.

"I think so," McLeod said.

"Who was that woman?"

"She's a postdoc in the chemistry department."

"Was this about the murder?" asked Victoria sternly.

"Yes, I guess it was. No, I know it was." She felt guilty. "But I wasn't trying to get information from her. She has to go to the police and she wanted me to go with her. But I have a class."

"Wasn't she here yesterday, too?"

Oh, God, thought McLeod. She must think I totally ignored her warning. "She came yesterday but that was before we had lunch," McLeod said. "And she called me this morning and wanted to come back. There was no way I could refuse her. And I have not forgotten what you said to me. Believe me."

"I'm sure you haven't." She looked at McLeod. "Are you all right? It can be exhausting dealing with people in a state like she was in."

"I know. But I'm all right. I've got to go meet an old friend of mine, a Florida journalist who's going to speak to my class. And I've got to take him to lunch at Prospect. But it will be relaxing compared to that conversation this morning."

"Good luck, my dear," said Victoria.

How could a woman who was younger than she was be almost motherly? It was amazing, McLeod thought as she went upstairs to get her purse and go meet Tow Sack Burlap.

LATE THAT AFTERNOON, McLeod walked home. Class had gone well, she reflected. Tow Sack had been suitably articulate with his tales of interviewing law enforcement officers, colorful legislators, reluctant governors, and several criminals at Raiford Prison. The students had listened raptly, laughed in the appropriate places, and asked him probing questions about his interview techniques.

"Everybody likes to talk—well, nearly everybody," Tow

Sack had said. "Just tickle 'em and let 'em talk. Then write down what they say."

He did use a tape recorder, he said, in answer to a question. "I didn't used to, but people were so eager to call me a liar I started taping interviews to protect myself. It's amazing what people will say to you—and then swear on the Confederate flag that they didn't say it."

Greg Pierre had appeared, the last student to arrive, and taken his seat just as Tow Sack started talking. He was the first student to leave and McLeod, busy with collecting papers—the assignment had been to write about somebody working in science—could not catch him.

She had walked Tow Sack down to the Dinky station, and now she was plodding homeward, her students' articles in her briefcase. She was worried about Greg, worried about Wesley, worried about explaining to Megan that she had given the copies of the letters to Nick Perry, worried about George, who was worried about the murders at the university.

AT HOME SHE checked for phone messages and found none. A look in the refrigerator confirmed her recollection of tons of leftover tetrazzini. So supper wasn't a problem.

She called Megan and asked if she could come around. Megan assented, and McLeod drove to Edwards Place. She had walked enough for one day, she told herself.

When Megan greeted her, she was once more wearing a large man's shirt with her jeans.

"I have to tell you," McLeod said they had sat down. "I gave those letters to the police."

"I know," said Megan. "They came back to see me today."

"Really? Who came?"

"Lieutenant Perry and Sergeant Popper."

"They're good," said McLeod. "You understand that I felt that I had to let them know about it."

"No, I don't, not really. I told them that the letters had nothing to do with the murder. And I told them that Owen had probably been helping her with her experiments and just wanted the credit he deserved. But then they said Wesley had changed her story. They said she had admitted fudging her data, and I said that maybe Owen had found out what she'd done and was trying to stop her—all in the interests of keeping science clean and the reputation of the university unblemished."

McLeod marveled at Megan's ability to put a good spin on what Owen had done. "What did the police say to that?"

"They seemed surprised."

I'll bet, thought McLeod.

"What made you turn the letters over? I thought we had agreed to let things ride?"

"Lieutenant Perry came to the house and I gave them to him. He was stunned. He obviously thought they were important. You know, we both could have been charged with obstruction of justice."

"I don't see how. The police saw them here and didn't pay any attention to them."

"Even the best police make mistakes. And it wasn't Lieutenant Perry or Sergeant Popper who went through Owen's desk, was it?"

"No, it wasn't. Oh, well, what's done is done. I'm not angry at you. People have to do what they have to do."

"I certainly hope you don't stay mad at me, Megan. You're a wonderful young woman and I value your good opinion."

"Thanks. Don't worry. It will all work out, I'm sure."

"Thank you." McLeod stood up.

"Don't go," Megan said. "Won't you have a cup of tea? A glass of wine?"

"I had better get home," McLeod said. "I'm tired. What a day. But thanks. Thanks for everything."

GEORGE WAS HOME when she got there and happy to eat leftover tetrazzini. "It was really good," he said. "You put in lots of chicken. But first a drink and I'll build a fire. Don't you want to get your knitting?"

"George, your concern is flattering. I just hope you like that sweater—if I ever finish it."

"You'll finish it."

"But maybe not in our lifetime."

"Sure you will. I found a room for Nick Perry to use on campus. Did you see him today?" George asked when they were ensconced before the fire with drinks.

"I didn't see him," she said, and told him about Wesley Bryant.

"I was afraid of that when I saw those letters—I knew it was yet another public relations problem for the university."

"Have another drink," she said, and wondered if Princeton continued to be a murder scene whether George would become an alcoholic.

Thirty-eight

❧

FRIDAY MORNING MCLEOD got up full of resolve to find Greg Pierre. As she came down the stairs, George was standing, looking up at her, ready to leave for work.

"Good morning, he said. "What's on your schedule today?"

"Good morning. I want to find Greg Pierre and then I want to talk to Nick Perry. And I also would like to talk to Wesley Bryant. I feel guilty that I couldn't go to the police with her. And I've got to grade the stories my students turned in yesterday, pieces on people in science, but I don't have to finish that today. How about you? What are your plans?"

"I've got meetings all morning. I'd like to talk to Nick Perry myself. I am going to take Polly out to dinner. Would you like to come, too?"

McLeod, who knew when three was a crowd, said she thought not. "But it's sweet of you to ask."

"Listen, be careful. I have an uneasy feeling about what's going on. If this business with that postdoc and Berman and that article ever gets out, it's bound to have serious repercussions for the university."

"Not as serious as the murder of two graduate students, surely?"

"Oh, yes, in a way. Murder doesn't reflect on the scholarship of the university."

"I see."

George stared at her. "You know what I mean," he said uneasily.

"Sure. I see what you mean. But murder trumps it all, doesn't it?"

"Certainly. I'm not a moral philosopher, but I agree that murder is beyond comparison with scientific fraud. Still it's my job to worry about the university's reputation in academia and in the scientific world. Anyway, that's beside the point. I'm very aware of the murders and their impact on Princeton. And I worry about you, McLeod. You're always the flash point somehow. Just be careful today—and every day. I'll be home before I pick up Polly, but you have my cell phone number. Stay in touch."

"Thanks, George. You're a good shepherd."

George looked puzzled.

"Baaa!" she said, but grinning.

George kissed her on the cheek and left.

MCLEOD, SMILING AT the kiss, put on water for tea and dialed Greg Pierre's telephone number in his room. Somewhat to her surprise, he answered.

"How are you?" she asked. "Is everything all right?"

"Fine," he said. "I guess. We've got a track meet tomorrow in New Haven. I'm getting psyched for that. I'm sorry about the conference Thursday, but next week will be better, won't it? Give you time to read the science papers."

"Sure," said McLeod. "I don't have my calendar here, but e-mail me when you'd like to come and I'll put it down."

"Will do."

"I just wanted to make sure you weren't in the clutches of the law," she said.

"Not right now anyway," he said. "Haven't heard anything from them in a couple of days."

"Let me know if you need—if you need a surrogate parent," McLeod said.

"Will do. Thanks."

She tried to reach Nick Perry but they told her he was at the university. George had said Nick had a situation room in Frick now, and she wondered if she could call him there. At any rate, she left a message at Borough Hall for Nick to call.

Breakfast over, newspapers read—no news about the murders—dishes in the dishwasher, McLeod went back upstairs, took a shower, dressed in jeans and her FSU sweatshirt, made up her bed, and feeling tidy and organized, called Wesley Bryant.

"Oh, hello," said Wesley, when McLeod had identified herself. McLeod could almost hear the unspoken words, "Why are you calling?"

"I was calling," she said in answer to those nonwords, "to say I'm sorry I couldn't go with you to see the police yesterday. And I want to invite you to lunch—so I can hear about that and how everything else is going."

"I understood why you couldn't go to the police with me," Wesley said. "It wasn't so bad. I can have lunch and tell you about it. Where?"

"Let's go to Lahiere's. I'll meet you there at twelve, if that's all right."

"Fine," said Wesley.

McLeod hung up and took her briefcase downstairs and settled down at the dining table to start reading the interviews with scientists.

Olivia's tale of the man who was working on animal domiciles was as good as she had thought it would be. She was hard put to offer more comments than she already had, and simply wrote, "Good work," and gave her an A.

A student named Mark Johnson, a blond lad with two gold rings in his left ear, had interviewed a professor in molecular biology who believed that viruses were the most abundant, highest evolved life forms on the planet. He brought the professor to vivid life, with all his intensity and fierce purpose laid bare. Mark seemed to have trouble dealing with the parts about cells and genetics, but who wouldn't? She indicated some places where he might improve things, wrote a note saying that it was otherwise very good, and gave him a B+.

Clark Powell had chosen another professor in ecology and evolutionary biology, a man who studied zebras in Kenya. This kind of biology, McLeod noted, was much easier to write about than molecular biology. Clark's sentence structure was sometimes shaky, but he was on the whole an excellent writer and she was sorry that he was going to be a doctor. Maybe he could use his considerable talent to write about medicine for laypeople, she thought, but what about his passion for the theater? She sighed. If she ran the world, she would arrange things so that every young person could follow the career path that most appealed to him or her. No parental choices for the vocations of offspring.

So far, the papers weren't bad at all—but then nobody in her class was devoid of talent. They had all worked hard, and she read their work with interest.

To her surprise, Greg Pierre had written about Sandy Berman, who had apparently taught him general chemistry. Greg had done a good job of interviewing Berman, McLeod thought, and had gotten much more out of him about himself than McLeod ever had. But then I was interviewing Berman about Shivers, she told herself in her own defense. She read on with interest.

Berman had grown up in a nonscientific family. His father had been an English professor and his mother a poet, and they had been completely bewildered at his interest in science and his refusal to work for a liberal arts degree. He had pursued his goal, graduated *summa cum laude* from Tufts, earned his Ph.D. at Michigan, and endured a post-doctoral position at a federal government lab for a couple of years before he came to Princeton. At Princeton, Berman began working to synthesize a substance that was extremely effective against tumors of all kinds in certain circumstances. (He was rather vague, McLeod thought, about exactly what the circumstances were.) "You can't imagine how thrilled I was when I succeeded," he had said to Greg.

Almost immediately, though, he fell into utter despair. He learned that a rival chemist at Colorado had beat him to it. Just as Berman was typing up his article, the Coloradan published an account of his discovery of the same thing. The man made millions, Berman nothing. "It was very disheartening," he told Greg. "Years of work, then at last success, and then to find out somebody else had done it first. The man who's first in chemistry wins the prize. The guy who's second—well, he comes in second. There's no red ribbon in chemistry. It's ignominy."

McLeod remembered that Berman had spoken to her sadly of the man who comes in second in chemistry, but she had not realized he was speaking from bitter personal experience. Berman went on to tell Greg that he was again working on synthesizing vital substances, that he enjoyed teaching general chemistry, and was stimulated by his work with graduate students. He said his wife was a graphic designer, and of their four children, none was interested in science. "I guess I'm the anomaly in the genetic chain," he said.

McLeod felt a surge of sympathy for Sandy Berman. This explained a lot—his apparent lack of ambition and his loose supervision of his laboratory, his jealousy of Earl Shivers. Poor Berman. She gave Greg an A and wrote him a note that said, "I know the man you wrote about, and I am very impressed with the job you've done. Congratulations."

Interesting as the papers were, she realized she'd better get ready for lunch. The world dressed down and further down every day, but she still couldn't wear jeans and a sweatshirt to Lahiere's nor even to her office on a weekday. She changed into a skirt and sweater and decided it was warm enough outside to wear only a jacket.

Wesley was waiting for her at Lahiere's, and they decided to eat in the bar, which was cozy and cheerful. They

ordered white wine and discussed the menu at some
length, a process McLeod always enjoyed. She finally decided on the scallops, and Wesley ordered the prosciutto
and fontina cheese sandwich on focaccia. (A cousin of the
cheeseburger at the Annex, McLeod thought.)

"Tell me how it went with the police," McLeod said.

"It wasn't as bad as I thought it would be. About like a
root canal, I'd say. I bit the bullet and told the truth and
shamed the devil, like you told me to."

"And they don't suspect you of murder?" McLeod
asked, after she'd nodded approvingly at Wesley's brief
account.

"They don't seem to regard me as any more than one
among many suspects."

"Did they ask you about Carey Srodek?"

"They had already talked to me about Carey. I really
didn't know him."

"Do you have any idea at all who killed him?"

"None. I told the police that."

"Do they think the same person killed Carey that killed
Owen West?"

"I really don't know. I guess I'm so centered on my own
problems I can't think about the murders. That's pretty
weird, isn't it?"

"No. You're facing a major dilemma, I know. Moving
on, did you talk to Berman about the article?"

"I did. At first he seemed abstracted, not really interested. Then he got really mad and said he had trusted me,
that it was monstrous—that was his word—of me to abuse
his trust the way I had. I said he was perfectly right. What
else could I say? I wanted to yell and scream at him, but
what could I say when I screamed? I made a mistake and I
have to take the consequences. I've processed that. Finally,
he calmed down and said I'd live through it. He said that
he was very glad I came to my senses before the article was
published. He asked me if I had withdrawn the article yet,
and I said I had not had time, that I would do it immediately. He urged me to call the editor, and I said I would.
Then he became actually rather sympathetic and told me

about an incident that occurred when he was a postdoc at the Medical Research Institute of Infectious Diseases at Fort Meade. It wasn't him, but a friend . . ."

Fort Meade? That rang a bell, McLeod thought, her mind wandering. But what bell? What chime, gong, carillon? When Wesley finished her anecdote, McLeod asked her about Fort Meade. "That's where they work on chemical and biological warfare—or defenses against them."

Their food arrived. McLeod tasted a scallop and found it cooked to perfection. "If only I could cook a scallop like this," she said.

Wesley seemed puzzled by such an intense interest in food, and chewed away on her sandwich. "Berman was as good as he could be, I guess, under the circumstances," she said. "Anyway, I'm glad that's over."

"And did you call *Science*?" McLeod asked.

"I did."

"Was that awful?"

"Not at all. They acted like I was a heroine. I explained that some further work had indicated a few fuzzy spots—I wanted to make sure we were on firm ground. I said 'we' so it would look like Berman and I were working together—which, of course, we aren't. I am just trying to salvage some shreds of respectability out of all this."

"I am sure you will," McLeod said. "I have to admire you."

"Hmpf," said Wesley. "Don't admire me yet. I've got a ways to go. I've got to get myself clear of a murder charge, clear myself of scientific fraud, placate my boss, and I don't know what all."

"Sounds like you're well on your way with all of them."

"Actually, I'm glad it's turned out that I'm not publishing a spurious article," Wesley said. "I think I'll make it eventually. And if I don't, I'll just go back to Waynesville and take a course in dental hygiene."

"I bet you fifty cents it won't come to that," McLeod said.

"I hope you're right. Anyway, I'm paying for lunch this time. Thanks for sticking by me."

Thirty-nine

FEELING MORE CHEERFUL about Wesley, McLeod waited on the traffic light at the corner of Witherspoon and Nassau, glancing idly around. There was a big mailbox on that corner, not the anthrax box—that was farther down Nassau Street—but it reminded her of something. But what was it?

She crossed the street and went to Joseph Henry House. When she went in the Humanities Council Office to get her mail, Frieda was grimacing at her computer.

"What's the matter?" she asked.

"Computers!" said Frieda. Then she looked solemn and intoned: "To err is human, but to really foul things up, it takes a computer."

"Very good, Frieda. Who said that?"

"I have no idea. But it has the ring of truth, doesn't it?"

"It does," McLeod agreed and took her mail upstairs, where she felt very efficient for at least an hour, tending to her mail, her e-mail, and phone messages.

She still hadn't heard from Nick Perry and decided she would go over to Frick and try to find him. She stopped in the chemistry department office to ask where the police situation room was and agreed with all the administrators and managers (they were no longer called secretaries) that it was a beautiful day.

The police were in two rooms near the side door of the building, the door that opened on William Street, they told her, and she set off. Sergeant Popper and a young woman she didn't know were working at computers. The young woman wore earphones. No Nick Perry in sight.

"Where's the lieutenant?" she asked Kevin Popper.

"He's interviewing somebody in that other little room," said Popper, pointing at the door. "We call it the closet."

"I think I'll wait for him. Will that be all right?"

"Sure."

She stood awkwardly for a while, then sat down in an empty chair. Restless, she stood up and waited by the door again. "Sergeant Popper, I'm going to see if Professor Berman is still here," she said. "Would you tell Lieutenant Perry I want to see him?"

"Sure thing," said Popper, not looking up. The young woman did look up but said nothing.

McLeod went upstairs and knocked on Berman's office door. "Come in," a voice said. McLeod. opened the door and began to feel uneasy the minute she saw Sandy Berman. He looked tired and worn.

"Hello," she said. "I just read a wonderful article about you that a student of mine wrote."

"Oh, was that one of your students? I wasn't sure what class he was in. Very thorough fellow. He talked to me for more than two hours. I couldn't get rid of him. What did he say about me?"

"For one thing, he said your family wasn't sympathetic with your ambition to be a scientist," McLeod said. "I always like to read about people's childhoods."

Berman almost began to preen. "He went all out, did he? Put in all those details? What else?"

"He told the most interesting story," she said, "about your discovery—the synthesized substance—and how somebody else did the same thing and published it before you could. That's a dreadful thing to happen. You came so close to fame and fortune, didn't you?"

"Did he put that in? I probably shouldn't have told him about that, but he was a good listener. Anything else?"

"Lots. It's a good article. He should be able to sell it. Maybe you can read it in print."

"If it's going to be published, I'd like to check it first."

"E-mail him and tell him," said McLeod. "But I wanted to ask you about something else. You did your postdoc at Fort Meade. Did you work on biological or chemical weapons?"

Berman looked as though he had been hit in the solar plexus. He stared at her. "How did you know that?" he asked. "I didn't say anything about that to your student."

He appeared to be so upset that McLeod did not want to involve Wesley. "I don't remember," she said vaguely.

"I worked on defenses against biological and chemical weapons, he said. *"Defenses against them,"* he repeated. "Do you understand that?"

"I wanted to ask you about anthrax. Fort Meade is where they purified some anthrax, isn't it? So I thought maybe you could tell me more about anthrax. The mailbox where those lethal letters were mailed a few years ago fascinates me. Right here in Princeton."

Berman's attitude had changed. "What are you doing here? What do you want?" he asked.

"I don't know what you mean. I don't want anything. I'm interested in you, and after I read that article, I decided the next chance I had I'd ask you about some of the things in it."

Berman was standing up now, looking at her with loathing.

She stood up, too. "Actually, I came to Frick to see Nick Perry," McLeod said. "He's a friend of mine," she continued, trying to sound like a lovesick Southern belle rather than a police informant.

Berman's hand was groping on his desktop while he continued to stare at her. "Don't threaten me," he said, picking up the heavy Bunsen burner paperweight. He started toward her.

A blunt instrument, McLeod thought as she stared at

him. Then she moved. He had to come around the desk before he could get to her and she was by the door. It was simple, if she could just move her feet. She did. She opened the door and shot out. Berman came after her into the corridor, but stopped when Binky Tate rounded the corner. "Where are you rushing off to?" she asked McLeod, who followed her, caught up with her, and passed her. Even as she scurried to what she hoped was safety, she thought about Victoria Sullivan and feared another lecture on harrying faculty members. When they were down the stairs and outside, on William Street, and she saw Berman had not followed her out—only then could she let out a sigh of relief.

"He was trying to kill me!" McLeod said.

"You're too much," giggled Binky Tate and walked toward the parking lot. "Have a good weekend!" she caroled over her shoulder.

McLeod looked around. The sidewalks were far from deserted. She supposed she was safe out here in broad daylight. But she wanted to see Nick Perry. Maybe I'm crazy, she thought. I should be hightailing it home, but I've got to see Nick. She rounded the corner on Washington Road and went in the front entrance of Frick.

Forty

❧

NICK WAS IN the situation room when she got there, standing by the young woman's desk.

"I have to talk to you," she said.

"Good to see you. I take it that it's about business?"

"Of course it is. I'm not here for gossip."

"Let's go in here," he said, leading her to the adjacent room. She looked around. "No wonder Sergeant Popper calls it the closet," she said. "That's what it is."

It was indeed a large closet, lined with shelves holding the detritus of some academician's life—books, scientific journals, files, boxes containing God knows what. A table and two chairs took up all the floor space.

"Sit down," Nick said. "It's a closet, but it suffices. I've talked to nearly everybody that works in Frick. And Sandra out there is transcribing the interviews."

"Any headway?"

"Lots," said Nick. "Slow and steady, that's us." He did not sound like a man on the edge of victory.

"I know who did it," McLeod said. "I think I know who did it. I'm pretty sure I know who did it."

Nick Perry looked at her. "Who?"

"Sandy Berman."

"How do you know he did it?"

"He just came at me with a Bunsen burner paperweight."

"What were you doing that made him come at you with a Bunsen burner?"

"I was asking him some questions."

"That's your SOP for getting yourself killed."

"Nick, Sandy Berman is your murderer. I'm sure of it."

"What makes you say so?"

McLeod told him all she knew about Berman. "He knows something about the anthrax, too," she said. "I know he does. I kind of suspected him, but when I found out he worked at Fort Meade, I was sure of it."

"What anthrax?"

"The anthrax that was posted in that mailbox on Nassau Street where University Place dead-ends into it. The anthrax that was mailed to the United States Senate and to television networks. That anthrax that killed five people."

"The FBI was all over the place five years ago and they never went after Berman." Nick paused. "Well, they may have thought it was somebody in the chemistry department. But they found nothing, nothing, to connect anybody at the university with anthrax."

"I know. Somebody told me they looked at all the glove boxes."

"And they were all clean," objected Nick.

"Couldn't Berman have gotten rid of his glove box? He's smart. I bet the FBI alerted everybody to what they were going to do. They didn't make a surprise raid on Frick or anything, did they?"

"No, I don't think so. Well, well, well. But why would Berman mail anthrax to people in the government? Why would any respectable college professor, a *Princeton* professor, do such a thing, McLeod? I have to pay attention, but this boggles the imagination."

"Nick, he's a mad scientist. Sort of. He performed a brilliant feat in the laboratory years ago—but he got nothing out of it. Somebody beat him to publication by a hair. So he was frustrated beyond belief. He's always been frustrated—by his parents and now by his wife and children. Not a one of them has ever understood what he's doing. He's jealous of other professors. He doesn't supervise his graduate students closely enough. And he just narrowly escaped being involved in a scientific fraud scandal—his name is listed as coauthor with Wesley Bryant, you know. Did you ask him about that?"

"I see what you're saying. He may be implicated in the anthrax caper, but the murders?"

"Of course he did them. Who else? I'll bet you anything that that scheming, nasty Owen West found out about the anthrax and was threatening to expose Berman. And then Carey Srodek probably found out something and Berman thought he was going to expose him and he probably killed Carey."

"Right," said Nick. "And he really came at you with a paperweight?" McLeod nodded. Nick opened the door and went out. "Sergeant!"

Popper stood up, seemed to stand at attention a moment before he came out to join the lieutenant. "We're going to go talk to Professor Berman again. McLeod, you and Sandra, go home. Do you hear me? Lock your door. Don't let anybody in. I'll call you."

McLeod heaved a huge sigh of relief as they set out. She looked at Sandra. "My name's McLeod," she said. "Let's go." And as was her nature, began asking questions. "Are you from Princeton?"

GEORGE CAME HOME and found her having a drink in the living room. "I don't think I ever saw you drinking alone before," he said.

"I know. I never do, but today I deserve it," she said. "Let me tell you what happened since I saw you last."

"Wait a minute," said George.

"I know," said McLeod. "You're going to say, 'Let me build a fire and get a drink,' aren't you?"

"Well, yes, I was, but if you want to sit in the cold while I shake helplessly because I need a drink, that's all right."

"No, go ahead. Of course. I was just teasing."

After she had told him all about Berman, he shook his head. "It's unbelievable," he said. "A tenured professor! Oh, God. But this is not definite, is it? I mean, is there any evidence to support all this? He hasn't been arrested?"

"When I left Frick, Nick and Popper were on their way to his office."

"Well, we can still hope it's not true."

"Who then do you think killed Owen West? A tramp? And who killed Carey Srodek? Another tramp?"

"I'm just saying, let's wait and see."

GEORGE ANSWERED THE phone when it rang. McLeod heard him say, "Sure, it's more than all right. See you . . ." He hung up. "That was Nick. He's coming over." He looked at his watch. "I wonder if I have time to go pick up Polly and bring her over? No, I don't. I don't want to miss a minute of this."

He poured a scotch so it would be ready for Nick when he arrived, and then he stoked up the fire. He went in the kitchen and brought back some potato chips. He was nervous, McLeod thought. But so was she. She had fingered a murderer. It was an unnerving act. Well, she'd done it.

Nick arrived. George greeted him at the door, handed him his scotch, and brought him into the parlor. Nick nodded at McLeod, and came and sat beside her on the sofa.

"How did it go?"

"He said he was sorry he threatened you with the paperweight. He really is just undone by the murders, you see. He apologized profusely for the way he treated you and sent his best wishes to you. He told me he was going to send you some flowers."

"Send me flowers! Whatever for? Because I turned him in to the police?"

"No, because he's sorry he chased you out of his office. He says you're a wonderful woman, but he was just at the end of his rope this afternoon. After all, two of his graduate students have been killed, and the killer is—"

"He's the killer! I told you that."

"McLeod, you're wrong. Dead wrong. I knew he hadn't killed those students. There was absolutely no evidence against him—"

"I told you that, McLeod," George said.

McLeod glared at each of them. "If he didn't do it, who did?" she asked.

"Oh, I guess you don't know." He took a big gulp of scotch.

"A tramp?" said George hopefully.

Nick ignored that, and looked at McLeod. "Wesley Bryant is the murderer."

"But I had lunch with her today." said McLeod. "She said she told you the truth and shamed the devil. She said she confessed to fudging her data, but she certainly didn't confess to the murder."

"She did later. I was questioning her this afternoon. When you were looking for me."

"But you went after Berman . . ." McLeod said. "You and Popper."

"We went after him because you said he had threatened you with that Bunsen burner paperweight. I thought I'd better get that sorted out. But he was so apologetic I let it go. He is really upset that his postdoc murdered two graduate students. You have to cut him some slack."

"But he did work at Fort Meade?"

"He did. So did lots of other people. Incidentally, the FBI checked his glove box at the time. It was here. Popper called them to make sure."

"I was so sure he was the one. It all fit," McLeod said.

"It all fit, but it was a fantasy," Nick said.

"But Wesley. She's a woman. She's a Southerner."

"Southern belles are lethal," George said.

"But she told me—"

"That woman is the best liar I've ever seen in my life," Nick said. "And act! She could star in *Hamlet*—play Horatio and make him believable."

"What on earth made you think she did it?"

"Forensic evidence. Good old hard evidence. Her fingerprints were all over Carey Srodek's apartment. When we confronted her with that, she said they were lovers. But we knew that was a lie. The other graduate students knew Carey's girlfriend. His landlady knew his girlfriend and saw her there all the time but had never seen Wesley Bryant there."

"Well, I'll declare!" said McLeod, reverting to an old Southern expression as she sometimes did in moments of real depression. Then she rallied. "I should have known. I should have known. That time I interviewed Carey Srodek, he kept saying, 'Talk to Wesley Bryant. Talk to Wesley Bryant.'"

"He seems to have known that Bryant killed Owen West from the get-go," Nick said. "He may have stumbled on her in the lab that Sunday. For some reason, though, he didn't tell us. Maybe he had promised not to. Maybe he was afraid to tell. I don't know about that. But we have a good case. She had motive, means, and opportunity. The state's attorney is confident it's a strong case. And as I said: She confessed."

George stood up. "Congratulations, Nick. I'm glad you found a murderer that wasn't a professor, at least. I've got to go pick up Polly. Why don't I bring her back over here? Is that all right with you guys? We can cook or get takeout or go out."

Nick did not look enthusiastic, and said nothing. McLeod shrugged, and smiled limply.

"Be right back," George said, and left.

"I feel like such a fool," she said when they were alone.

"You shouldn't," Nick said. He moved closer to her on the sofa and put one arm around her. McLeod shivered and huddled against him. "That was a great case you spun against Berman."

"Oh dear, I thought Wesley Bryant had changed so much—and for the better," she said. "She even bought my lunch today!"

"Good for her! I'll buy your dinner tonight—but remember that doesn't make me a murderer."

McLeod laughed.

• • •

WHEN GEORGE AND Polly arrived, they found them still sitting on the sofa, McLeod sheltered in Nick's arm. "Why aren't you knitting on my sweater?" George asked. "I'm kidding, of course," he said.

It was actually a very pleasant evening. George and Nick went out and bought champagne and Chinese take-out.

"The food's not up to our usual standard," said George, "but who cares?"

"I'll toast that!" said McLeod, raising her flute.

Forty-one

❧

NEWS OF WESLEY'S arrest was in the Trenton paper on Saturday; it made the other newspapers on Sunday. Television cameramen came back to campus and took endless pictures of Sandy Berman, his lab, the university apartment building where Wesley had lived, and of Lahiere's restaurant, where the accused had had lunch before she was arrested. They took McLeod's picture, too, and quoted her at length about how much she had liked Wesley Bryant.

But this fuss died down and Wesley stayed in jail awaiting trial.

Greg Pierre won the 3,000-meter event in New Haven that weekend and he got his own blast of publicity the next week when his whole history was revealed by the Trenton paper and picked up by the world's press. Greg hated it, but behaved admirably.

He told McLeod he had decided to give up competitive running. He was too old, really, for collegiate competition, he said. He might as well acknowledge it. If Isabel Pittman could come clean, he could at least play it straight. He was going to concentrate on school. He would be a senior in the fall with a senior thesis to write, and he wanted to make it the best one ever written. He polished his article on Sandy Berman, added the part about Fort Meade, showed it to Berman, and sold it to the *Princeton Alumni Weekly*. Like Olivia, Mark, Clark, and the other students in the class, he began to work on his final paper for McLeod's class, a lengthy story on Nick Perry. He had wanted to write about McLeod, but she threatened to give him an F in the course if he dared. He and his roommate, Ted Vance, had jobs on a ranch in Wyoming for the summer.

Scott Murphy moved in with Megan Snowden and they both appeared to be blissfully happy.

McLeod finished knitting George's sweater. George thought it was beautiful and he was disappointed only that the weather was getting too warm to wear it often.

McLeod started a sweater for Nick but didn't have any hope of finishing it before the semester was over and she went back to Tallahassee. She interviewed Earl Shivers about his needlepoint, did a little more research, and sold the article about him to *New Jersey Monthly*. Sandy Berman became her good friend and suggested she write a book about protein folding. McLeod said she'd cut her throat before she wrote anything about science.

Victoria Sullivan said nothing more about McLeod's relations with faculty and invited her back to Princeton to teach again.

McLeod accepted.

Author's Note

My heartfelt thanks go to Stefan Bernhard of Princeton University's Department of Chemistry for his encouragement, advice, and generous help. This book would not exist without his aid. And thanks, too, to three of his graduate students, Angie Sauers, Karl Oyler, and Mike Lowry. Jeffrey Schwartz and Donald McClure, Russell Wellman Moore Professor of Chemistry Emeritus, also answered questions.

Richard O'Brien patiently coached me on track and field; Susan Emerson provided information about the Department of the History of Art at Yale; Lieutenant Nicholas Sutter was very helpful about procedures in the Borough of Princeton Police Department.

Jim Merritt provided other information, as did Tom Waldron and Kent Miller.

And special thanks to editor Susan Allison, agent Elizabeth Knappman, and copy editor Joan Matthews.

Lolly O'Brien and Amanda Matetsky, faithful and true, as always, read the manuscript. Marcia Snowden read the proofs.

Let me say that the characters in the book are entirely fictitious, not nearly as interesting as the real people at Princeton University.

Recipes

Baked Sea Bass with Eggplant

1/4 cup olive oil
1 onion, chopped
1 teaspoon chopped garlic
1 small eggplant, cubed, but unpeeled
1 cup chopped tomatoes, canned or fresh
1 tablespoon grated ginger
1/2 cup white wine
salt and pepper to taste
chopped coriander or parsley
4 sea bass fillets
1/4 cup lime juice

Heat olive oil in a saucepan over medium high heat. Add onion and garlic and cook, stirring, until onion is wilted. Add eggplant and tomatoes. Cook about 2 minutes. Add ginger. Add wine and salt and pepper to taste. Stir in the coriander and bring the mixture to a boil. Cook for 10 minutes.

Oil a baking dish and arrange the fillets skin side down. Spoon some of the sauce over them, sprinkle with lime juice, and bake at 450 degrees for about 10 minutes. Serve the rest of the sauce with the fish.

Arugula Salad

fresh arugula
orange sections
black olives, pitted

Toss all ingredients with dressing of olive oil, vinegar, salt, and pepper.

Vondelle's Mother's
Can't Wait Apple Cake

4 cups diced apples
1/2 cup cooking oil
2 cups sugar
2 eggs, well beaten
2 cups flour
1/2 teaspoon salt
11/2 teaspoons baking soda
1 teaspoon cinnamon
1 teaspoon vanilla
1 cup chopped nuts

Combine apples, oil, and sugar. Add beaten eggs. Add flour, salt, soda, cinnamon, vanilla, and nuts. Bake in a 375-degree oven for about 45 minutes.

GET CLUED IN

Ever wonder how to find out about all the latest Berkley Prime Crime and Signet mysteries?

berkleysignetmysteries.com

- *See what's new*
- *Find author appearances*
- *Win fantastic prizes*
- *Get reading recommendations*
- *Sign up for the mystery newsletter*
- *Chat with authors and other fans*
- *Read interviews with authors you love*

MYSTERY SOLVED.

berkleysignetmysteries.com